THE LEONOIDS
FALL OF LEOTUS

The Leonoids: Fall of Leotus

Brett Goetz

For GOD; I can do all things with YOU by my side.

Thanks to all those who have offered their skills in helping me finalize this book and lent their love and support along the way. Special thanks to my Wife, my Mother, Amber Goetz and Cleion Morton.

CHAPTER ONE
Havenbrook

HAVENBROOK IS A small town in the heart of Kansas surrounded by corn and wheat fields, but occasionally one will get lost on a summer drive and find himself in the middle of a sunflower field. It's beautiful in mid-June to watch the summer breeze blow through the golden wheat like a great ocean on the plains, or seeing a field of sunflowers stretch for the morning sun. As one drives into downtown, from K-69 onto Main, he'd notice the streets are still lined with red bricks and old stone storefronts. Some of the buildings have been renovated and modernized, but the town's history and age can be seen in the crumbling stone of others.

On the corner of Avenue A and Main is Miss Mayfield's Diner. Dad said the building was a bustling train station when he was younger, but the passenger trains stopped coming through here long ago. Miss Mayfield only serves one kind of pie, Berry Rhubarb, but it's the first thing you smell when you walk in and the last taste on most folks' tongues when they leave. I prefer my pie a la mode, with a large scoop of Miss Mayfield's homemade vanilla ice cream melting on top. The berries come straight from her garden during growing season and the cream, from the Johnson's dairy farm, two counties east. Folks say Miss Mayfield brews the best sweet tea this side of the south.

As one continues north on Main Street he'd pass the old courthouse, a limestone building kept up by taxpayer dollars. The Ten Commandments stood on the front lawn until some yuppie, in a monkey suit, caused an uprising a couple years ago. My family has never attended church on a regular basis, but the statue seemed to keep the peace with the older generation. Since it was torn down, they haven't stopped ranting about how all of us young folk have "lost our way" and how "disrespectful" we are. They watch us from their windows and porches and push the city council for earlier curfews and a city dress code.

Across the street is the county credit union. Mr. Fickler is the bank president; a real orderly man that will be at one's front door if they're a day late with their payment. He organized demonstrations against the town's decision to do away with school prayer and many anti-abortion rallies across the state. The only time I have seen him out of a suit is at the gym, where he still wears his slacks to exercise in. He is not the odd ball in town though; many people are more perplexed by the man with nine cats who goes around town hissing at the locals. He is a rugged man with tangled red hair that needs trimmed and a belly that certainly lets one know he is not going hungry. No one really knows his name and most just call him "cat man." There are many stories about how he came to be the way he is, but the one I hear most often is a bad trip on LSD.

Turn east on Sunset, go two blocks, and one will run into the only grocery store in town, The Fancy Apple. Passed down from my great grandfather to my father, the store is our little piece of Havenbrook. It used to bear our last name, Fosters' Market, but when dad remodeled the store he also changed the name. It is sleek and modern; the exterior rusty red and beige and the entry way lined with natural stones. It's not as large, or cheap, as the chain stores, but the employees are friendlier and the service is great. Lit by sunlight and track lighting, one can usually see his reflection in the laminate flooring. The walls are lined with murals of vibrantly colored, peeling, red and green apples and the words "fresh" "crisp" "fancy" and "delicious." I have worked in the store for my father ever since I was twelve. Since I started high school, my main responsibility has been to unload produce and meat. It is hard work sometimes, but has allowed me to build the strength I need in my arms to throw the football well.

Three more blocks east and two blocks north, at the intersection of Tiller Lane and Jeremiah, is Brooks High School and the Tiller Family Stadium. The street and the stadium were named after Tyler Tiller, a wealthy oil man that contributed millions to the construction of the stadium and other projects in town. Mr. Tiller is a lonely old man that has dedicated his life to building a fortune. He has a beautiful home, but no wife or children to share it with and he is rarely seen with company.

The football stadium sits just north of the 3-story, red brick, school. It is where you can find most folks in town on Friday evenings in the fall. Bucks football has accumulated a record of 59-7 over the last six years and five straight state championships. Last fall, as Brooks first-ever starting freshman quarterback, I led the Bucks to a 35-21 state victory over our rivals, the Mission East Eagles. Many in town doubted me, standing only 5'9" and 159 pounds, but after an injury to the starter and a season of stellar stats, I proved my pundits wrong and won the town's confidence and affection. The night of the state championship is one that I will never forget and it is where this story begins.

The morning started like any other, with mom shaking me from a deep and pleasant sleep. "Jayden Foster, I swear, if you don't get up I am going to douse you with a pitcher of cold water!" It was either the third or fourth time she had come upstairs to wake me that morning; honestly, I had lost count in the intermittent sleep.

I stretched and rubbed my eyes. "Just five more minutes" I pleaded as she walked out of the room. My legs were sore from two practices the day before. I buried my head under the pillow and closed my eyes.

"Now Jayden!" she demanded with authority from the hallway. Her voice was unusually high pitched for a woman her age, but even shriller in the mornings. It was always difficult to differentiate the anger in her voice over the southern charm she had developed growing up in Carolina. I was happy to have a pillow to muffle the sound. She was a good mom, but found her way under my skin at times, always demanding perfection.

I had a tendency to stay up too late and it never worked well when rising with the sun. I much preferred the comfort and warmth of my down comforter to the ice-cold temperatures dad kept the house at. None the less, I knew it was time to get up, so I drug myself out of bed with a cotton blanket wrapped around my body. I looked in the mirror and wiped the curly, brown hair from my eyes as I rubbed the sleep from the corners. I ran my fingers through my hair, but it was knotted and needed combed. The whiskers on my face offered proof that I had not shaved for days and the rings under my eyes said something about the amount of sleep I had been getting; they were so dark that I almost looked like the raccoons that dug through our trash almost daily.

My room was large and spacious, but every corner was usually filled with clutter; I could never find the time to clean it up. My blinds were always pulled and KSU blankets covered the windows to keep light out, against my mother's wishes. I almost tripped on a pair of denim jeans that were strewn across the floor as I made my way to the door, catching myself on the dresser as I fell forward. Half empty bottles of sports drinks, water and an open bag of chips cluttered the top of my dresser. I opened the bedroom door and a ray of sunlight momentarily blinded me. I quickly shaded my eyes until they could adjust. I had asked dad to tint the windows for years, but he insisted the sun warmed the house and brought nature's brilliance in. The only thing that came from the outdoors I wanted to see that early in the morning was the bacon on my plate.

Our home is large, six bedrooms, and the perfect mix between a southern plantation and an old Victorian home. It is white, with red shutters. Brick pillars support a large balcony that overhangs the porch. There are three bedrooms on the second floor and a family room that overlooks the first floor. My room is at the end of the hall, on the right. I made my way across the hallway and down the spiral staircase to the living room.

Frying butter and the sweet, warm scent of fluffy pancakes filled the air. My stomach growled and my mouth salivated to the smell of sausage caramelizing on the griddle. I quickly closed the blinds on the six large windows that allowed the morning sun in and made my way into the kitchen. I sat down at the breakfast table to a large country breakfast: scrambled eggs with cheddar cheese, browned sausage links and hash browns, pancakes with apple marmalade, toast with melted strawberry jam and butter and, of course, chocolate milk. As often as Mom and I disagreed, there was no denying that she was a fabulous cook. Her mother taught her everything she knew about southern cooking and I was sure my arteries would be clogged by thirty.

As I stuffed my face I looked out onto the patio and dozed off, watching the horses play in the pasture; they seemed so free, wallowing in the grass and trotting around. There were many mornings I wished to trade places with the horses; to break out in stride through the pasture, towards the morning sun. Dodge

5

put his head up to Jasper, as if to give her a morning kiss and Dorado chased Thunder off into the valley.

Startling me, mom snuck up behind "Eat all that you can, you're going to need all your energy today," as she piled a second helping of eggs on my plate and kissed my forehead. I shoveled them into my mouth along with a few pieces of sausage.

I tilted back in my chair and gulped down half the glass of milk. "Where is dad?" I asked, already knowing the answer.

She looked over at me and put on her best fake smile, which was more of a smirk, "He went in early to work. He apologized for not being here this morning, but promised to be there tonight." I wasn't ever surprised not to see him at breakfast; he was rarely around. He usually left for work around six and did not make it home until after the sun set. However, he always made it a point to make it to my games and never missed church when we went. The only time he and I spent together those days was mending the fences and our annual fishing trip.

I finished some hash browns and half a pancake, as mom started on the dishes. She was a clean freak and had a thing about getting the dishes done before she ever sat down to eat. Often, Dad and I started without her on Sunday. An overly full sensation crept up on me and reminded me of how I felt those mornings we enjoyed the brunch buffet at Miss Mayfield's. It was a good thing I was in the comfort of flannel pajama pants rather than tight slacks. I got up and grabbed the rest of my milk to bring upstairs with me. About halfway up the stairs, mom shouted "Get some clothes on; Katie is on her way over."

Katie and I grew up next door to each other our entire lives. We got in plenty of trouble as children, messing with the neighbor's cows and running off to the creek for a swim. As we grew older we spent time cramming for tests, fishing and riding the horses. I was half asleep when I invited her over the night before and I had completely forgotten, but could not wait to see her.

Katie is funny and random; I cannot count the times we played in rain puddles together, skipped class to swim in the pond and all the silly notes she left on my car. Perhaps those traits contribute to her success as a cheerleader at Brooks; at the time she was a freshman on the varsity squad. We did almost everything together and my parents loved her like she was their own. I ran upstairs and sat the milk on my dresser with the rest of the mess; I was sure that if I took one more drink I would vomit.

By the time I heard the front door open I already had my boots and jeans on. I could hear Katie talking to my mom downstairs, the two of them giggling about something. I grabbed my cowboy hat and crept down the stairs quietly. Hoping to surprise her, I tiptoed my way to the kitchen only to hear from behind me "Hey handsome, who you looking for?" She giggled as I picked her up and spun her around. She was petite but toned; easy to lift into the air.

She looked gorgeous as always, the perfect mix of class and country. She had on a pair of tight, worn jeans and a belt buckle with plenty of green rhinestones to match her eyes. Two French braids met in the back and her curly, brown hair hung on her shoulders. I grabbed her hand and pulled her behind me as I asked "ready to ride?"

She grinned and her dimples grew deep "Always!"

I led her out the back door and down the dirt path to our stables, which are large and red with enough room for 12 horses. We had never had more than eight until Jasper gave birth to our first colt last May; Dad and I were up all night by her side. At one point, she had lost so much blood we thought we might lose her, but she pulled through. Katie grabbed Dorado and I Dodge, named after Kansas towns that existed since the days of the Wild West; both Tennessee Walkers with a fast gate and a smooth ride. Dorado is brown with white on his hooves and snout and Dodge is all black.

Katie was short enough that I had to boost her onto Dorado's back. I put my hands under one foot and boosted her up as she swung the other foot over his back "Up you go smalls."

She laughed "You know, I remember when we were young and your daddy had to help you onto that horse too. He'd put me on right behind you and caution us to ride slow. He always looked so worried as he watched you kick your heals into the horses side and ride off with me."

I laughed too "Yah! He was never worried about me, just what your daddy would do to me if I ever let you get hurt." Katie was definitely a daddy's girl and no boy was taking her out without shaking his hand first. Her dad was a kind man, but he was sure to let you know what would be coming to you if you let anything happen to his baby.

We led the horses out the back fence and rode them bareback into the pasture. Our land sits on 380 acres. Two hundred acres of pasture leads into a large valley, densely planted with trees, followed by rolling, rocky hills that overlook everything that is ours. The land has been passed from generation to generation, like a family heirloom.

The crisp November air blew through Katie's hair as we rode across the hard ground. The sound of the horses hooves reminded me of lessons in history class; stories of a time when men rode this way for the adventure of a new start. I always felt free when I rode, like I was outpacing the chaos and ugliness of the world.

As we left the pasture and headed into the valley, tall cottonwoods and red maples grew more numerous. We neared Chisholm Creek, the shallow water we played in often as kids while looking for lost arrowheads and dinosaur bones. The water ran murky after heavy rains, but its stony bottom was normally visible. There weren't many fish, but we did see an occasional box turtle or snake and swarms of minnows. We took an old wooden bridge, covered in moss and vines, across the creek and past an abandoned cottage. The old building was the home of a groundskeeper that did work for my great grandfather, but it became our childhood fort. Katie and I still visited the fort occasionally when we skipped class or stayed out late.

Old, abandoned farm homes are a mainstay on the Kansas countryside. Many are engulfed with vines or missing shutters or roofs, blown off by the constant wind and stray twisters. As the land sloped up, the trees began to thin out again. The leaves and vines that covered the ground quickly traded place with a grassy hillside, spotted with limestone rock. We took the dirt path to the top of the hill, avoiding the stone.

At the top of the hill there's an old hammock, nestled between two trees that my father planted when he was young. Close enough to the hammock to feel its warmth was a fire pit that Katie and I built out of limestone rocks; a pile of wood lay nearby, that we had gathered from the valley. I quickly got a fire going to take the nip out of the cold air. Katie took the horses to another set of trees and tied them up; they chewed on the prairie grass and eventually lied down for a short nap. Yes, before you ask, horses do occasionally lie down for a nap or just to sun bathe.

I crawled in the hammock and Katie joined me. She curled up next to me and rested her head on my chest, looking down on the land. The air was quiet and peaceful; the only sound was the wind rustling through the dead leaves on the trees. Katie looked up at me and into my eyes, grinned, and asked me a question that startled me "Why do you suppose we have never been more than friends?" It was a question I had thought of many times, but had never expected to answer.

I looked down into her eyes; I had always wanted green

eyes but was stuck with brown like ninety percent of the rest of the world. There was so much about her that I loved; things that normal people don't notice. I loved her smile and her deep dimples. I loved her freckles; my mom always called them angel kisses. I loved that she never wore enough makeup to cover them up. I loved how free she was, like a wild mustang blazing her own path. I loved her kind heart and how sweet she was to everyone. I loved how funny she was and how she always giggled so loud. Still, I did not know how to answer her question.

I nervously chuckled and smiled and then gave her the best answer I could "Katie, you're my best friend; you have always been there for me when the times are tough. I love so much about you, but what I love the most is that I can always turn to you for anything. It is not that I could not see us being something more, it's just, I am afraid of losing that, of losing this."

She looked up at me and smiled. As she pulled me in closer, I wondered if I had said the right things. I laid my head softly against hers and closed my eyes. I remembered a time in grade school when she was chasing me around on the playground. I ran to hide from her under a wooden jungle gym set, but she found me and kissed me on the cheek. She ran off giggling with her friends and the boys teased me all day about having cooties. I acted disgusted by it, but even then a part of me wanted to run up and grab her hands and kiss her back.

We lay on that hillside until the fire burned out without many more words. Her hand in mine let me know that we were ok. Once we got home, mom and Katie spent most of the rest of the afternoon making "Puppy Chow" and cookies for the team. I relaxed and called up a few teammates to give them pep talks and snuck a few treats while Katie and Mom weren't looking.

Luckily, 4A state was played in Havenbrook for the last two years and would be for the next three, so the commute from our house to the stadium was not far. Mom left early to get a good seat, while Katie and I left about an hour before the game. We both had our black and red uniforms on and were ready to go. A red bow held back Katie's curly hair and the glitter on her face matched the silver stars on her uniform. The black under my eyes matched my jersey, and the crimson red seven on my back matched my pants. We were cute and tough, that year's homecoming king and queen.

By the time we got to the stadium we were pumped up. Our heads bobbed up and down as we belted out the lyrics to an old Bon Jovi song "It's my life, It's now or never, I ain't gonna live forever, I just want to live while I'm alive..." She always had a way of picking out the right songs and this was no exception. It was one of the biggest nights of my life and it felt like it was "now or never." We beat our fist on the dashboard and Katie laughed out loud as I reached over and tickled her. She reached over and tried tickling me, but I did my best to hold it in. "Not fair!" she pouted.

It was about forty-five minutes until kickoff when we pulled up; the parking lot and stadium were full. The smell of burgers and brisket on the tailgate, and the sounds of a large crowd, filled the air. We pulled into one of several spots that had been saved for athletes, near the locker room. My red F150 fit in perfectly with most of the other vehicles. Trucks are the norm in small Kansas towns like Havenbrook, where most students are the sons and daughters of farmers. Right before heading into the locker room Katie left me with a big hug "kick some butt out there Jayd, but don't let it get too boring!"

I laughed at her "I'll try hard to keep you on your toes. Cheer hard for me!"

She smacked me on the butt and hustled off to meet a group of giggling girls that had been waiting for her. I never blushed anymore; I was too used to having her around and doing things like that! Part of me knew it was her way of saying he's mine and I liked knowing it. I headed into the locker room without a worry, weightless.

The locker rooms are the only part of the stadium Mr. Tiller did not renovate. Musky, old, and rusted, the metal and sweat combine to form a foul odor that is always present. The common area is small and allows for an intimate bonding experience before games and during halftime. The cement walls and lockers always left me feeling claustrophobic when the team crowded together. The walls are covered by inspirational quotes and posters that Coach Pelosi put up. My favorite is a poster of my idol, Troy Aikman, with the Theodore Roosevelt quote "Believe you can and you're halfway there."

The common area is where I found most of the team, huddled around the office door where Bones usually spoke. He was a clean shaven man, but walked with a limp from a bad fall on the ice a few years back. After his retirement from college football he could not stay away from the game, so he became our source of inspiration. He was stern but emotional and formed a bond with every player on the team. He had a story for every circumstance: love, death, winning, loosing, overcoming and falling down. Most of his stories made us laugh, but some made us mad enough to inspire greatness. He knew how to strike a chord and touch the soul.

Moments after I had walked into the locker room, Bones walked in with coach Pelosi wearing matching red button-ups and black slacks. The outfit was an upgrade from Bones' usual polo shirt and jeans. He was clearly dressed for the big night and was ready to deliver his best speech. As he got closer to the team, I could not help but notice that his eyes and face were red and it looked like he had not shaved for days. He made his way to the center of the huddle with coach Pelosi by his side.

Everyone looked around questioning what was wrong. Tears rolled down his cheeks as he began to speak. "Not many of you know, but earlier this week I lost my only son in an automobile accident." His voice was haggard and crackling and his eyes were wet. The team gasped and scooted in closer to Bones, listening intently.

Pelosi put his arm around Bones' shoulder as he continued with a deep breath. "I'm here tonight because you boys are the only family I have left. You are my pride, my inspiration, and my legacy." He paused as he got choked up.

Breathing deeply, he tried to keep the tears from falling as he continued, "His life was taken too soon, but tonight you have the opportunity to rise above death and remember him with your play. You have this moment in time to cherish all you have accomplished and to be at your best." A smirk came across his face and his voice grew stronger. "Today, I cannot help but remember his first game and touchdown as a Buck. This rivalry goes back to his days in a red and black uniform and I know he is here watching you tonight. Go out there and play as brothers and beat some Eagle ass. Live in the moment! These are the memories a life is made of! Go Bucks!"

The team rallied around Bones after that speech, not only in the locker room, but throughout the entire game. Hugs and tears were exchanged as he led us onto the field with a new passion for life and the game. We did not rush onto the field that night; instead, we marched onto the field behind Bones and Coach Pelosi, holding hands as teammates and as brothers. The crowd erupted with a rhythmic chant as they saw us, "Bucks, Bucks, Bucks!" I was proud to march out behind Bones after the endless hours he had spent that season teaching me about poise in the pocket and throwing the ball correctly. He knew how much it meant to me for him to be there, but I put my hand on his shoulder and let him know again "Thank you Bones!"

He just looked back at me and mustered up a smile as he put his arm around my pads and whispered in my ear "It was never me Jayden, it was you. Your determination reminds me of him. Go out there tonight and remind us all why you're in this position."

I nodded and smiled "Yes sir!"

My eyes were red and my face wet. I was anxious and my palms were sweaty. Goose bumps radiated down my core and there was a knot in my throat. I saw Katie smiling and cheering on the sidelines, but I had tuned out all the noise; I was focused. We made our way to the benches. After a short huddle, some stretching, and further encouragement from Pelosi, we were ready for the game.

The Eagles lost the coin toss and we elected to receive the ball. Hackeim Smith, our leading receiver and kick returner, brought the ball out to our 38 yard line with a few spins and a juke. At 6'3" and 235 pounds he could outrun and out power most defenders. His dreadlocks hung on his shoulders and he was almost always dressed in athletic apparel. He was known by most as the "Gentle Giant" because he looked like a beast, but was always willing to offer a helping hand.

Hackeim's parents had moved from the Ivory Coast of Africa when he was just three years old to escape civil war and to provide Hackeim and his sister with a better life; so far they had done just that. Hackeim was being recruited by several DI colleges, not just for his athletic ability in football and track, but also for his intelligence. He was so driven to have a 4.0 that he retook Geometry during the summer to replace a B grade with an A. He is not only my leading target on the field, but also a good friend off the field.

As I marched our offense onto the field, I couldn't shake a feeling I had endured my whole life. It felt as if there was some-one walking beside me, hanging over me, watching my every move. Not like big brother with a camera; it was more like a shield around me, a weight on my shoulders. I could almost hear their footsteps' next to mine, the beat of their heart. It was something I often felt when I was alone in my room or out on an evening run. Sometimes it left me scared and anxious and other times it left me feeling secure and sure of myself.

The first offensive play of the game I handed off the ball to our running back, Travis Barber, who broke free and ran twenty-seven yards before being pushed out of bounds. The next play Barber ran the ball fourteen yards which put us on the Eagle's twenty yard line. After a sloppy first down and a sack, it was third and sixteen; I looked over at Bones and called the previous play again. Then I looked over at Smith and said "Hackeim, go up and get this one for Bones!"

Hackeim signaled he had heard me with a thumb up and I knew I could put it anywhere and he would find it. The ball snapped and I could immediately see my pocket breaking down; the defense had opted for a blitz. I rolled out of the pocket, planted my feet and launched one high in the corner of the end zone. The defender was stride for stride with Smith and the safety was coming across. I saw both men go up for the ball and the defender grabbed it. Before the defender hit the ground, Smith ripped the ball from his hands, pulled it to his chest and fell into the end zone. I pumped my fist, ran to Hackeim, and jumped into his arms. We knew who the ball belonged to; Hackeim and I quickly ran it over to Bones and Hackeim hugged him "This ball, this moment, is for your son!" Bones smiled, raised the ball in the air and the crowd roared.

Our defense held the Eagles to three-and-out on their first possession and only allowed three third down conversions in the first half. I tossed two more touchdowns, one to Smith and one to our tight end Bobby Hays. Barber ran the ball into the end zone to end the first half 28-0. We had played hard all season, but it was clear this game meant more to the team.

Back in the locker room everyone celebrated and prepared

themselves for the second half, but I could not help but let my mind wander as Pelosi tried to keep the team focused. I remembered what Bones had said about living in the moment and thought of Katie. I thought of everything she meant to me and of a life with her; it made me smile! I made my mind up that I would ask her to be my girlfriend that night. As the end of half time approached and we made our way back onto the field, the feeling of a presence with me intensified. It was stronger than I had ever felt, almost suffocating. For as surrounded as I felt, a feeling of isolation from the team and crowd intensified. It was like I was standing apart from the team, watching the game from the sidelines.

I looked over to Katie and tried to focus. As I ran by her I grabbed her arm "I have something to tell you after the game!" She giggled "What silly?" I smirked at her and continued down the sideline as she put on her best puppy dog face.

The Eagles got the ball to start the second half, but our defense made sure they were not on the field long. After six plays and a punt return, I led our offense back onto the field and we started the drive at our 35 yard line. We quickly drove the ball down to the Eagle's fifteen yard line, but on third and goal my night began to take a wild turn.

I took the snap and dropped back in the pocket; as I planted my feet to make the pass, all the sounds around me grew silent and my vision became blurry. Within moments my vision cleared, but I noticed something odd. I could not make it out very well, but among my teammates was a man in the end zone. I closed my eyes and opened them back up; he was still there. He wore a robe, lustrous and white. I could not make out his face, but his hair was long and gray, as was his beard. What was he doing on the field? Had a distraught fan from the audience made his way into the end zone? I dropped the ball to my side and looked around to see what was going on, only to notice that the world around me had slowed to a halt, except for the man in white who was walking toward me. I closed my eyes and shook my head. As I opened my eyes, I was slammed to the ground and the ball popped loose; an Eagle's defender swiped it up and brought it 85 yards for the score.

Hackeim pulled me up from the field and we walked to the sidelines. He was by my side stride for stride as I grabbed the back of my head "Dude, what was going on out there? You just stood there and took the hit. I was wide open. You ok?"

I just nodded "I'm fine, sorry man!" I took my helmet off and grabbed a cup of water and splashed it on my face. I closed my eyes and ran my fingers over them. Who was the man in white? It had all seemed so real. In fact, it seemed like it was only him and I on the field at all.

As special teams took the field, coach came over to see if I was ok and what had happened. "What was that Foster? You ok? You took quite a hit. Why don't you sit out for a bit? Sam can take a few snaps."

"No, no, I am fine. It was just an accident!" I assured him. I could not let Sam on the field after a momentum shift like that; he had not taken a snap with the first team all year. The defense would surely pick him apart.

"Just one series!" he promised, as he signaled Sam to get ready. I shook my head and covered my mouth to keep from saying anything disrespectful. I was furious and scared to lose the lead I had built, but I couldn't blame coach, my ears were ringing and my mind was foggy.

I could not tell them what I had seen. They would call me crazy and sideline me for the rest of the game. As I sat there thoughts ran through my head. What was wrong with me? Why could I not shake the feeling that someone was watching me? Who was the man on the field? Surely, he was not real. I must have been hit hard and imagined the whole thing.

I was anxious to redeem myself, but also shaken and nervous. I could feel the blood pulsing through my neck and legs and could hear my heart beating in my chest. I looked up to see an Eagles receiver come down with the ball in the end zone.

I jumped up from my seat "Damn it! Coach, I'm going back in as soon as we get the ball back!" I was not going to talk about it. As I saw it, it was my season and my team. I picked up my helmet and put it on and stood there with my arms crossed. I hadn't meant any disrespect, but the look in coach's eyes told me what he thought; I was being a poor leader. I looked to my right "Sorry coach! It's just, I practiced for this moment all year and now I got to go out there and win!"

I had provided the Eagles with a glimmer of hope and it had inspired them. They took advantage of me being out and now I had to make it right. The score was 28-14 with 1:05 left in the third quarter; too much time was still on the clock. The Eagles kicked the ball off and Hackeim had an electrifying return to the Eagles fifteen yard line causing four missed tackles and breaking another! Our team was ignited as I led the offense back onto the field and two plays later Barber pounded the ball in for a touchdown. It was the end of the third quarter and the score was 35-14. I held my head high as I marched back to the sideline. I looked over to Katie and smiled and she returned the gesture.

Our defense went back into the game and played strong after a pep talk from Bones. They held the Eagles to thirty-five yards and forced a punt. The last drive had restored my confidence, but I was still shaken as I led the team onto the turf. I came out strong with three straight completions for thirty-five yards. On first and 10 from the fifty yard line I handed off to Barber who was hit behind the line for a loss of two. I had thrown to Hackeim all night so I went back to the huddle and called a deep pass for our tight end Hays. I dropped back and took the snap. I looked up and Hays was running down the field without a defender. As I stepped into the pocket and threw the ball down the field, I was smashed to the ground from my blind side.

When I opened my eyes I did not notice my teammates around me, instead the man in white loomed above me. He looked down at me with an expression of concern in his eyes. He examined me, moving his head from side to side. I noticed detail I could not see before. His skin was tan and smooth; there were no wrinkles to match the gray in his hair. His eyes where soft and blue. He appeared to be very tall. I was not anxious anymore, instead I felt secure and unafraid. He reached his hand down to help me up and I reached for him. I closed my eyes and opened them only to see coach Pelosi by my side. As quickly as the man had come, he was gone. I became more alert and as Pelosi helped me from the ground, the crowd cheered!

The last thing I could remember before the hit was throwing the ball to a wide open Hays, so I was shocked to find out the ball had been intercepted. Pelosi said I had thrown the ball into the arms of the defender covering Hays.

I angrily replied, "That's not possible, there was no defender within ten yards of Hays. I saw him streaking down the field with my own eyes." I threw my helmet on the ground and shut my mouth. I had already given him enough reason to not put me back in.

Coach looked at me concerned; "Jayden, the defender was on him the whole time. You got sacked and were out for several minutes. I'm taking you out of the game. Even more, I think we need to have the medics check you out!"

I replied "Damn it coach, I know what I saw. I'm fine!"

I walked over to Hays and threw my arms up "Bobby, what happened? It was just you man." I left my mouth open and my arms up, waiting for an answer.

He just looked at me with a concerned look and smirked

"You ok Foster?" He stood up and offered me his seat, but I walked down to the end of the bleacher and sat by myself.

What was going on with me? It was too much to have seen the same man twice. Why did no one understand? Why could no one else see what I saw? Maybe coach was right, maybe I had been hit too hard earlier in the night. My head hurt and my nose was bloody! Maybe it was the stress, confusion, or the hits I had taken. I agreed with coach and my dad, who was on the sidelines by that time, to allow the medics to look me over. I wanted to talk to Sam first though, and I still wanted to talk to Katie after the game.

I walked over to Sam and pulled his helmet into my face "Sam, go out there and play with confidence, play like we practice every day. Give the ball to Barber and pass only if you have to. We have a nice lead; you just need to control the clock and prevent turnovers." With the few words of advice, I patted him on the shoulders and turned my attention to the field.

The medics checked my eyes and reflexes as the Eagles marched the ball down the field and scored a touchdown to bring the score to 35-21. The touchdown brought a grimace to my face; more points because of me. They attempted the onside kick, with only 2:30 remaining in the fourth quarter, but our special teams recovered. Sam went in to finish the game. A few runs and a quarterback kneel and it was over. It was not as exciting a finish as it could have been, but the students rushed the field anyway.

A reporter from the local newspaper met me on the field for an interview as the medics cleared me, but I declined. I even sidestepped my mom as she stepped in front of me. I felt nauseous and I wanted to find Katie. I noticed her on the sidelines, talking with her parents and looking over at me with a smile. I ran over to her and she jumped into my arms!

My head got light and everything was spinning. The nausea

turned to pain in my chest and everything got blurry. I tried to say her name but the words would not come. I heard her ask "Jayden, are you ok," but I could not respond. I felt the weight of my body fall to the ground, but I was still standing. What was happening to me? Was I dying? I was confused, but my pain and anxiety were replaced with a calm comfort that surrounded me like a warm blanket on a cold night. My vision cleared and I felt rejuvenated.

I turned around only to see what I already expected, the man in white standing in the distance. We stood for a moment just looking at one another. I began to walk towards him and he opened his arms wide. I had to know who he was; I had to get to him before he disappeared again. As he spread his arms, something very strange began to happen; a small light that radiated from behind him began to grow and transform into something new. I stopped walking and stood still. From all directions, it was as if the particles that composed this world broke apart to build another. They raced past me as beams of light, at first slow but then faster and faster. Color filled the air and everything old turned new. A new horizon of orange, red and pink formed and the heavens could be seen in the middle of the day. The things and people I had known my whole life dissolved to build something beautifully brilliant. In the center of it all, the strange man remained.

Towers and steeples emerged from the ground to form a great palace that towered above everything. Its walls, so white that the sun glistened off them like the sand on the beach. There were more windows than one could count and golden balconies adorned every steeple. There was no gate to protect the castle walls and wild animals roamed free in the pasture. The most beautiful lions, tigers and horses one had ever seen, all living in harmony. There were also many beasts I had never seen before, all beautiful and different. The one I remember most resembled a horse that was as strong as a grizzly bear, with a coat as long and white as a polar bear. He had small antlers that grew from the back of his head and he was able to stand on his hind legs.

On both sides of the castle was a body of water so clear that one could see the large creatures that inhabited it. White sand and sea shells glimmered from the beach. The trees were sparse, but enormous; the leaves were bigger than my head and the most brilliant shades of crimson red and dark orange. The pastures were deep green and flowing and the trees swayed, but there was no wind. Everything was alive and had a motion to it. There were no billboards or flashing lights to cause distraction. No cars, or horns, or stoplights. It was a mesmerizing and peaceful place as far as one could see, but the horizon had a darkness to it that made me question what was beyond the light.

As the last of what I called home vanished, the man began to walk towards me. I looked to my left, and then slower to my right, and gasped in awe. Standing among me where hundreds of others just as mesmerized as I. Some were young, but most were about the same age as me. They were of different ethnicities and races; people from around the world. I did not recognize any of them, but I felt at ease with them all. No one spoke; everyone just looked on to the man in white who was now within fifteen feet of us. As he made an effort to make eye contact with all of us, one could not help but feel a connection to him. He smiled and spoke the first words I had heard from him all night, "Welcome home Leonoids, welcome to Leotus!"

CHAPTER TWO

A New Home

THE MAN CONTINUED to talk, but it was hard to pay attention to everything he said. Everything was so new; there were so many things I had never seen before. Trying to listen to him was like trying to listen to my parents the very first time they brought me to the toy store. I was torn between a desire to know who he was and the distracting beauty of the land in front of me. I looked him in the eyes and tried to focus as he continued.

"I know that all of you are excited, nervous and confused and that you have many questions. After dinner there will be a celebration and I will try to answer some of your questions; it will take time to answer others. For now, know that you are safe and that you may call this place Pax Leotus or home."

His tone was strong but calming. He spoke clearly and confidently and joy resonated in his voice. He did not make hand gestures or pace back and forth. He spoke only through his eye contact and words. "Take some time to explore Leotus and to get to know one another, but do not stray too far from the castle. I must warn you that in the darkness your imagination might stir the things that nightmares are made of. If you have any questions there are many among you, in white, who are able to answer them. Dinner will be served at six-thirty in the dining hall; the chef has prepared something special! Lastly, if an emergency should arise, and you should need something from me, I can be found in the headmasters' suite. My name is Alcaeus." With that, he turned his back to us and headed up the road towards the castle.

I looked around and noticed others begin to wander aimlessly, like rats in a maze. There was not the type of chaos one would expect in such a situation; instead a strange cheerfulness seemed to have overcome most everyone but me. Fear and anxiety were replaced with a joy so resonating that most could not help but belt out in laughter. Some set out on their own and others gathered in groups and spoke of their experiences and how they got to Leotus. They talked of where they were from and what they were doing in those final moments. Strangely, everyone could understand one another.

I had always been shy around new people so I decided to set out on my own. Besides, I did not want to end up in a group of babbling fools. I did not know where I was heading, but I began to walk briskly away from the group when the beautiful blue water caught my eye. I had only seen the ocean in pictures, but the beach was close to the castle and I had always wanted to feel the sand between my toes. I headed in that direction, but quickly came to a standstill as I felt something tugging at my pants.

I looked down to see a young girl at my side. She must not have been much older than five or six and was short, a little taller than three feet. She had light red hair, in pony tails, which hung slightly below her shoulders. A face full of freckles made her fair skin appear tan and her light blue eyes sparkled with a joy for life. Her dimples made me think of Katie for a moment.

Was Katie at the game, crying over my dead body, or was all of this a dream? Was she there to comfort my parents? Was she wondering what I wanted to say to her? I should have told her how I felt about her at half time. I should have told her years ago!

My thoughts were quickly interrupted "Hey mister!" Her voice was soft but her face was filled with expression as she squinted her nose and eyes, demanding attention. I could tell from her accent that she was from Ireland. Every year, at Brooks, we had a few exchange students from that country.

I knelt "What's wrong?"

"This is desperate! Do you know where we are? Are we dead? Am I going to see my ma again?" She asked with a trembling concern in her voice. The first thing I noticed was that she had not been overtaken by the babbling laughter that surrounded us.

They were all questions I had too and I did not know how to answer her. Luckily, before I had to, a girl about my age came running towards us screaming "Chloe, Chloe!"

She grabbed the little girl with tears in her eyes and pulled her in close. "Why did you scatter? I thought that I had lost you. You need to stay near me; this place is jammed with plikes. It was awfully thick of you Chloe. We don't even know where we are or what is going on. For all you know he could be a mentallar!" Her hands shook and I could tell she feared for the child and our circumstance.

"A mentallar?" I asked, with what must have been a puzzled look on my face. I had never heard the slang from any of the Irish kids I had gone to school with.

"Cop on, Caiohme! I'm fine! Don't go off your nut" she exclaimed as she let out a sigh and then a slight giggle.

The little girl then looked up at me and smiled "She was just saying you could be crazy, like everyone else here."

Crazy, I thought; at least I was not the only one wondering if I had fallen off the rocker. I figured the two must have been sisters the way they argued. They shared many of the same traits and were close enough in age. The older girl, Caiohme, had darker hair that was closer to brown than red. A nice tan accented her light blue eyes and white teeth. She had fewer freckles than Chloe, but the two shared the same dimples. She looked up and our eyes met. She was beautiful and there was an immediate attraction. We stared at each other for a moment and I felt that I could see much about her in her eyes.

She smiled. I smiled back and for the first time she spoke to me "I am sorry if she was bugging you or throwing shapes. It's just, we don't know where we are and we are both scared. One moment we were at her dance recital and the next we are here. Everyone seems to be off their nut, except us. I was actually beginning to wonder if I was the crazy one or if they're just all polluted. Her name is Chloe and I am Caiohme. We are from a village outside of Dublin; Dalkey. What is your name? Where are you from?"

I didn't understand the expression, but I joked anyways "Well she has not been throwing circles or squares at me."

Both the girls laughed and it helped take the edge off the tension as Caiohme explained "It means showing off, something she is quite good at!"

I shrugged "She's fine. I'm just as frightened as she is and these people are only making it worse. I don't know whether to laugh at them or run from them. My name is Jayden. I'm from a little town in Kansas." I looked behind me and saw others approaching "Maybe we should distance ourselves from the others, head to the beach?"

Before Caiohme could even reply Chloe grabbed my hand and started pulling me "Yes, yes, please! Let's get away from them!" She was not shy and it seemed she had taken up a liking for me already. Crazy or not, Caiohme seemed to agree as we all took the next steps together.

We walked north, towards the castle, on the same road that Alcaeus had taken. Instead of street lights, the road was lined by black poles with hanging lanterns, each lit by fireflies that glowed even in the daylight. The road was surrounded by pasture and wild flowers of the oddest colors; cerulean, neon fuchsia, cinnabar, persimmon, cyan, deep carmine pink, guppy green. Occasionally, a wild beast grazed near us and frightened Chloe enough for her to hide behind me, but she was quick to come around.

Chloe had so many questions that Caiohme and I barely spoke. "Where is Kansas? What is it like? Do you miss it already? Why do you think we're here? Do you have a girlfriend? If not, neither does Caiohme. A boyfriend I mean."

Caiohme giggled in embarrassment; so did I. I looked over to see her blushing. She grabbed Chloe and wrestled her to the ground, tickling her "Stop twistin' hay Chloe; you're making my cheeks scarlet!"

They both laughed so hard that I forgot I was in a strange land for a moment. I took in a deep breath of the fresh air and the deep floral scents wafted through my sinuses. The sweet scent relaxed the tension in my neck and shoulders and made me hungry for farmer John's honey, which I always used to sweeten my lattes at Miss Mayfield's. The echo of a strange beasts' roar startled me, reminding us to be cautious in this strange new land. I looked around, but saw nothing to stoke my fear.

As we got back on the path, I told the girls stories of Havenbrook, the prairie, and the Wizard of Oz. I told them about Kansas twisters and the Wild West. We talked about sunflowers, how I play for the Bucks and Miss Mayfield's ice cream. I told them about my family, the horses and how I was an only child. Chloe asked if it was lonely and I told her of Katie and how she was always around.

"Oh, so you did leave somebody special behind?" Caiohme

laughed, but I could tell that she was curious to know more by the way she continued to look at me for an answer.

"Yah, she was my best friend." I smiled.

"Oh!" She replied with skepticism.

Things were awkwardly silent after that, but I wasn't ready to tell a stranger all the things I was just figuring out for myself. I felt at ease with the girls, but for all I knew they could have known more than they were telling me; they could have been the reason I was there. I knew that I needed to be careful, even around them.

The walk was longer than I had expected. The vast size of the castle made everything seem much closer than it was. As we approached the castle walls, we came upon a town square and housing that we had not noticed from a distance. I let Chloe down from my shoulders; about half a mile back she pouted on the ground and refused to go any further without a piggy back ride. She had grown increasingly hungry, tired and fussy.

The square was surrounded by a semi-circle of homes on the north and south ends with the east and west ends exposed. Behind each semi-circle lay a smaller semi-circle and a smaller one behind that. The layout formed somewhat of a diamond shape with the fronts of the homes facing the square. Everything seemed to have a sameness and order to it.

The homes were all similar in architecture; small, with the entry way as a focal point and no garage. Come to think of it, at that time I had not seen a single car in Leotus. The walls were rustic red with wood shake roofs. The clay walls gave the homes an earthy texture that fit in well with the gardens that surrounded them. Large windows, without screens, cranked open to allow fresh air in. The beautiful lawns and gardens did not stop at the homes' walls. Many homes had vines growing up them that produced the most vibrant purple and orange flowers.

The town seemed to embrace nature, incorporating it in their homes, rather than tearing it down to build.

As I looked over to see what Chloe and Caiohme thought of the homes, I noticed they were not by my side. My stomach shifted, as I looked around frantically for the only people I had met in Leotus up to that point. I looked past them once, but on a second sweep I noticed the two of them walking toward the town square. I snuck up behind Caiohme and grabbed her shoulders. She jumped as she turned around.

I laughed "Had enough of me already?"

She looked at me with a dirty stare that said she wasn't amused. Then, she laughed and stuck out her tongue "Haha, got ya! I saw people, and the food smells so good. I'm starving!"

"So am I" Chloe whined.

I agreed with them; the food did smell good. "Let's see what it takes to get a bite to eat around here."

The square was filled with vendors. Some sold clothing and blankets, some food, others jewelry and accessories. Many sold the white garments that all the locals wore, but there were also garments and blankets that were bold and colorful. There was art, and food, and music. The locals danced, ate, and sang, as if there were a festival occurring. They all seemed happy and carefree, but like the homes, there was a certain sameness and order to everything they did. They danced the same, laughed the same, and talked the same. As we passed them, they noticed us and smiled and waved, as if we had been neighbors our whole lives. Some stared and others whispered; I would have felt uncomfortable had they not all seemed happy to see us.

As Caiohme and Chloe looked for a place to eat, I browsed the other vendors. I came upon a garment of dark red, orange and yellow material all woven together. It had a texture much like wool, but was a lot softer and resembled a hoodie or poncho.

I had seen similar clothing on a mission trip to Mexico and I wanted it.

I approached the woman that ran the stand "How much for this item?"

"For you, child, it is free." Her dark eyes opened wide and her smile grew. Her white gown brought out the green specs in her brown eyes. She seemed excited and surprised to see me, to speak with me, but her excitement quickly grew to a fearful awareness as she looked from side to side to see who had noticed our conversation. Something odd was going on in town between the locals, and I was sure she had a part in it.

"What, why is it free for me?" I asked; confused, but appreciative of her generosity.

She grabbed my hand, looked me in the eyes and pulled me close. I pulled back some, as she spoke quickly with a soft tone, "We have waited for your arrival for too long. You children bring us hope again. I pray you will do much for Leotus and the Leonoids, so it is the least I can do for you. You are our guests, the children of Leotus. Don't forget the people as you learn why you are here. I cannot say much more than that. Please, take the garment and be on your way."

Her answer only caused my mind to stir. My insecurity grew as questions blossomed in my mind "What do you mean we will do much for Leotus? Where are we and what are we here for?" I raised my voice in anger and frustration.

As others took notice of the commotion I caused, she grew more frightened to be seen talking with me. She walked away from me, to another table in the opposite direction, and began folding garments. She did not face me or reply to my questions. It enraged me in a way I had never experienced. I walked over to the table and squatted in front of it so that I could see her eyes.

"I need a better answer. I need to know what's going on. Why will you not tell me anything? There are people at home that care about me!" I asked slower and louder than before, emphasizing every word.

"Just leave me, you have no idea the danger you are putting me in, the consequences I will face if I tell you anymore. Your answers are coming, but they cannot come from me. I can tell you, there are people here who care for you as well Jayden, and soon you will see that your purpose here is great" she whispered.

She stepped back from me. Her hand shook nervously and she tapped her foot against the ground. I could see the fear in her eyes. Why was she afraid? What did she know? Maybe it was more than she could tell me, but I was not one of those laughing fools, I needed to know what danger I was in. I grabbed the corner of the table, but before I could do something I would have regretted Chloe came up from behind me.

"Jayden, we got lunch. Come have a picnic with us; it's so good!" I could not show my anger in front of her, and I didn't know what would happen to us if the situation escalated.

I grabbed Chloe's hand and lowered my tone "Oh yah, what did you get for me?"

I didn't listen to the answer. I was distracted by a concerned man that approached the woman. He was shaking his head and covering his eyes, as he whispered something in her ear. He knew something too, something I was sure he would not share with me. I was a prisoner, without knowledge of my whereabouts or sentence. I was hostage to the information they refused to share. I looked up at them one more time, making a mental note of their location and identity. I would visit them again, without the girls; I was sure they had the answers I needed to free myself, to get home to Katie.

I looked back into her eyes as Chloe led me away; the man embraced her as they saw me off. I was reminded of her initial generosity when the colorful poncho fell from my shoulder and I had to bend over to pick it up. As I grasped the soft garment in my hand, I found myself momentarily torn between the shame of striking fear in such a kind individual and the anger of my circumstance.

Chloe pulled me towards the center of the square, where Caiohme was sitting near a fountain. The sun radiated off her, forming a halo around her head. I starred at her, forgetting all the reasons for my anger and shame. For the first time that day, I felt nervous that I might say something wrong or that it might all just be a dream. She made me want it to be real. I quickly found myself fighting those feelings. How could I think of her like that when Katie was probably mourning my loss? It was wrong. No more, I told myself. Still, I could not help but smile at her as we approached.

"Thanks for getting me food and for coming with me today." I said kindly.

She shaded her eyes from the sun as she looked up at me "Nah, don't say thanks. I'm glad to have you around. Should bad turn to worse, at least I have a fella with me. Now sit down and eat before I gain ten pounds." She laughed.

I was thankful to have the two of them by my side as well. It was nice to be around sane people when everyone else seemed so mindless. Chloe made me laugh and relax in the middle of all the hysteria. They were both optimistic, finding ways to look at the situation and make it seem better than it was. Both the girls had found a way to relax and enjoy the food and music, while all I could do was find more things to question.

Why had Alcaeus brought us to Leotus and left us to find our own way in a strange town? What was expected of us? Why did all the locals look at us like they recognized us? Why had we not caught a case of the giggles like all the others?

As I sat down I noticed that Caiohme was sitting on a blanket made of the same material as the poncho, only it was every shade of blue I had ever known. There were several fruits strewn across the fabric that I had never seen, along with sandwiches and bottled drinks. She handed me a piece of fruit that had been cut in half "Try it, it's rapid!"

I had no idea what she meant by "rapid," but I was too hungry to question her slang. I took it in my hand. Its' skin was soft, but it was covered with blunted spikes. It was bright yellow and about the size of a grapefruit. Its flesh was red and firm. I cautiously examined it for a minute. I was nervous to eat it; what if it was poisoned?

"Just take a bite you big sap," chimed Caiohme with a giggle. Chloe giggled too. They both seemed relaxed and easily amused. I worried they were coming down with the same hysteria that had affected the others, but maybe a good laugh was what I needed. An escape from the chaos seemed inviting. I dug a piece out with the spoon and shoved it in my mouth.

I closed my lips around the fruit and it slowly melted on my tongue like cotton candy. The fruit overwhelmed my senses and the smell took me back to a peaceful place; the horse and I, riding through the prairie flowers on a warm Kansas day; the air, so sweet and pure. One bite left me craving another until I had eaten the whole half of it. It left me feeling rejuvenated, satisfied, overwhelmingly happy and then relaxed. It made me laugh and laugh. The relaxation began as a weightless feeling, a sense of carelessness, a thoughtless void. The relaxation grew progressively until Chloe's eyelids drooped and she finally passed out.

Chloe curled up in a ball with her hands under her head. It was the most peaceful she had been all day. Caiohme was lying on her back, hands under her head, with her face to the sky. I lay down beside her and stared up to the heavens "What was that you gave me? I think it was poisoned! Where did you get it?" I asked.

"Isn't it great?" she smiled slowly. "I got it from one of the venders, he called it Lucula. He gave me an entire basket of food for free and another vendor gave me the blanket. They are good people."

She was quiet for a moment. The fruit seemed to slow down her thought process "He said something about being anxious, thankful that we are here."

The thought didn't quite register at first, but it eventually caught my attention. I grabbed the hoodie that was lying beside me and showed it to her. "A woman gave me this for free too. She said something about us bringing hope and doing much for Leotus. I questioned her, but she wouldn't answer me. She knew something, but she was afraid to tell me. She knows why we are here."

She pondered it all for a moment, wiping the hair from her face "I am sure, whatever the reason, Alcaeus will explain it all tonight and we'll be back home soon."

She seemed content with the lack of explanation and the fruit began to leave me in the same state of mind. I laid back down "I suppose you're right. Why worry about the things we cannot change; Might as well enjoy the free food and gifts while we can!"

As we lay there, I forgot about everything that was going on around us. The music calmed me, each note dancing through the wind like a melody from a song bird. Caiohme scooted closer to me and laid her head on my chest. I put my arm around her shoulder and ran my fingers across her back. I brushed the hair from her face and ran my fingers through her soft brown curls, letting myself pretend I was next to Katie.

The stars were bright and there were more than I had ever seen, even in the country sky. They were brilliant enough that not even the light of the sun could dampen their glow. A few planets were visible, shinning bright red and yellow. My hand came to rest in her curls as I began to drift away. The smell of her hair was as intoxicating as the wild flowers that grew on our land in the spring, sweet lilacs and honeysuckle. As my eyes closed, I caught a glimpse of a flaming white ball shoot across the sky, a shooting star. I breathed in deeply and fell asleep to the sweet smell of her skin, as I kissed her forehead.

Startled by footsteps near my head, I awoke to a man who had stopped in his path in front of us. My head wasn't groggy or pounding; it was sharp and quick to react. As I jolted to a sitting position I woke Caiohme. She rubbed her eyes and looked over to Chloe who was still asleep. We both looked up at the man as he looked down at us with a smile. For a moment there was an awkward silence. His hair was brown and his skin was fairly light. His teeth were very white and straight. He did not have any facial hair or wrinkles and appeared to be about thirty-five. A single tear began to roll down his cheek as he spoke.

"Hello Jayden, Caiohme! I see that the two of you have already met, that is good. I came as soon as I heard the news that you had made it to the square. I had to see you with my own eyes." His voice was soft and calm and he spoke with joy, as if I was not supposed to be alarmed by the fact that he knew our names.

"Who are you? How do you know our names? Did the woman vendor send you?" I asked with suspicion. It would have been simple for him to have known that we made it to the town square; everyone seemed to take notice as we approached. What concerned me was how he had come to know our names.

He came closer but I scooted away from him. He kneeled. "None of that is important right now Jayden. I know of you the same way you know of me. Think about it. Look me in the eye and it will come to you."

He put his hands on my shoulders and looked directly at me. First I looked off in the distance, then at Caiohme. I looked up at him for a second then back down at his chest. It was awkward, looking a stranger in the eyes, who does that? I looked up at his chest, then his neck, his chin, and finally starred into his green eyes. All at once I couldn't pull my eyes away from his as my mind raced; electrical currents jumped from one synapse to another. Information flooded my brain, but I couldn't connect any of it. I pulled my chin down to my chest and covered my eyes.

I shared the same type of connection with him that I had earlier shared with Caiohme. Looking in his eyes I could see his character, I could tell he was a good man. I did not know who he was or where he had come from, but I knew his name. I whispered it, as if to inquire if I was correct "Excadeus?"

He smiled. He knew I would remember him. The question then became, how did I know him or Caiohme? How did I know any of them and how did they know me? I sat there puzzled, examining my thoughts. How did I know anything about a man that I can't recall meeting, who lives in a place I have never been? How does he know me and what does he want of me? Almost as if he could read my thoughts, he spoke again.

"The three of you, and everyone else here, have nothing to worry about. You are here because you are a part of who we are and what we will become. All of you will do great things for our people and this land. You have been treated uniquely because you are unique; you have special gifts and attributes. You must learn what is good and use them justly. I only hope that you can understand our sacrifices, when it comes time to make your own."

We both looked at him more confused than before. I could see the agitation and anger I had felt for the woman growing on Caiohme's face "What do you mean special gifts, attributes? What is all this about sacrifices? I did not ask to come here. I do not even know where here is and you talk about sacrifice. Sacrifice? What the hell am I supposed to sacrifice? I'm already without my ma. Don't think for a second I'll ever let any harm come to Chloe." Her voice was loud and angry. You could see every word on her face, as her eyebrows dropped and her nose wrinkled.

He looked her in the eyes and grabbed her hand, but she pulled it away. "Caiohme, I did not mean to scare you, only to prepare you. You have incredible talent; I only hope to have you as an ally and friend. Listen to what Alcaeus has to say tonight and make your own decisions. I would never stand in your way and I would never let anything come of Chloe either. For now, finish your trip to the beach; you are almost there. I will show you the quickest route. You will need to get to the castle soon." His gentle voice was calming and he had a way with words that left me trusting him; or maybe the Lucula hadn't quite worn off.

He reached out his hand and pulled me to my feet, then Caiohme. She knelt down and rubbed Chloe's shoulders to wake her. Rolling around with her eyes still closed, Chloe said "Ma? Ma, is that you?" Her soft voice longed for home, for the comfort of her mothers' arms. It made my heart ache for Katie, for my own family and home.

"No Chloe. It's just me, just Caiohme, but I am sure we will see her soon."

For the first time that day I saw a tear roll down Caiohme's cheek and I wondered what she was thinking. Did she really think she would go home again or did she lie to keep Chloe strong, to keep herself strong? The more I knew of her, the more I knew she would do anything to protect her little sister. Caiohme squeezed Chloe tightly, as she woke up and rose to her feet. It wasn't the type of hug one receives daily. It was the type of hug a mother gives her son when he first comes home from war, warm and tight.

Chloe smiled. "Since this wasn't all a dream, when is the celebration? I want to play games and eat candy and have fun!" We all laughed as she jumped up and down with excitement.

The reality of everything had clearly not set in for her; she was too busy enjoying the beauty and splendors of Leotus.

Caiohme took her hand and walked her over to Excadeus "Soon Chloe, very soon. This is Excadeus; he is going to walk to the beach with us." She acted excited to know him, not wanting to instill any fear in Chloe, but I could tell she felt uneasy with him around.

"Who is he?" she whispered. Caiohme pulled her close and whispered back in her ear "I don't know, but I think he is our friend! Now gather up your things."

Chloe quickly gathered some of the food and drinks and put it all in a large red bag that she must have gotten at the market. Caiohme grabbed the blanket and I grabbed my hoodie. Within minutes, we had exited the square and were back on the road towards the beach.

It was not a long walk from the square to the beach, five or ten minutes. Along the way Excadeus, or Ex as he preferred to be called, told us little more. He told us that Leotus had been there for thousands of years. He told us that it had been a peaceful place through much of its existence, but like all empires, greed and hate planted seeds that had begun to blossom. In the darkness there hid tribes and a great city, a city so corrupt and broken that its people killed for sport; he called them the Farrians. He warned us not to stray into the woods, that some had adopted cannibalism. It seemed unreal, like we were on the set of a horror movie. I wondered if he stretched the truth to keep us away from something, something they were hiding. After all, it did seem like there was a lot to be hidden.

As we got closer to the beach he pointed to a plant that grew in the sand "These are the plants that the Lucula comes from." It was knee high and bushy, with thick orange and green leaves and big pink flowers. On some of the plants, the flowers had shriveled and died and little yellow fruit had sprouted.

I laughed "We had some for lunch. It was amazing, relaxing! I could really use a couple of those plants at home."

"We have long used Lucula for its calming and rejuvenating abilities, but in concentrated doses it is a poison that is very dangerous. It can be used to force ones tongue and has put grown men in a permanent coma." Sleeping forever didn't sound so bad in the moment. Maybe I could get a few days' rest, wake up and find this all to have been a bad dream.

Ex picked up the sand and let it run through his fingers. The sand was so fine that as it fell to the ground it almost floated, like the snowflakes that fall in the calm of a storm. The grains clung to his skin and his hands glistened in the sun like glitter "The walls of our castle were built by the sands of this great sea and its' waters have fed our people for thousands of years."

We stood there and looked out onto the ocean for a while. I watched the waves lightly break on the shore, washing away the foot prints and seaweed. Chloe ran down to the water and let the waves run over her toes. Reaching down, she let it run threw her fingers. She giggled as a larger wave splashed against her calves and she ran to shore. Caiohme watched her run on the beach and splash in the water. She was soaked, but the sun would dry her quickly. Once again, Chloe had brought out the beauty of Leotus during trying times.

Caiohme smiled as she watched her "It is nice to see her happy and having fun. Everything is so beautiful that it doesn't seem real! I wish that I could be so simple minded about it all." She sat on the dune and ran her fingers through the sand.

Excadeus smiled "This is what you're here to save. Not just the people or a way of life, but a creation. To save the beauty of something so simple that it can bring peace to the heart and calm to the soul. To be part of something so untouched by man that it can reach inside of you and connect you to the bigger picture. Some fall victim to the things that these sands can build, but I have always just enjoyed the sands for the creation they are." He took a deep breath of the fresh air as he stretched in the sun. An expression of relief and satisfaction grew on his face. He seemed able to appreciate the simple things, a passion we shared.

The silence was soon broken by excited shouts down the beach "Come here guys, come here!"

Caiohme ran down to the dune and onto the beach frantically. Ex and I walked slower in her path. When she was far enough from us not to hear our conversation, Ex looked over at me with a smile "I am glad you met Caiohme. The two of you share a bond that will hold your hearts close and test your convictions."

"What do you mean?" I asked as I wiped the hair from my face and looked to him for answers.

He rubbed his eyes and moved his hand from his forehead down to his chin, where he held it as he thought for a moment. With the same delighted smile he had when he woke us, he answered "It's like the bond between a brother and sister. You both share characteristics that will allow you to understand one another in ways that others have not been able to. Your whole life you have felt as if you were not alone, like there was someone watching over you. Part of that feeling was a bit of her that has always been with you. She has felt the same presence. You don't know it and neither does she, but you have both carried a bit of one another with you your whole lives. That is why you feel like you know her even though you have just met. It's the reason you finally feel whole!" He stopped speaking about it as we approached the girls.

Caiohme lightly shoved me as I came up on her right side, "About time slowpokes! She would not even tell me what was going on until the two of you got down here. What were you fellas gossiping about?"

Ex laughed and I just smiled as we looked down at Chloe, who was holding something in her hands, close to her chest. She was giddy, jumping up and down with a huge grin on her face.

"Well, what is it then?" I asked.

She reached her hands out towards us and opened them up. "Isn't it awesome?" she squealed as she dropped it in Caiohme's hand. Caiohme flinched with a look of disgust "Ewww, its slimy!"

It was bright green, about five inches long and a little larger than the width of a nickel. It had two large black eyes, a mouth, and thick blue hair that stood a quarter inch off its body. Tiny suction cups on its bottom side allowed it to move.

"What is it?" Caiohme asked with interest.

I looked over at Ex for answers but Chloe jumped in "It's a caterpillar, of course! I was walking and looking for shells, I picked a big pink one up and she was under it. She's just different."

Ex laughed as Caiohme and I waited for his answer. He put his hand next to Caiohmes and let the creature crawl into his palm "I have not seen one of these in years! He is actually not a caterpillar Chloe, but a distant relative. He is a sea worm, or as we like to call them Weed Walkers. They can usually be found crawling and feasting on seaweed as it floats atop the water. Occasionally, one is found rummaging through weeds on the coast, but they usually stay offshore. You see, if they stay out of the water for too long they have been known to explode. It's really quite sad."

Chloe looked at him with a sad face "Awww no, let's hurry and get him back in the water!" Caiohme looked terrified, but all she had to say was "disgusting."

Ex handed the worm back to Chloe and she walked it down to the water. About the time she had said her goodbyes, and bent over to free him, the sound of a siren filled the air. For a moment, it was a buzz so soft that I thought it was a large bumble bee, but it soon turned to a roar. Chloe jumped into the air, probably thinking the poor thing had exploded in her hands.

"What is that?" I screamed as I covered my ears.

Before I had even finished the question, I turned and noticed Excadeus run down to the water and sweep Chloe into his arms. Startled, Caiohme ran towards him as he bolted back in our direction "Hey, what are you doing? What are you doing with her?"

He grabbed Caiohme's arm with a panicked look on his face and pulled her alongside "There is no time to explain, we must hurry."

The smile he had worn all day had turned to an expression of fear. There was an urgent quickness in his step as he practically drug Caiohme from behind him. The panic spread to Chloe, who had tears streaming down her cheeks. Agitation and anger worked its way back into Caiohme's expression; her cheeks bright red, as she struggled free from Excadeus' grip. She attempted to tear Chloe from his arms, but he held her tightly and kept running.

"What is going on Excadeus? Where are we going?" she pleaded with him.

I looked behind us as the sirens continued to roar and saw nothing. "What are we running from?" Still, he did not answer as we approached the castle walls.

He reached for the handle on the castle door. As he pulled at the handle, it became obvious that the door was not going to budge. It was locked, or someone held it shut from the inside. Either way, we weren't getting in. He pounded on the door repeatedly with one fist as he handed Chloe off to Caiohme. The girls were both scared, their faces red and wet with tears that streamed down their cheeks. Chloe was coughing from crying so hard and Caiohme tried to calm her. "It's ok Chloe. We are going to be ok. Aren't we Ex?"

I looked behind us as he responded "I do hope so, but we must get inside!" His whole demeanor, the way he appeared so shaken and frightened, only made things worse. His fear spread like a sickness between us.

As I looked over my shoulder again, the fear on Ex's face grew inside of me. The sky that had been beautiful all day was quickly becoming black, not by nightfall, but with a swirling cloud that approached quickly. I grabbed Caiohme, who was holding Chloe, and pulled her towards me. I doubted I could protect them from whatever approached, but I wanted to give them something to hold onto in the darkness. Chloe buried her head in Caiohme's chest and Caiohme in mine.

Ex wrapped his arms around all of us with the cloud within twenty feet "We must stay strong and hold onto one another. Do not let the darkness play tricks on your mind. Fear and manipulation are its greatest strength. Shut out the fear and you shut it out."

As it approached so did the sounds of howls, cries and grunts. The door rattled and Caiohme cried "Help us please!" Ex screamed "Let us in. It is not too late yet."

He pounded on the door again, but it was too late. Darkness, so dense that I couldn't see Caiohme standing next to me, overtook us. Caiohme's grip tightened around my fingers as howls echoed off the castle walls.

CHAPTER THREE

The Life Tree

FOR A MOMENT, the darkness grew so quiet that all I could hear was the pounding of my heart in my chest. Thump, thump, thump, it beat in faster and faster succession. Caiohme's breathing was deep and heavy on my chest. Chloe coughed and cried intermittently, but Caiohme continued to reassure her that everything would be alright while she rattled the door handle. "Chloe, it's okay sis! We will figure out a way to get in the door or we will find another way. I will not let anything happen to you!"

"You promise?" Chloe asked as she sniffled.

"I promise." Caiohme said with confidence.

It was no use, the handle was not going to give and no one was going to let us in. As she continued to rattle the handle and knock, I heard whispers that grew louder "Jayden, Caiohme, Jayden, Jayden" I grabbed Caiohme tighter and screamed "What do you want? Leave us alone!"

The voices came from all around us. They spoke faster and faster, until words could barely be made out, eventually it all just sounded like a loud buzz. I was panicked and knew we had to get inside.

"Ex, what should we do?" There was no reply. "Ex?" Nothing. Caiohme screamed "Ex, where are you?" Still, there was no reply.

Had he abandoned us to save himself? Had something gotten hold of him? Thoughts raced through my mind as something brushed strongly against me from behind, knocking me off balance "Ex?"

I jumped, released Caiohme's hand, and turned around. It was not Ex, but there was someone wandering, faintly visible in the distance, a girl. Her hair was long and her build was small. "Katie, Katie is that you? Katie?" I screamed, louder as she got closer.

I took off running towards her. She looked in my direction and I stopped in my steps. She was frightened and alone. Had she been brought here at the same time as me or was this just one of the tricks Ex had warned us about? Was she real or was it my imagination? I couldn't help myself from going after her.

I turned around as I heard Caiohme cry "Jayden! Jayden! Where are you? Please don't leave us."

I wanted to run back to Caiohme and Chloe, wrap them back up in my arms and tell them it would be all right. It was the right thing to do; I even found myself turning around to take a step back in their direction, until I heard Katie's voice "Jayden, help me. Where am I? What is this place? "

It was her; I knew that voice. I was selfish. I turned and ran towards her "Katie, Katie," but as I got closer I began to doubt what I was seeing. How could I see her when I could not see Caiohme right in front of me? How could she see me? I closed my eyes and opened them and as fast as she entered my mind she was gone.

I could no longer hear Caiohme calling for me and I was

turned around. I did not know what direction the castle was in or where I was. I panicked "Caiohme, Chloe? Ex? Caiohme?" shouting their names with my hands cupped around my mouth.

No one answered, but why would they? I had abandoned them. I had left them to fend for themselves in the darkness. I hoped they had found a way into the castle; but that would mean I was all alone. I felt awful for thinking of myself, but I did not want to be alone in the darkness. The air was heavy and foul smelling, a fog that slowly ate away at your mind. I agonized about the people I cared about as I walked with their voices filling my head.

I wandered aimlessly, hollering out for the girls, breaking to listen for a reply "Caiohme? Chloe? Caiohme?" At first I walked, but as panic grew a slow jog turned into a clumsy run. I almost tripped twice, once over something in my path and a second time over my own feet. Somehow, I managed to catch myself both times.

I was ready to collapse and hope everything would work itself out when a faint voice grew stronger and stronger in the dark silence "Jayden, Jayden, we're over here! Hurry, we found a way in!"

I began to run towards them when something hit me from behind and slammed me to the ground. My forehead bounced off the grass and it felt like a brick wall had fallen on top of me. Caiohme and Chloe had found me and I was so close to them, then all of a sudden I wasn't. I tried to lift my shoulders, but something had me pinned to the ground. It bent over me and I could feel its warm moist breath on my face. Its rough skin was like sandpaper on mine. I turned my head and closed my eyes as my body trembled. Not now, this isn't happening. I kept telling myself it was not real, trying to drift off to a different place, to the pasture.

From what I had seen, the beast was not human. Its skin

was scaly like a reptile. It had slits for eyes that glowed yellow in the darkness. Its nostrils were large and wet with mucus that dripped onto my face. The beast's lips where rough and dark.

As the beast drew closer to my face, others joined it. Their hands traced over my body and I could feel their breath on my skin as they examined me. I felt like an experiment on an alien ship, something foreign to them. I tried to lie there silently, hoping they might think they had killed me, but the tears that streamed down my cheeks soon turned to cries for mercy "Please don't hurt me. Please, I'll do anything!"

The beast that had been holding me down put his mouth to my ear and spoke with a loud and raspy voice that rattled my ear drum "So you are the one that has brought hope. You are nothing but a coward. You lie and tremble with fear in my presence, too afraid to defend yourself. Get up and fight for your people." His words were moist in my ear. I wanted to turn away from him, but I didn't dare.

He grabbed me by the shoulders with his large, rough hands and tossed me to my feet. I back peddled as I hit the grass, but I could feel the ground shake with each step he took towards me. I limped, as pain shot up my torso from my left hip. His voice, like thunder, boomed down on me "This is the one they call Jayden, the one that is to bring hope and peace. Look at him cower. Kill him. He is not one of us. He is nothing to us."

He shoved me into the air and again I hit the ground and slid across it. I laid there, curled up in the fetal position and barely able to move. My body so tired and beaten that I was void of any emotion.

I tried to crawl away, fighting for my life, but the ground shook and I fell back to my chest as they approached. It was like a stampede of rhinos and I was an injured rabbit in their path. In that moment, I thought I would die and all I could think of was the fact that I had left Caiohme and Chloe to the same fate.

In despair, I looked up and pleaded for mercy from the God I had shut out most of my life "Please God, please," but I was distracted by a flicker of light that began to grow. I watched it as the beast kicked me across the ground. Was this the end for me, the proverbial light at the end of the tunnel?

A figure approached as the light grew, like a dark spot in the sun. The light was intensely bright; all I could make out was his form. The light burned away the darkness, and his voice boomed from all directions "Leave the boy you beasts and crawl back to your forest and your caves. Tell your master he is mine and you will never take him from my side."

He spread his arms and the light burst out in all directions and then I could see him. It was Alcaeus. The heavens appeared and the stars shined bright again. I sighed in relief and let my head fall. My energy was gone and I could barely breathe.

For the first time I could see all the beasts, eight or ten of them, as they scurried away in fear. They were even bigger than I had thought, perhaps ten feet tall. They stood like humans and were strong like oxen. Their entire bodies appeared rough and leathery, covered in scales. They had tails like dinosaurs that drug across the ground with spikes that lacerated the earth. Their feet were huge and left footprints in the dirt as they walked away. They were truly the beasts of nightmares, but they ran in the presence of Alcaeus, even as other Leonoids stood back in fear.

Alcaeus knelt down beside me with tears in his eyes and picked me up. I could feel his energy pulse through my body and his heart beat in unison with my own. He ran his hand across my face and closed my eyelids. He kissed my forehead and with a whisper spoke only to me "I am sorry Jayden, you are safe now. Let me heal you. You must be strong for the others. Close your eyes and rest; you will not feel a thing."

He ran his palms across my body and I could feel the pain

leave me. It was a sensation I had never experienced, like stitching being pulled from a doll or a blanket being unwoven. The only comparison I can leave one with is the way it feels when the doctor pulls a stitch through your skin, without the pain. What they had done he undid. He pulled the darkness from me and it accumulated in his palms and traveled up his arms. His body shook as he pulled it from my body into his own and I could see the pain on his face.

The crowd of spectators grew larger and they looked on with wonder and sadness. When he had pulled all the damage and fear from me, he sat me on the ground and began to expel the darkness from his skin. It accumulated into a ball between his hands where it spun like a planet on its axis. He looked over to me and smiled as he took the ball and forced it into the ground "You are healed and one with Leotus. Your fibers are the fibers of this land."

As he removed his hands a seedling sprouted from the ground and grew several feet into a sapling. Its branches sprouted many orange and red leaves, like the giants I had seen when I first arrived in Leotus. I could feel its energy inside of me, growing and soaking up the sunlight. Just as its leaves stretched towards the sun, I too rose to my feet and stood strong in front of the crowd. They cheered.

Alcaeus stood and spoke loudly to all "This tree is the Life Tree. It knows the pain that evil can cause, but it grows with the same spirit of strength and survival that is in this boy. The tree will grow as this young man grows and its' story will be the story of our people." The crowd cheered and a feeling of energy and excitement spread through the air. I felt like a celebrity, but I knew they cheered at the amazing things Alcaeus had done, not for me.

Before I could ask about Caiohme and Chloe, they burst through the crowd and ran towards me. They fell onto me and wrapped their arms around me, almost knocking me to the ground. With a red face and a scratchy voice Caiohme looked me in the eyes "I'm so glad that you are ok. You had us scared for a while."

She hugged me tightly, putting her head on my chest; then pulled back and looked me in the face again. Her hair was a mess and her cheeks were dirty. Her tone changed from one of relief to a stern one "Don't ever leave us like that again!" she demanded.

"I won't!" I promised, as I put my hand behind her head and pulled her cheek up next to mine. Her hair was sweaty, but a faint, sweet scent still lofted off of it. I breathed in deeply as her curls brushed against my face. I wanted to kiss her cheek, but was distracted by Chloe yanking on my pants, the same way she had when I met her earlier that day.

I knelt down and she flung her arms around my neck tightly "Thanks for keeping the monsters away from us. Now let's go to the carnival!"

I smiled at her "It's about time for some fun isn't it?"

I grabbed Chloe in my arms and stood up. I was hungry and ready to get inside, then I thought of Ex. I looked to Caiohme who was still wiping sweat and tears from her face "Have you seen Ex?" I asked.

She smiled as she pointed to a crowd of people that were parting to let a man through; it was him. He walked with a limp and his clothes were tattered. His arms were bruised and his lip was bleeding, but he smiled like he had when I first met him earlier that day. The blood stained his white teeth. It was clear he had fought to protect us, while I had questioned his integrity.

I put Chloe down and walked toward him, so he would not have to walk as far. As I approached him I reached to shake his hand; he grabbed mine and pulled me in for a hug. He wrapped his cold arms around me and whispered in my ear "I am weak but I am glad to see you strong brother. Someday I hope that we may fight together."

I looked at his bruised arms and black eye and wondered how he could think of fighting "Looks like you stood up to battle better than I did. Maybe someday we could play a game of ball together instead." He laughed, but as he did he coughed up blood.

I offered him my shoulder "Let's get you inside buddy."

I turned around, supporting the weight of his hurt body, and we slowly made our way to the castle door. The crowd parted to let us through, honoring us as if we were warriors just home from battle. They fell in line behind us as we approached the towering oak doors. A Leonoid opened the door for us and for the first time I entered the castle, with Ex on one side and Caiohme and Chloe on the other.

Upon entering the building, a Leonoid woman summoned a medical attendant to meet us near the door. She quickly took note of our condition and urged us to allow her to take Ex to the clinic for care. I carefully handed him over; the woman assured me he was in good hands. He coughed up more blood as I transferred him to her arms. I promised to come and check on him later that night. I watched him limp away until he disappeared from sight. I worried about his health and wondered how safe we all truly were.

My attention turned to the castle; we were in a center court of some type. There were tables surrounded by a full circle of shops and eateries. The open circle rose several levels, capped by a glass ceiling that let the sun light in. The levels were supported by a ring of nine towering, timber poles that appeared to be the trunks of old Sequoia trees. Growing up the timber, and all around the court, were vines with vibrant flowers, which moved flowingly, delicately twisting around the railing and tree branches.

The vines were so beautiful and lively in their movement

that they left me dazed. I reached my hand out to touch one and it wrapped around my fingers and my wrist. It tickled and I could feel its energy as it calmed me. Life pulsed through its veins and through me, but I noticed the vine begin to shrivel up and die. I pulled my hand away, but even as I released it a large portion turned brown. My gaze broke and I stepped back.

I looked over my shoulder, hoping no one had seen what I had done, and noticed I lost Caiohme and Chloe as the crowd scattered around the court. I turned away from the dead vines to find Caiohme, when a voice from behind me whispered "You must not touch the Zoe Vine with fear or hate in your heart. The vine feeds off of ones' emotions, relieving you of them but sacrificing itself."

I turned around to a Leonoid woman with a stern look on her face. She grabbed the vine with both hands "Perhaps it is not too late. Often, life still flows through the wounded and abandoned."

At first it seemed futile, then one bud bloomed; then five, then twenty. As life raced through the veins of the vine the woman's' breath grew shallow. Her tan skin turned pale and her red hair gray. She pulled her hands away as flowers began to bloom. Soon, her color returned "It only took life from me because of my willingness to sacrifice it. It is important that you learn quickly what sacrifices you're willing to make Jayden."

There was that word again, sacrifices. Everyone seemed to expect them from us. She was older, perhaps in her sixties, but her voice was strong and passionate. I looked her in the eyes momentarily, but her stare was bold and I could tell she was disappointed in me. I looked back down at the ground "Yes ma'am!"

I did not notice immediately, but the court had grown quiet around us. I lifted my head and saw only a few children and locals still wandering through the court; even they walked at a pace that said they had somewhere else to be. I looked to the woman confused, too nervous to ask where everyone had gone. There were four hallways connected to the court; one to the north, east, south and west. She pointed to the North hall "Take Boreas Hall all the way to the end. Take the staircase up to the third floor and take a right. Enter the boy's dormitory and look for your room. Your name should be on the door. Get ready for dinner promptly. You don't have long. Now, off you go."

Her directions were more like orders. She did not exchange any pleasantries, not even a smile. I looked to the hall and then back to her. She stood sternly, waiting for me to leave, as if I would do more harm if she left me alone. I said thank you and began to walk towards Boreas Hall.

I did not get far, perhaps twenty feet, when I heard her harsh tone ring out from behind me "Jayden."

I stopped and turned around. "Perhaps it would be best to keep your hands in your pockets and not let your curiosity get the best of you along the way. We wouldn't want any more unfortunate events to occur." She then waved me on my way with a hand gesture and kept watch over me until I reached Boreas Hall.

The hall was not long; maybe a hundred to a hundred-fifty feet. It was well lit, but not with any type of lighting I had ever seen. Color danced and swirled on the wall, green and blue, purple and pink, much like the Aurora Borealis does in the northern skies. Everything in Leotus seemed to be composed of energy and life. I wanted to touch the walls, but remembered the stern warning I had received against it.

On my left there were many offices with windows. The wooden blinds were pulled, but the entry ways were left open without doors. It seemed counterproductive, but everything seemed strange in Leotus. To my right was a single, huge room, a gym, with glass windows from the floor to the ceiling. It was deserted, but it was filled with equipment and a rock climbing wall. It had a pool, with a waterfall that was surrounded by the same stone that composed the rock wall. It looked more like a Colorado landscape than a gym, but it seemed peaceful.

As I reached the end of the hall I approached the staircase, which was like everything else in Leotus, different. Each stair appeared to float, without railing or beams for support, only connected at the wall. I was hesitant to step onto them, afraid that they may collapse from under me. I put one foot on the first stair and it lit up with the same colors as the walls. I brought my next foot up and bounced to check the strength; it didn't break, must be sturdy I thought. Each stair lit up as I stepped onto it and dimmed as I stepped off it. The flights were tall and steep, twenty or twenty-five stairs each.

About the time I reached the third floor several boys, around thirteen or fourteen years old, jogged past me down the staircase. They were either in a rush or a lot more confident of the stair cases sturdiness than I. They dressed in similar garments as the Leonoids, but theirs were green. I entered a door that opened to the third floor, marked with a large number three etched in its surface. To my left was a hallway that led back to the open circle. To the right, about ten feet in front of me, were two oak doors with the words "Boys Dormitory" etched in them.

I walked up to the doors with a sense of nervousness bearing down on me; It was the first time I had went anywhere in Leotus without Caiohme and Chloe. Who would be inside? What if it was some sort of trap? Would I share the room with another boy? If so, who? I sighed and slowly opened the doors.

Inside the two oak doors was a large, square living area, surrounded by doors on all sides. It was bustling with boys around my age, playing card games and other board games. The boys relaxed on the couches and sprawled out on the floor, telling

stories and laughing. All the boys had the same green garment on and many hurried past me, leaving the dormitory as I
walked in.

Large, pristine oak boards stretched the length of the room
and white fur rugs laid under all the furniture. Oil lamps were
set up in the corners and on the tops of end tables. There were
many plants that grew under the sky lights that lit the room. The
walls were bright yellow and the bedroom doors were white with
two to three names carved in each.

Few were distracted as I entered the room, but those who
did notice dropped what they were doing and stared. I acknowledged them with the nod of my head and they quickly went
back to talking and having fun. A few looked up every now and
then to see if I was still there, but quickly looked away when I
noticed them.

I made my way around the perimeter of the room, touch-
ing each door as I looked for my name. I found it in the back
left hand corner, on the back wall. There was only one other
name on the door, Malachi. I reached to open the handle and
two younger boys approached me from behind. Both boys were
quiet for a moment, until the taller one elbowed the smaller one
in the side. "Umm Jayden, we were just like wondering, what
where the monsters like that you fought?"

They both seemed nervous and frightened, waiting to hear
my answer. I looked at them and smiled "They were a bunch of
big sissies. Didn't you see the way they ran off?" I laughed and
the boys did too. I knew I had set them at ease. No need to have
them worry, we had all been through enough that day.

"Well, I have to get ready for dinner dudes; it was nice to
meet you. What are your names?"

The shy boy responded first as he pushed his straight, blond
hair from his eyes "I'm Henry!" The other boy reached his hand

out and shook mine "I'm Cordell. Henry is my younger brother. We are both from California, but our parents are from England."

Both boys had the same sandy hair color and blue eyes, along with many other common traits. It was easy to tell they were brothers, possibly twins. I grabbed the door handle "Henry, Cordell, hopefully I will see you later on tonight!" I turned my back, twisted the handle and walked in.

I stepped into the room to see that my roommate had arrived before me. As I closed the door, he glanced at me without a smile, and then went back to what he was doing without saying hi. His skin was dark brown and he looked like he was probably from somewhere in South America. His hair was dark and buzz cut, longer on the top and shorter on the side. He was a little taller than me and probably a little stronger. The bed closest to the balcony doors had its sheets pulled back and a welcome basket strewn across it; clearly he had chosen it. Beams of light shined down from the skylights onto his tan skin as he fidgeted with things inside his dresser.

I sat down on the other bed and, in an attempt to end the awkward silence, said "Hi, how are you?" There was no reply. He grabbed a blue garment from the bed and walked right by me into the restroom. I questioned if I had somehow done something to anger him already.

The room was symmetric on both sides and lightly furnished. The right side of the room was much deeper than the left. Two large beds were separated by a central walkway, which lead into the bathroom. A railing down the center of the room allowed a curtain to be pulled to separate the two sides. There was a dresser to the right of the first bed and to the left of the far bed. On the left wall there was a desk in each corner, with books stacked on top and a clock. Next to each desk was a closet door. There were no televisions or computers; the lack of electronics was a common theme in Leotus. The floors were composed of the same oak boards as the living area. A black rug ran in front of both beds and down the center, to the bathroom door. Wooden beams ran parallel to the entry door across the ceiling. Each bed had blue and green flannel comforters with blue sheets and pillows. On my bed was a wooden welcome basket with an envelope attached; I reached for it and opened it.

The note was handwritten on brown stationary. The introduction "Dear Jayden," glowed energetically, like the walls in the hallway. As my eyes met each new word, they too lit up. "We are all very pleased to have you with us and to speak with you about why we have brought you to Leotus. Please put on the garments that can be found in your closet and meet us promptly, at six-thirty, for a dinner celebration. You will find us in the dining room at the end of East, or Eurus, Hall."

I read the salutation "Sincerely, Alcaeus," and the whole page began to swirl with color. Then, without warning, the pages burst outward into thousands of tiny pieces. I jumped as particles flew toward me and were absorbed by everything around me until there were none left.

I looked to the clock on the desk, 6:20. I jumped off the bed and looked over at Malachi's clock; it turned over to 6:21. I ran over to the closet and flung it open, as Malachi came out of the bathroom. I looked over my shoulder to notice that he had on a blue garment. Strange, I thought; all of the other kids had on green robes. The blue made his skin appear even darker than he was. I looked into my closet and saw three of the garments hanging there, all blue as well. I wondered if color varied by age, but knew I didn't have the time to think about it.

I looked over to Malachi, sitting on his bed, as I took my shirt off "Dude, did your letter say six thirty too? We better hurry; it's already 6:25!" This elicited a deep glare and smirk.

He looked away and shook his head, mumbling something in a language foreign to me.

I slid my pants off as I pulled the garment down. It was warm and comfortable on my skin, like my blankets after sleeping under them all night. I walked over to Malachi's side of the room and looked down at him "I don't know what your problem is, but all I am trying to do is be friendly. I understand that we are both in a place we know little about, but would it kill you to try a little harder. Who knows, we may even need each other if things turn bad."

He just looked down at the bed. Maybe he couldn't understand me or maybe he was shy. Maybe I was mistaking looks of confusion for glares. Or maybe he just didn't care to know anyone in Leotus; that was the attitude I had before I met the girls. I looked at the clock again, 6:28, and I turned to leave the room without even being acknowledged "Whatever man."

I walked to the door and a voice came from behind me "You may know nothing about here gabacho, but I know plenty. Things are already bad, don't start thinking you can change that!" He spoke slowly and softly, with a strong accent, but good English.

I turned around to see him standing by his bed staring at me, half expecting him to charge me into the door. He looked down at his bed, shaking his head and rolling his eyes as he bit his lower lip. I too looked over at his bed, just in time to see objects rising from its surface; a wallet, a pair of shoes, a t-shirt. He held out his hands and the objects spun, suspended in the space above his palms. The objects began to fall apart, much the same way that Havenbrook had. The particles accumulated to form something new; a football. Before I could even comprehend what had happened, he tossed it at me "Think quick!"

I caught the ball and let it fall from my hands as he walked up to me. He got so close that his chest was almost against mine.

He looked me in the eyes and brought his mouth close to my ear. "You see Pendejo, I know all about you, Caiohme and Chloe, Leotus. I know the bullshit storyline and what they want from us. Truth is, I'd rather be clueless at home with my music and friends then stuck in this place. He will make sure you have nothing left to go home to though, things will never be the same for you again."

He brought his hand up to my head and thumped my skull with his finger. "So next time you want to be friendly, use your brains and leave me the hell alone. Now get out of my face. Get downstairs so you can learn about all the great things Alcaeus has in store for you. None of it makes a difference anyways. "

He stepped back and smirked, tossing his chin up in the air. Something had made him hate Leotus, hate me. I wanted to know more of what he knew, but he clearly wanted his space. I shrugged it off and walked out the door, hoping I would get the answers I needed at the celebration! I hoped that he wasn't right, that things weren't already bad.

CHAPTER FOUR

Descendants of the Gods

I JOGGED DOWN the stairs, through Boreas Hall, and into the center court. The restaurants and shops were all closed and the evening sun didn't shine through the glass like it had a short while before. It was so quiet that I swore I could hear the vines growing in the dim starlight. A creepy feeling came over me, like the kind you get when you're walking alone in the dark. I felt like someone was watching me and I kept turning around to make sure I wasn't being followed. I quickly tiptoed across the court towards Eurus Hall, trying to avoid being noticed by whatever might be hiding in the dim starlight.

About halfway across the court, I looked over my shoulder and tripped over a chair that had not been pushed back to its table. I cursed as my calf smacked the corner of the chair and I fell to the ground "Ouch, damn it!!" I grabbed my leg and pulled the robe up to my knee; my shin was already bruised, black and blue. I rolled over onto my stomach to push myself up, but as I did I heard footsteps coming from South, or Notus, Hall. I collapsed to the ground and lay there silently, only looking up to see who was around. The tables and vines blocked a lot of my view, but I could see well enough to recognize the individual. It was the Leonoid woman who had been so stern and passionate about the vines.

She was light on her feet as she walked into the court. Her red hair moved from left to right several times as she surveyed the area. She moved toward the set of doors, located between Notus Hall and Zephyrus Hall, which I had first used to enter the castle. I quietly repositioned myself so that I could see what she was doing. Once she reached the doors, she surveyed the area again. Her head came to a rest as she starred in my direction for several seconds. I lay still as a board, afraid I had been seen. My heart raced and my palms grew sweaty as she took a step in my direction. I was breathing heavy, but I covered my mouth so I wouldn't be heard. She took another step towards me, but quickly jerked around as someone lightly tapped three times on the door.

She grabbed the door handle, but seemed to hesitate for a moment as she looked back again and let out a deep breath. I too exhaled the air I had been holding in and took a shallow breath. Two louder knocks echoed in the court and she opened the door frantically. The dark figure of a man stepped into the door frame and she leaned forward to whisper in his ear. She stepped back from him and spoke louder, but I could not make out what she was saying. The man appeared to grow irritated and became aggressive, shoving her backwards. As she regained her footing, she pulled a rolled up piece of paper from under her robe and tossed it at him. She followed him outside as he stepped back from the door frame, closing the door to just a crack.

I turned around and quickly crawled on all four toward Eurus Hall. My knees burned as I emerged from the tables. I pushed myself to my feet and quietly ran into the hall just in time to hear the center court door close. I was close to the dining hall! I could hear the applause and laughter of a room full of people. I ran down the hallway, past professional portraits, art work, and a large room filled with books. My heart pounded in my chest with fear. Would she see me before I could make it to the entrance? No, I was there! I tripped on a rug, but caught my balance in time to shove through the double doors.

Stomping into the room was cause for a lot of unwanted attention; everyone turned around to see what all the commotion was. Luckily, salad was being served and no one was on stage. I looked for Caiohme, but only noticed several sets of eyes locked on me like hawks. The children starred at me as if I was to be the guest speaker; their whispers like soft wisps of wind on the sea, visible, but barely audible. I was used to attention on the field, just not the quiet, secretive type. I felt awkward until I saw her sitting in the middle of the room, the girl that had been by my side all day, Caiohme.

She stared at me from the center table, waiting for me to notice her. Once I did, I couldn't have peeled my eyes away if I tried. Her blue garment hung from the edge of her shoulders and I could see the definition of her collarbones as they curved toward her slender neck; a beautiful sapphire pendent hung in the middle of her chest. Her hair lay behind her shoulders in loose, large curls and her tan, freckled skin stood out against the light blue color. I was so fixated on her that it took me a moment to notice her motioning me to the table.

I maneuvered between the chairs and tables, excusing myself as I went. I finally reached the table, so excited to sit down next to Caiohme that I pulled my chair out in front of a server and nearly caused him to drop a tray full of salads. The server apologized profusely for not paying attention. I assured him it was my fault and excused myself. He quickly went on his way.

I sat down at the table and Caiohme smiled at me "fashionably late eh?" The radiance of her smile seemed livelier than at any point in the day. She looked refreshed and enthusiastic. Surely she didn't have the time to rest and get all dolled up, I had not been away from her that long. I was jealous; I wanted to look as radiant as she did. I wanted her to look at me with the same lustful attraction.

I looked at her and rolled my eyes "You have no idea. First, I got lectured for practically killing the strangest vines I have ever seen. Then, I found out that my roommate, Malachi, is not only a jerk but that he is capable of some of the same things as Alcaeus. Then…"

Before I could finish, Caiohme shook her head no and puckered her lips "Sshhhh!" I looked behind my back, no one was there. Why had his name drawn such a stern warning?

A voice came from across the table and I looked up. "It's ok Caiohme. Malachi can come off as a bit self-centered and uncaring. Don't worry though Jayden, he will grow on you." She was calm and reassuring, but she must have seen a different side of him than I.

I looked at her and laughed "A bit?" To me, self-centered and uncaring were not the words to describe the man that had just cursed at me, threatened me, and told me to leave him the hell alone. The words that came to my mind were asshole, jerk and, perhaps, racist.

Caiohme looked at me with big eyes and lightly nudged my shoulder "Hey, be nice! This is my roommate Samarra. She and Malachi have been together through everything today." I looked up and across the table again and noticed she was still looking at me. Was she expecting some sort of apology, I wondered? Maybe I owed it to her after an entire day with Malachi!

"Well, hi Samarra! If you don't already know, I'm Jayden. I hope we are ok, I did not mean any harm in what I said." It was a half-ass apology, but it was all I could muster up. After all, I was only describing the side he had shown me!

She smiled "Yes, I have heard quite a lot about you! Don't worry about it Jayden. I think you will see a different side of Malachi tonight. He was probably just tired; it was a long day." Her voice was soft and soothing and her etiquette led me to believe she had come from a wealthy background. Her skin was darker than Malachi's and her eyes were as blue as the garment she wore. The dress fit tightly on her shoulders, less revealing then Caiohme's.

It was hard to shake the impression Malachi had given me, but I hoped she was right and that he was just tired. I did poke my nose in his business; who was I to tell him what to do? Maybe I should have just let him have his space. I decided to just let it be and hoped the night would ease the situation before we slept.

The table was set for six, with an empty spot by Samarra marked for Malachi. The setup was very formal with hand embroidered, white lace tablecloths covering the table. Glass stemware with a gold rim and white china sat on top of coral colored placemats; matching napkins lay beneath our silverware. Crystal chandeliers hung from the ceiling and supported different sized, boldly colored, pillar candles. Candle light flickered and bounced around the room as it reflected off the crystal.

I looked to the other two individuals, Adrianna and Carmine, and greeted them "Hi, how are y'all?" They both had olive skin and dark hair. Adrianna's lips were full and deep red. They both had large black eyebrows and appeared to be very natural. Neither wore many accessories or pieces of jewelry and Adrianna's makeup was minimal.

Adrianna and Carmine replied "Hello!" at the same time, then looked at each other and laughed. They seemed to be comfortable with each other and to have formed a unique relationship, similar to each of us at the table. Aside from hello, they did not talk much with the rest of us; they seemed to mingle only between themselves. I turned to Caiohme and Samarra, who were giggling and gossiping about others around the room, but before I could get Caiohme's attention the door swung open and we all turned around.

It was the Leonoid woman. Most everyone quickly turned back around without a thought, but I watched her walk around the perimeter of the room and join Alcaeus at a table in front, near the stage. Who was she to sit at Alcaeus' table? Did he know of her secret meeting with the hooded man? I doubted that he knew anything of it.

I watched her walk around the room, but something odd broke my stare as she sat down. Green, green, white, green, white; there were plenty of green and white garments scattered around the dining room, but our table was the only one that wore blue. Come to think of it, we had all developed bonds and been with one another during the day. We shared rooms and a table with one another. I didn't have long to try to piece it all together; when I looked up I noticed the Leonoid woman staring directly at me. I quickly broke my gaze and looked toward Caiohme.

Malachi joined the table, but greeted no one but Samarra. It didn't seem like dinner was going to be any more pleasant than our first encounter. I looked at him and he looked back at me "What's up Jayden?"

He spoke like nothing had occurred between the two of us. "Not a lot, just looking for someone to play ball with after dinner."

He took the innuendo lightly, mostly laughing it off, but throwing it right back at me "Shouldn't be hard, I heard there's talk of a team forming between the lightweights. Word is that real men play rugby or soccer though."

I didn't feel it was a good time for another distraction, so I shook my head "Whatever!" and turned my attention to Caiohme. I nudged her in the side a couple times to ask her if she knew anything about the blue garments, but by the time she turned her attention from Samarra to me, a man from Alcaeus' table had gotten up and began to walk towards the stage. The room grew silent.

A young boy quickly became the center of attention as he knocked his stemware off the table and it shattered on the floor. He went to pick the glass shards up, but cut his hand wide open. A nurse that was on hand had to rush him off to get his hand stitched up after he spurted blood across the floor and onto the girl's shirt that sat next to him. Naturally, she freaked out and ran from the room in hysteria.

The man from Alcaeus' table had rushed to help, but resumed his walk to the stage as the nurse escorted the boy out. The room grew silent again. He stepped onto the wooden stairs and I could hear them creak. He walked up to the granite podium and his white robe glowed against the red curtains. He was younger than Alcaeus, but not nearly as tall or strong. His skin was firm and olive and his dark brown hair had little gray. His jaw was square and his shoulders were wide. As the mystery man approached the microphone, Alcaeus and the other man and woman at his table, applauded. The room erupted with cheers and applause as he stood for a moment smiling "Thank you! Thank You! Thank you! Please, take your seats. Thank You!"

He stood, looking out on the crowd for a moment and then he spoke "Boy, what an eventful day we've had! Don't know that I could stand any more excitement. My name is Deseus and it is my privilege to welcome you to Leotus! I am the assistant head-master of education and health and I hope that you had the opportunity to enjoy the beauty of our country and the hospi-tality of our people today. I know that you have seen a lot, and the day has been long, so I will get straight to the point. You are here because this is our home and we have long awaited your arrival. Our country has thrived, undivided for centuries, but

history has proven that men cannot forever be satisfied by con-
tinuity and peace. Our country is now facing a time of trial and
division and you have been brought here because of your ability
to create change. The choices you make will be your own, but it
is important that you understand the situation and how you will
influence it. So, without further ado, it is my greatest pleasure to
introduce our headmaster, Alcaeus."

As Alcaeus stood, so did all. The applause that Deseus
received was magnified tenfold as Alcaeus walked to the microphone. The sound echoed off the ceiling and vibrated the chandeliers. He stood at the podium for some time before everyone
took their seats and stopped cheering. He did not speak until the
room was completely silent. A smile grew on his face as his eyes
moved from one side of the room to the other. He looked down
at the podium for a moment, but quickly brought his teary eyes
back to the audience and began to speak.

"Hello children! It is great to be with all of you tonight! I
know that the day has been long, and unexpected things have
occurred, but it has only given you a glimpse of what we are up
against. I know that all of you are tired and hungry so I will try
to be quick, but it is important that you listen closely. What you
know will shape your decisions, and it is your decisions that will
shape our future together."

With that, he turned his back to the audience and walked
up to the red curtain that stood behind him. He stretched his
arms out, grasped the cotton in his large hands, and pulled it
down. Cries and gasps came from the audience as he revealed
two of the beasts that had beaten me earlier that day. Caiohme
grabbed my hand and pulled her chair closer to me as I took a
deep breath. She wrapped her arm around me tightly, but part
of me wanted to cower off into the hallway. Why had he brought
them back to Leotus, to the festival? Didn't we deserve to have a
moment to relax, free from terror?

The beasts huddled in the corner of the cage with their faces tucked in their chests. They breathed heavily, but not as heavily as those in the audience. Alcaeus turned his back to the beast and walked to the microphone. "Do not be afraid of these beasts. They are a harmless distortion of reality, a fragment of your imagination. They are fear. Overcome your fear and you will overcome them. Reality is different for each individual based on your experiences and knowledge. It is with knowledge that you can learn to change reality." He grabbed the microphone and walked off the stage and into the audience.

He stopped in front of the stage and looked out on all of us. "Long ago, Leonoids and Humans lived together as one people and the world was much like the place you have seen here today. Existence was simple and other life and creation was valued. Over time, humans grew arrogant and were fueled by greed and hate. War broke out and natural resources were depleted. A constant need for progression polluted the waters and killed the land we had lived on for thousands of years. Our people faced a fear of extinction and we could no longer coexist. The creationists among our ancestors cleaned the water and the lands, destroyed the technology and erased memories of the past. They eased the human heart and returned them to a simple life. They left them with free will and walked away from them for good; living by their side, but this world and the things of it no longer visible to them." He paused for a moment and leaned against the stage.

"In time the humans went back to their old ways, fighting bloody wars for wealth and resources as they grew further apart from the land. Now, they compare themselves to their neighbors and always want more. They are never content. Most wander around with an empty feeling, fighting within themselves over a piece of their heart that still remembers what it was like to be free from it all. That is the world you live in; a world where you can't break free from the bars that imprison you. With each accomplishment, you have been conditioned to only want more. Expectations are always on the rise. It is a place where a false perception of reality clouds your ability to live freely."

He walked to the right of the stage and stood to the left of the table he sat at earlier. He put his right hand on Deseus' shoulder and sighed. "We have spent years coexisting with humans, without their knowledge of our existence. They do not know of Leotus and they no longer remember us or who we are. Legends and books have been passed down, but few look at them as more than myth. We have lived in peace and content- ment for hundreds of years by their side, but now old problems threaten our way of life. The lands are polluted and we have been pushed to the sea. Several years ago, many Leonoids broke away from Leotus and began developing a new community that is growing quickly; it is a dark place. They have begun drilling for resources and developing dangerous technologies. They have plans to commit genocide, they want the humans dead. They say they are a waste of space and resources. Thankfully, they lack a creationist and without one they cannot enter the human mind or change reality. There is rumor that they have attempted to persuade the creationists among our ranks to join them and I fear they will not stop until they have what they want."

He took a deep breath and made his way through the crowd, towards our table. I looked up at him as he approached and he looked down at me and smiled. He walked behind Caiohme and I, putting one hand on each of our shoulders as he began to speak again "About twenty years ago we began a project. Embryos were created and transplanted into human wombs. You are the products of this program, you are our children. I know this will be hard to accept, but time is a luxury and deci- sions must be made quickly."

He grew silent as a look of astonishment grew on many faces. Some covered their mouths with their hands and some had tears streaming down their cheeks. Some sat their silently, processing it, and a few looked on with disbelief. Personally, I didn't believe any of it, it was all lies. Cannibalizing beasts, a hellish city, genocide, embryos; how could any of it be true? I expected to wake up from the nightmare at any time. Alcaeus grabbed Caiohme and I by the shoulders and gently pulled us to our feet, then signaled for the rest of our table to rise and follow, as he led us toward the stage.

He began to talk again as we slowly walked toward the stage. I felt anxious and nervous as everyone's eyes focused on us. It reminded me of Thanksgiving Day parades in Havenbrook. The high school band and football team, local business men, farmers on old tractors, the fire and police departments; all marching down Main Street in front of crowds of residents. One year my father decorated his Ford truck to advertise for the market and I got to ride in the back, tossing out candy. I was terrified at first, lying in the bed of the truck where no one could see me. That was how I felt at that moment, but there was nowhere to hide.

"Few of you have been here, but many of you have seen us or felt our presence with you as we watched over you all these years. Humans have many names for us: angels, demons, spirits, ghosts, deities, and gods, to name a few. Most humans see us only as a blurry spot in a picture or a dark shadow, but there are few that have found something inside of themselves to see glimpses of Leotus, of us. All of you children have the ability to walk among humans and Leonoids; to live in their world and ours. Some of you have the ability to look inside the mind. Some can alter emotion and thought, but there are a few among us that can do much more."

As we walked onto stage he declared our names, and for the first time I understood all the hospitality, the healing of my body and the reason for the different colored gowns. "Meet Jayden, Caiohme, Malachi, Samarra, Carmine and Adrianna. These six are the descendants of the great creationists and they will be your leaders. They have the ability to alter reality, to create and destroy existence."

He looked at the six of us "You all have a decision to make. Join us and fight for existence and those you care about, or go home without a memory of this place and wait for the fight to come to you. These decisions must be made quickly, our time is short. Try not to think about all of this tonight; instead, enjoy getting to know one another. In a moment the servers will bring out a special meal. First, we have a fun treat for you." He turned to Malachi and then walked off the stage.

How could we make a decision with such little information? Who did he expect us to fight, for how long? The Farrians, the beasts; how did he expect us to win? They were immensely more powerful! How did he know Malachi and why had he nodded to him? Did they have a personal relationship? Was that how Malachi was capable of the same abilities as Alcaeus? Had he taught Malachi before he taught the rest of us? I had so many more questions that he had not answered.

Malachi turned and walked towards the beasts in their cage. He stood in front of the cage for a moment, without fear, and looked at them as they quivered in the corner. Then he walked up to the cage and grabbed the bars which disintegrated as a gold shimmer in the air. The beasts did not run as he walked up to them and put one hand on each. They seemed to be paralyzed, in some type of stupor. He closed his eyes, leaned his head back and pushed down on the backs of the beasts. When he pushed down, the beasts crumbled into hundreds of colorful birds that took to flight in the dining room. They flew low, slightly above the heads of everyone in the audience. Without warning, the birds began to burst like piñatas in the air; candy, confetti and streamers of all colors rained down. The streamers folded themselves like origami on the tables and began to dance

71

around as dinosaurs, elephants, monkeys, and many other animals. As the streamers continued to rain down, servers burst through the kitchen doors, skating in colorful pinstripe uniforms, and delivered trays of food to the tables.

The crowd erupted with applause and laughter as Malachi led us off the stage; he did not smile and seemed to take little satisfaction in the excitement he had created. He shrugged off several children that tugged at his pants with laughter and walked back to the table without speaking to anyone. I noticed Chloe playing alongside the group of children that confronted Malachi. Filled with sugar, the children jumped around and laughed at the origami animals as they danced.

We sat down at our table to a feast. Carved red meat and purple potatoes lined a silver platter. The meat was done perfectly, juicy and red in the center with a charcoaled crust and brown gravy on the side. Wild rice with cherries, almonds and bananas in a sweet, creamy sauce tempted my senses. Lucula and other fruit lay on top of the table, surrounded by streamers as the origami collapsed. Our cups were filled with juice. The half empty bottles sat in the middle of the table.

Before filling my plate and taking a bite, I looked around the room and noticed everyone enjoying their meal and laughing with those at the tables next to them. They all seemed so happy, as if they had forgotten the world they were snatched from. It was like Alcaeus came in the night, kidnapping us from everything we knew, drugging us so we wouldn't notice; it seemed that some hadn't. Looking around the room, I wondered exactly what it was that we were all capable of. I thought of the colorful birds and wondered what else Malachi could create. I imagined dinosaurs hunting their prey, centaurs blazing across the prairie, flying unicorns, mermaids and mermen and dark beasts!

I woke up from the day dream to hear Caiohme ask Malachi with excitement "That was awesome! Could you teach me how to do it?" It angered me to see her intrigued by him, to show interest in what he was able to do.

He looked up at her after hesitating for a moment, his voice angry "I don't have to teach you. It is innate to who you are, who we are. It's how you will fight his war, and in that, you will lose everything you ever cared about. Life will become an empty void. Your purpose will be their purpose."

Samarra shook her head in agreement "I am sure Alcaeus has a plan for you. After all, he was the one that taught us." It shocked me and caught my attention. They had been to Leotus before, they knew Alcaeus?

"So, you and Malachi have been here before?" I asked.

Samarra looked over at Malachi, who shrugged his shoulders, and then back at me "Not just Malachi and I; everyone at this table, except you and Caiohme, has been to Leotus. Alcaeus wanted to wait to bring the two of you. There is something different about you. There is something he would not tell us."

I was confused and distressed; I rubbed my eyes with a sigh. If they had fought without us before, why did they need us at all? Why did Samarra need to look to Malachi for approval? Was he special, more powerful? I wanted to stand up and scream, demand answers, but I dug my spoon into the wild rice and stuffed my mouth full. The cream was heavy and sweet on my tongue.

As we ate our meal a feeling of relaxation and carelessness came over me. I found myself laughing about the silliest things and noticed others doing the same. The more I drank the more relaxed I felt and I soon realized that the juice must have been made from the Lucula. After all, it did have a very similar taste to the fruit.

A band set up and began playing and everyone sang to the music. As they ate and conversed, the Leonoid woman snuck onto the stage without being noticed. Without applause, she tapped the microphone twice and the music came to a halt. It took a moment for the room to grow quiet, but I immediately turned my attention to her when I heard her voice "Hello Leonoids, children! My name is Flora, Assistant Headmaster of living and activities. The meat you had tonight was roasted Leucrocota, a dangerous, wild beast that roams these lands and can imitate human voice to lure its prey. It is rare to see one and even rarer to catch one. The juice is a Leonoid favorite, Lucula. As you find yourself in a state of relaxation, please join us on the dance floor and continue to get to know one another."

With the short introduction, she walked off the stage and the music started back up. Many of the candles blew out as a light breeze swept across the room and the dance floor lit up. I wasn't much in the mood to dance, but could not say no to Chloe as she pulled Caiohme and I onto the dance floor. "Come on guys, it will be so much fun!"

Chloe did not release our hands until we were in the middle of the crowd. Caiohme looked at me and I at her; with a grin and the shrug of her shoulders we all danced to the reggae beat. The band reminded me of the ones in Jamaican vacation commercials; dread locks, colorful shirts and beads, and bongo drums. Caiohme and Chloe looked so lively after the exhausting day. As the beat picked up, I began to sweat, so I took a moment to rest and look around! Chloe had run off with her new friends, dancing wildly near the band. Malachi and Samarra were nowhere to be seen. Adrianna and Carmine sat casually at the table, talking and laughing. Alcaeus, and those at his table, laughed as they pointed towards Chloe and her friends on the dance floor. Everyone was having a good time.

I turned around to find Caiohme, but as I did she fell into my arms. With her back against my chest, she grabbed my arms and wrapped them around her. Her body moved slowly against mine as the beat slowed down. My hands moved up and down her waist as she danced. I could feel her heart beat against my chest as she breathed in deeply. She leaned her head back and my lips met her neck. The smell of her skin was intoxicating and I softly kissed her collarbone. My hands moved down her waist to her thighs and she grabbed my hand and ran it across her stomach. I ran it up her stomach, then her arm, and through her hair. With one hand on her waist, I turned her around and pulled her into me. I ran both hands through her hair and looked into her eyes for a moment with her chest against mine. She smiled and I pulled her in and kissed her lips. I froze for a moment as my heart fluttered and my lips tingled. It was like nothing I had ever felt. A sense of breathlessness moved down my throat to my stomach. I felt weightless and euphoric. I grabbed her hand and whispered "come with me," as I lead her off the dance floor.

We left the dining room and jogged down Eurus Hall to the center court. She looked at me with a nervous grin and giggled "Where are we going? What if we get in trouble?"

I kept walking, but looked over at her "We won't get in trouble. If we do, what are they going to do, send us back home?" I really had no idea what would happen, but I did not care.

She looked back at me and laughed, shrugging her shoulders "Whatever!"

I pulled open the same doors we had used to enter the castle and we ran outside. The weather was perfect, clear and about sixty five degrees. I turned around and kissed her lips playfully "Muahhh! Hop on my back."

She giggled "No way! I'm too heavy."

"You're crazy! Just do it!" I laughed.

I turned around and she threw herself on my back and laughed as I almost fell forward. I grabbed her thighs and went running towards the beach. She screamed as we ran "slow down, we are going to fall." I just laughed and ran faster.

I lost my footing as we reached the loose, white sand and we both fell onto the beach. She punched my arm with a pouty face "See, I told you we'd fall!"

I sat up and she fell back between my knees with her head against my chest. I wrapped my arms around her and grabbed her hand as we looked out onto the ocean. The moon reflected off the still water and the sand glistened under the starry light. As we lay there, I looked up to the stars; without the distraction of city lights you could see thousands of them, like Christmas lights in the sky! It was so peaceful until Caiohme screamed with excitement "Oh my God! Look Jayden! Look!"

She pointed out to the ocean, where two dolphins were playing about a hundred feet from shore. They jumped in and out of the water and nudged each other around. We watched them play and I thought about how simple their lives must be. Nature always seemed to provide peace for me in chaotic times.

I ran my hand up and down her arm and kissed the back of her head as I took a deep breath. She smelled amazing and all I wanted was to lay there with her the whole night. I leaned back a little and supported myself by placing my hand in the sand behind me. "I am so confused by everything Caiohme. Right now I feel like I could stay here with you forever, but I miss home too. I love how peaceful it is on the water, without the distractions and chaos of everyday life, but Havenbrook is peaceful too. How are we to forget the people we grew up with, our families? My heart is content in this moment, but my mind is pulling me in a million different directions. I don't know what is real anymore or what to believe."

She turned around and pushed me on my back. She lay down beside me, her hand intertwined with mine on my chest, and kissed my lips. She pushed herself up and looked me in the eyes "I'm real Jayden. I'm real."

She ran her fingers across my lips and a hand through my hair as she kissed me again. I rolled her over on her back and locked my fingers in hers, stretching her arms out above her head. I kissed her forehead, then her cheek, then her lips. They were soft and moist against my cracked lips. I kissed from right below her left ear all the way down to her collarbone. We were both breathing heavy and I was nervous. My heart pounded in my chest and my stomach was filled with knots. I pulled back for a second, but she grabbed my shoulder and pulled me towards her. She ran her fingers through my hair and smiled as I kissed her lips again. She bit her lower lip as I ran my hand across her forehead and down her cheek bone.

I ran my fingers down the sides of her waist. I rolled half way on top of her and looked her in the eyes "You have made me feel more in a day than I have ever felt. I feel like I have known you my entire life."

There was a voice in the back of my head that was whispering "No, don't do this! What about Katie?" but in the moment it all felt right. I was about to tell her what Ex had told me on the beach earlier that day, but then I heard footsteps running towards us. "Do you hear that?" I whispered.

"Hear what silly? It is probably just some animal in the dunes."

She laughed as she reached up to kiss me, but pulled back as a loud bang echoed in the distance. I jumped off of her, helped her up from the ground, and pulled her close to me as the sound of footsteps crept closer. I stood in front of her silently, in fear that the beasts had returned. The Farrians would take us to the dark city and have a feast of their own.

As the sounds of steps neared, we heard voices, a guy's and a girl's. At first we could not make out what they were saying, but as they got within fifty feet of us it was clear "Jayden, Caiohme! Where are you? Jayden, Caiohme?"

The voices echoed with a tone of panic and fear, but how were we to know it was not a trick, that it was not a Leucrocota?

The voices grew closer until Caiohme recognized one of them. "Samarra. Samarra is that you?" she shouted out!

We both took a step towards them as Samarra and Malachi ran onto the beach. They approached us in a frenzy, breathing shallow and fast, sweat dripping from their foreheads. Malachi looked at us with a concern I had not seen earlier "Alcaeus would kill you if he knew you were out here. I should tell him myself." He paused to catch his breath. He was angry, but seemed concerned as well.

"You need to head back to the castle Jayden. Something bad has happened."

I looked deep into his eyes and could sense real concern. I grabbed his shoulders "What is it? Has something happened to Chloe? Have we been attacked?"

He hesitated for a moment and looked at the ground and then back up at me. "It's Ex. You should go now! He does not have much time. His pulse is weak and he asked that you come to his side. Go!"

"What?" I froze for a moment in disbelief.

I shook off the shock, grabbed Caiohme's hand, and started running towards the castle until I heard my name from behind me "Wait, Jayden!" I stopped and turned around.

"What Malachi?" I shouted impatiently.

He ran up to me with a genuine concern in his voice and put a hand on my shoulder "There is something else you should know. He is your brother Jayden. Now go!"

CHAPTER FIVE

Warning Signs

CAIOHME AND I ran to the castle with our fingers locked tightly. We did not talk; I don't think either of us knew what to say. I didn't think about anything, except the fact that I had left Ex to die alone while I celebrated. I felt horrible and I blamed myself. If we hadn't walked to the beach maybe the beasts would have never came. If I had stayed with Ex and the girls, things could have been different. What if he was my brother and I never got the chance to know him? What if he died before we made it back? I ran faster, practically dragging Caiohme, and burst through the castle doors panting.

Caiohme and I fell into Deseus' arms as we pushed through the castle doors. He caught me and wiped the sweat, sand, and tears from my face as he brushed the hair from my eyes. His touch was gentle, like a mothers'. He was inches from my face and looked straight at me "Slow down Jayden. I will take you to his room, but you must be calm and strong. Breathe and collect yourself. We need that from you. Your father needs that from you."

Deseus put his left arm around my shoulder, his right around

Caiohme, and led us toward Zephyrus Hall. He looked over at me as we walked "So what were you doing down at the beach anyway?" I took no notice of his question. I was consumed by the tragedy; the fact that a man lay dying because he fought to protect my friends and I. I was lost in the words that raced through my head: death, brother, father. I gazed off into space and saw his bruised face.

I almost walked into the wall as we reached Zephyrus hall. Deseus grabbed my arm and I looked up to see five or six Leonoids gathered outside a room. I heard the castle doors open; it was Malachi and Samarra. I didn't want them to see me like that, weak and dramatic. I wiped my face and began walking down the hall. As we approached, I heard the sniffles of bystanders and the soft cry of a man coming from inside the room. The cries shifted to bartering and anger. "Why, why have you done this? He did not deserve this. It should have been me. How can you kill your own kind, you wicked men? My son, I will avenge you. I will not rest until it is right."

Was his the voice of the man they called my father? It filled me with sorrow to hear him grieve for his son. Where was Alcaeus? I wanted to look him in the eyes and curse him for not bringing me sooner or for even bringing me at all. I wanted to know why he was not here to save Ex like he had me. Malachi and Samarra joined the group and we all stood silently outside the door until the cries faded. Why had Malachi come around; why the sudden shift in demeanor? He didn't seem to give a damn about me or Leotus just hours ago! It disgusted me to look at him; his fancy tricks hiding his true personality.

Deseus tapped lightly on the door and Caiohme and I followed him into the room, slowly and quietly. A knot quickly grew in my stomach and chills shot up my body as I noticed the sheet had already been pulled over his head. I was too late. I covered my mouth as the knot moved into my throat and my eyes swelled up. Deseus pulled Caiohme and I in tightly and wrapped his arms around us as tears fell down our cheeks "It will be ok children. He would tell you he died for a purpose, for something he believed in. He rests in a better place."

I tried to hold the tears back, but sniffles turned to cries as our heads rested on Deseus' chest. I put my arm around Caiohme's shoulder and pulled her close to me. We stood in each other's arms for a few minutes, until I let my arms fall to my side and turned toward the bed. I grabbed Caiohme's hand and looked towards the man they called my father, slouched over the bed with his hand resting on top of Excadeus' lifeless body.

He still sniffled as we approached from behind, but grew increasingly silent. I walked to his side and put my arm around his back. I let my hand rest on top of his and stood silently for a moment. It was strange trying to console a man I had never met. Before I could find the words, he began to speak to me in a light tone "Thank you for joining me. It saddens me for you to find out that I am your father under these circumstances."

His voice sounded familiar, but nothing would have prepared me to discover who the grieving father was. Caiohme and I gasped as the man turned around and looked up at us. It was none other than Alcaeus. I pulled my hand away and stepped back. I shook my head in disbelief. How could I be his son? He was powerful and I knew nothing. I dropped Caiohme's hand and looked at him in denial and anger "If you are my father, if Ex was my brother, why did you not bring me sooner? Why did you not save him like you did me?"

He stared at me with tears on his cheeks and I could see the sorrow in his red eyes. I began crying again, not for him, for Ex. He grabbed me by my waist and pulled me in close to him. He breathed heavy, trying to hold back the tears. I tried to pull back, escape his grasp, but he pulled me in tighter.

I put my hands on his shoulders and looked down at him, he

made me sick. A secret life, a brother I never knew and questions that still weren't answered; it all made me sick. Before I could push him away or ask him anything, he pulled my head to his mouth and spoke with a hoarse voice "Be strong Jayden, son! It is what he would have wanted from you. He longed to meet you his whole life. I would have saved him if I could, but some things cannot be changed. I too grieve as you grieve and my heart will mourn for our loss. Nothing will change the time we could not share together, but you must trust that I brought you at the right moment. I have brought you to Leotus on the cusp of a dirty war. Our time is shorter than I feared. Your brother was strong, but naïve. He believed reason and compromise could change an evil man's heart. So many times, I watched him bow at their feet to talk of peace. He insisted it was the right thing to do, but his life is what he paid. What is worse, they could not have done this without the help of a creationist; the help of one of our own. Someone that I trust is betraying us Jayden. The time for talk is over. The day for compromise and mercy has passed. We must stand united and fight; fight for our land, our people and the ideals of humanity. I need your help."

He released me and slowly rose from his seat and looked down at Caiohme "Do you mind if I have a moment with Jayden, alone?"

She shook her head no and looked down to the floor "Of course not." What else could she say? With what we knew at that time, there was no telling what he was capable of.

I stepped toward her and hugged her. I did not want to let her go. Her company had kept me strong through the day and I knew that we had developed a special bond, no matter what happened next. She whispered in my ear "Meet me in my room when you're done; Notus Hall." I smiled as she walked out the door.

Alcaeus stood by my side and we watched her leave. He

looked down at me "She's a great girl Jayden. I am glad that you seem to be getting along. Let's take a walk." I looked up at him filled with anger, then anticipation, then sadness, and lastly, remorse. Who was I to talk that way to a man who had just lost his son; a man that had saved my life just earlier that day? It was selfish and rude.

There were so many things I wanted to know, but my stomach was churning so badly that I only asked the most important question "Are you really my father?"

He looked down at me and his eyes opened wide "Yes Jayden, you are my son, my own creation. Walk with me and I will tell you more."

We walked out the door, past those grieving in the hallway, without many words. Alcaeus shook Deseus' hand and gave him a hug as we left. The group had grown to ten or twelve, few of which I recognized. Alcaeus patted Malachi on the shoulder, as we walked past him and Samarra, and spoke only a couple words "Thank you."

Many consoled us as we walked down the hallway and into the center court. As we left behind the crowd he spoke to me "I am sorry Jayden. Sorry that you did not get to spend more time with Ex. He had a huge heart; I see much of him in you. It has been difficult for me not to hold you and teach you as you grow, but the timing had to be right. Things are not as beautiful and simple here as they seem. I struggled, watching you struggle to find your place in the world, but it has made you stronger. You are a leader and that is what I needed from you. You are different then Malachi and Carmine; you are different than them all." He stopped speaking as we came to a stop near the end of Eurus Hall. We entered a corridor on the right, before the dining hall, and took the staircase to the second floor.

We exited the staircase and entered a room across the hall; the headmaster's suite. Alcaeus unlocked the door and opened it. My jaw dropped, it was beautiful. The entire North end of the room was glass that opened up to a large golden balcony. A chandelier composed of coral and colored shell hung in the middle of the room, lit by candle light. Bright, earthy-colored tile covered the floor. A large beige couch and loveseat sat on top of brown fur rugs, facing a fireplace on the east wall. Abstract sculptures and paintings filled the room. My favorite was a piece that sat near the balcony; three, fragmented human figures intertwined as a globe. The piece was carved from wood and smooth to the touch. I looked up at Alcaeus; he was standing near a desk, on the West wall, cluttered with open books and papers. He smiled. "Most of us are never whole. Some of us lack knowledge, some suffer from physical ailments, some lack courage. It is when we come together that we can change the world. The three bodies represent the Leonoids, Farrians, and Humans, and a hope that we can all be peacefully united one day; a hope your brother held. That was his favorite piece. What do you think of the room? "

I looked at him and laughed "Are you kidding? I love it. How about we trade and you can live with Malachi?"

He chuckled, "Someday Jayden. Someday it will all be yours. I know that Malachi can be rough around the edges, but he will be a resource to you in the future."

I walked up to the glass and looked out. Darkness shrouded much of the view, but the moon light glistened off the ocean water. I thought about how precious life was and how easily it could be taken from anyone. I thought about how Ex fought for Leotus, for peace, and it cost his life; it weighed on my heart. My body grew heavy and tired from the stress of the day. I wanted so badly to sleep. I turned and walked back towards Alcaeus. I looked up to ask him a question, but several figures on his desk caught my attention.

Three, different sized horses lie on the right hand corner of the desk. They were black and lustrous, carved from Hematite. I picked one up and looked up to him "You like horses, or are these just another piece in your collection?" There was anguish in my voice, but I did not mean to direct it at him. I had never been in a situation like that; I did not know how to grieve.

He picked the largest one up "They are a love that we share Jayden. They have lain on my desk since you were born to remind me of you. Even as a small child, I watched over you as you watched the horses in the pasture with curiosity. I built stables in Leotus long ago, hopeful you would come and stay one day. If we have the opportunity, I will take you to see them tomorrow. There is a horse there that waits for you, its skin as black as night. "

I smiled as I sat the horse down. "What did you mean when you said I was different than them all?" The question stirred in my head since he made the statement in the hallway. It was clear I was not powerful like Malachi, but what about Carmine and the rest of the children?

He looked at me and then over to the couch "Come, join me on the couch." I walked over and sat down as he threw a couple logs on the embers. The warmth would have put me to sleep if I was not so anxious for answers.

He rekindled the fire and spoke to me "You are more powerful than Carmine and Malachi combined; able to tap the energy of everything around you, to draw it out of nature and into yourself."

He stood up, sat down on the loveseat, and looked over to me. "When we created the embryos, they were created from a donor mother and father. Carmine and Malachi are the sons of two of our most powerful creationist. Carmine is Deseus' son and Malachi is the son of the other man at my table tonight, Erebus. They will be strong resources, but their mothers were not creationists."

I tried to take it all in, understand it. For the first time it hit me that the mother I had known my whole life was probably not my mother. Anger and rage pulsed through my body again with each beat of my heart "You have not told me about my mother? Is that another surprise tonight, something else you kept from me? Is there anything else I should know Alcaeus?"

He stood up, walked over to the couch, and sat down beside me. "I cannot express how sorry I am Jayden, that I have not been able to tell you all of this sooner. This will be hard to understand because it is not how you have learned that things work, but you do not have a mother. I created you in my own image, from my flesh and the earth of this land, from the beasts and the water and the sands. You are part of me and a part of Leotus. My blood is your blood and it is pure. You have all my ability, but a connection to the land much stronger than I. It has been hard for you to find peace at home. You feel chained down by the possessions that other men wage war over. Your heart is wild and that is why you find the greatest happiness with the horses or on the football field. Men are meant to be free. They were built to run, and hunt, and search for adventure. Most have lost their way, but it is innate in you. Once you learn how to use it, it is this connection that will allow you to control the wildest beasts."

He took a breath and I used the pause to ask him a question "Why me? What makes you think that I can even do what you are asking? Yesterday, I was just a football player. Today, you are telling me that I will lead a war to save man, to save the Leonoids. "

How could I be so powerful and not know it? How could he raise me from the land? Children were not just created; children and formed, by a father and a mother.

He put his hand on my knee and smiled "Yesterday you were a leader and tomorrow you will be the same. You will win this war because if you don't then your family and friends will parish and Leotus will fall. My father told me that one day my son would lead us in a great war. He had visions of you and prophesied your victory. I took his visions lightly until the talk of genocide began. You will win because of your leadership, passion and determination. You will win because you are my son. If I did not believe in you I would not have brought you here." He stood up and walked over to the glass doors; I followed him.

We both looked out onto the ocean. I opened the door and walked outside "This view, the land, it is what could keep me here forever. Too me, this is what is worth fighting for. When we were down by the ocean with Ex, he talked about what we were here to save. He mentioned the ocean and how it could bring peace to the soul. I could not have agreed more." Alcaeus was right about one thing; in the woods, the pasture, under the stars, that was where I felt the most free.

Alcaeus looked up to the stars and I could see a tear fall down his cheek "Ex loved the ocean and the land. He would spend hours on the beach watching the sun come up. I love this land. Our people love this land. We have fought to keep it before and we will again, but I wonder how many must die? You give me hope, your passion for the land, your humanity."

He reached over and put his arm across my shoulder "You should get back to your room and try to get some rest. Tomorrow morning will come sooner than you think. Learning about your abilities can be taxing. Erebus and I will spend time working with you."

Learning to do the things he could do scarred me; I didn't know if I was ready to learn his ways. I sympathized with his losses, with the vision he had, but I was so angry at him for all the things he had kept from me. In the back of my mind, I wanted to know myself, what I was capable of, but I did not want to be flung into a war that had already taken the lives of those who knew much more than me.

Really, all I wanted to do was see Caiohme before bed, but I still had many more questions. "Ex had mentioned on the beach that Caiohme and I share a special bond. How so? What has happened to me at home? Did I just disappear? Am I dead to my Mom, to Katie?" These were thoughts that made me particularly nervous. I wanted to see my home again, my family, Katie.

He turned and I followed him into the room and towards the door "Caiohme is a part of you. When I created you, I too created her. She is from the same water and land that gave you breath and life. In that, her flesh is your flesh. You are almost identical. You share physiological connections that allow you to understand one another like no one else you will ever meet. She understands your passions, your fears. Her heart beats in unison with yours and she knows the depths of your soul better than I; and you hers. She will give you strength when you are weak. She was the cause for the emptiness that lived in you before I brought you here. She makes you whole and to lose her would mean to lose a part of yourself."

He opened the door to the hallway and looked down at me "Do not worry about your family and friends Jayden. They will remember nothing of the time you spend here, but what you wish for them to know. Reality is only as strong as the memories that comprise it. Alter the mind and you alter reality. Go, try and get some rest. We will talk more tomorrow!"

I turned my back to walk away and he began to close the door behind me. I quickly turned around and stepped in the way. I looked up to him and wrapped one arm around his back "Goodnight Alcaeus." I owed him that.

I made my way down the staircase, across the hall and into the center court. The lighting was dim and the crowd of mourners had gone home. It was quieter than before dinner, but I was not afraid. The strong walls of my new home, and the knowledge of my connection to Alcaeus, had put my fears at ease. I walked slowly, noticing things I had not seen earlier.

An archery shop stood among the stores. Wooden bows and slingshots were displayed behind the glass windows. A coffee shop sat in the corner; not with the fancy machines of big chains, but with pour over brewers and French Presses. The flowers that hung from the vines glowed golden amber in the moonlight. What surprised me most though was a wooden door in one of the Sequoia trunks. It blended in very well with the color of the trunk and there was no handle. I would have never noticed it had it not been cracked open.

I slowly walked up to the door, glancing into the small opening to see what lay behind it. It was no use; not a single ray of light shined through the crack. I got close enough to touch the door, but hesitated. I looked from side to side and behind me. I was afraid of being caught doing something wrong again, but no one was around. I reached out and pulled the door open. It was so dark inside that I could not see the other end of the trunk. A strong musty scent infused the air around me. I plugged my nose, but the smell was so thick that I could taste it on my tongue, like a mouth full of lake water. I feared what I might find inside or that someone might see me, but a strong curiosity led me to take another step forward and poke my head through the opening.

At first, I saw nothing as I looked straight forward, but then a dim glow caught my attention. The light came from deep in the ground; fifty, maybe a hundred feet. I couldn't make out what was below. The constant flicker only allowed me to see the ground for a second or two at a time. I looked down at my feet and noticed a rope ladder hanging down the wall of the shaft as far as I could see. I knelt down and squinted, trying to see deeper. I brought my head closer to the shaft and something jumped in front of my face and over my head. I fell straight back and screamed. For a moment I could not move. I was in shock as I watched the creature dash behind a table to hide. I only saw the animal's backside. It was maybe two-and-a-half feet tall with a hunched back. Its body was covered in long, matted, gray and brown hair. My heart raced, my breathing was rapid and shallow. Sweat dripped from my face. Panic overcame me and I thought I might faint.

I didn't take the time to catch my breath. I sat up and pushed myself away from the tree, using my legs to slide across the floor. I kept my eyes on the table where the creature had hidden. Bringing my arms down to the floor, I prepared to push myself up and run, but as I tried to stand something grabbed my ankle. I turned around to see a vine wrapped around me. I hopped on one foot and jerked my leg, but that only seemed to irritate the plant more. It grew rapidly up my knee and thigh, twisting and coiling. It grew so tight that I could feel the blood pulse through the arteries in my leg.

As the vines grew longer, they twisted around my other leg and pulled me to the ground. My chest hit the tile and it knocked the air out of me. I tried to scream "Help me, help me," but I was short of breath and choking. I clawed at the ground, trying to pull myself across it with the strength in my arms, but the vine overtook my stomach and chest. I again tried to scream for help; the vines tightened around my chest and grew around my mouth "Please, help me!" I lay helpless, my arms and legs bound and my mouth gagged, and watched the creature slowly peer at me from behind a flower vase. His face was leathery and free of fur, like a rat's tail. Fear grew in his beady eyes as they dilated and his nostrils flared. He shook, as did I.

I tried to shake free, but the vine only grew tighter the more I moved. The creature hid behind the vase as footsteps approached me from behind. I wondered what would come of me; had someone come to save me, hurt me, teach me another lesson. Whoever it was, they approached slowly. The steps grew louder as I focused on the sound and tried to gauge how close they were to me. The sole of the shoe thumped against the floor like a baseball falling into a new leather mitt "thump, thump, thump." It must have been a man or a large woman; the steps were heavy and clumsy. They stopped right above my head, but I did not dare turn around.

After several seconds, I wondered if I had been left to the vines. Perhaps the footsteps were never real at all. Perhaps they were a manifestation of my fear. I let Alcaeus' ideas about reality consume me. I wanted to shout or turn around and look, but the vines restrained me. For a moment the vines loosened to the point I thought I might be released, but then they grew tighter than before and whipped me into the air. I closed my eyes and took in a deep breath through my nose. I was certain they would plunge me back into the ground, to my death. Instead, the vines held me up, suspended in air.

A gust of wind blew through my hair and against my eyelids. I tried to let my mind escape to memories of home, remembering the way storms would roll onto the prairie and how the wind felt on my face. I opened my eyes, almost expecting to see a lightning bolt or a willow swaying in the wind. Instead, I hung helplessly suspended in front of the faceless creature that had stood behind me moments ago. Surprisingly, it was not a beast or some magical creature, but a human figure in the same white robe that the locals wore. I was tired of being restrained, of being the victim. I shook my body and kicked my feet. It was no use. I drew deep breaths in and out of my nose, but I couldn't get enough air. I was suffocating as my heart raced in my chest. As I hung my head in exhaustion, the man finally spoke; his every word a long drawn out whisper.

"I am not here to hurt you, but to encourage you to stay on your guard. You have seen Leotus today and Alcaeus has taught you about reality. Remember though, reality is not always what it seems. Fear is often used for oppression, and oppression will make good men fight. Good and evil does exist here, but I encourage you to look for both in every man. It is true that you are strong Jayden, stronger than I. It is important for you to know the true intentions of those you call friend, or you might just lose all you have been chosen to fight for. We were once a nation of men, not a nation under one man."

With his warning spoken and his veil still on, he turned his back and walked away. His footsteps still heavy, like the weight he carried on his heart. His back wasn't straight and his arms hung at his side like a tired soul. When he was about thirty feet from me, the vines loosened and I fell a few feet to the ground. My body collapsed as I hit the tile floor. My body was weak as I gasped for the air I had been denied. I pressed my chest off the ground and looked up as he walked away. I could only muster a few lines, clinging to every word "If you are a good man, if I should trust anything that you say, then why do you hide behind a veil? Show your face, coward!"

He stopped to listen, as I used all my breath to push the words from the bottom of my chest. As I fell back to the ground he turned around. He put his hands to his neck and grabbed the veil in his fists. He stood for a moment, contemplating what to do, then he turned around and dropped his hands to his side "Jayden, soon you will understand why I cannot reveal my identity to you. To do so would cost my life, which I would gladly give it if I believed you were ready to fight for our people, but I am not sure you are. Know that I call you a friend."

He took a few more steps and then disappeared from the center court in the same way that I had watched Havenbrook disappear from my life that morning, in an explosion of light and color. His energy filled the room and strengthened me as my body absorbed it. I did not know if he was a good man, but for a moment I could feel the righteousness of his heart upon me. I longed to know more about him; who he was, where he was from, why he had come to warn me.

I pulled myself off of the ground, much stronger than I was moments before. The grip of the vines had wrinkled my robe, like the clothing I often let lay in the laundry basket for weeks. I looked to the Sequoia trunk, but the door had been closed. The creature must have made it back inside in all the commotion. I walked up to the trunk, but no longer saw a way inside. What had once been a cracked-open door, now appeared to be a solid tree. I walked around to the other trunks thinking I might have had the wrong tree, but they were all the same. I was tired and confused and decided to just head up to Caiohme's room.

As I made my way toward Eurus Hall, I thought about all the events of the day: the state championship game, Katie cheering on the sidelines, our horseback ride. I wondered if I would ever get the chance to tell Katie how I really felt. I already missed her dimples and the simple ways she found to make me smile. I thought of Leotus and all the things I had seen. There was beauty in the simplicity of the street lights, the homes and the land, but elegance in the castle. I felt like I could build myself a home on the water and live happily ever after. I thought of the evil, in the darkness and the beasts, and where else it might lay. I wondered what was behind the door on the Sequoia trunk and who I could trust. I was nervous to continue with the experience, but excited to learn who I was and what I was capable of. What I thought of most though was Caiohme and Chloe, and I was excited to continue to build a relationship with them.

Before I knew it, I was standing in front of the doors that read "Girls Dormitory." I had been so deep in thought and tired that I didn't notice anything along the way. I walked through the doors and received a nervous stare from a group of three young girls that were still awake. They weren't as young as Chloe but could not have been much older than twelve or thirteen. One had blond hair and the other two brown. They pointed at me, giggled, and whispered among themselves until the blond asked in a timid voice "Can we help you find something, Jayden?" She looked up at me, as the other two exchanged googly-eyed-giggles back and forth.

I looked over at her and smiled "I am just looking for Caiohme's room. She is a friend of mine." She pointed to a room in the opposite corner as mine "It is right over there."

"Thank you!" I whispered.

As I walked over to her room, I noticed that the lobby was set up much the same way as ours. Board games sat on a book shelf and lay strewn across the rugs. Plants sat under the sky-lights and brown leather couches sat in front of a stone fireplace. Instead of black rugs, beige rugs lined the floors and white blinds covered the windows. The walls were light purple and stars covered the ceiling.

I approached the door with Caiohme and Samarra engraved in it. I tapped lightly on the door twice, hoping to not wake Samarra. After a couple minutes, no one had answered so I tapped again a little harder. Still, there was no answer. I didn't want to go to sleep without seeing Caiohme. I put my hand on the door knob and gently turned the handle. It opened and I walked in slowly, whispering her name "Caiohme you awake? Caiohme?" The lights were on, but there was no answer.

As I entered the room I could tell there was no one in the far bed, but a short entry way blocked my view of the nearest bed. I peeked around the corner and could not help but smile and let out a little giggle of my own. Caiohme and Chloe were both lying on top of the covers, fully dressed in their formal wear. Caiohme was on her back with her arms and legs sprawled across the bed. Chloe was lying at the bottom of the bed with her head on Caiohme's stomach and her arms around her waist. Chloe's mouth was wide open and Caiohme's robe was wet with drool. I was sure that was exactly how I looked after a hard day of football practice. I stood, looking over them for a while. They both looked so peaceful after a long, stressful day. That was, until Chloe started babbling about some nonsense. I couldn't make out much of what she was saying but it had something to do with Dalkey and flying dogs. I laughed hard, but put my hands over my mouth so that I would not wake them.

As selfish as I wanted to be, I could not wake her just to say goodnight after the day we had been through. They both needed their sleep. I turned around and quietly opened the closet door where I found a couple extra blankets. I grabbed them and pressed them to my face. The scent reminded me of a time when I was little. I would hide in sheets that my mother put on the clothes line to dry in the hot Kansas sun. She would pretend she couldn't find me shouting my name "Jayden, Jayden where are you?" then sneak up on me and tickle me until I almost peed my pants. As much as she perturbed me at times, I could not imagine not seeing her again.

I walked over to the bed and unfolded the blankets. I spread one over their bodies and put the other at their feet in case they got cold. I stepped quietly up to the head of the bed and looked down at Caiohme. I softly brushed her wavy hair from her face and tucked it behind her ear; it was as soft as the cotton they grew in southeastern Kansas. She hadn't gotten all the sand from her hair and ears, but all I could see was beauty. I bent over and put my lips to her forehead and lightly kissed her. I let them linger for a moment, until her head rolled my way and I was afraid I had woken her. I pulled back, expecting her to be startled, but she did not open her eyes. I pulled the blanket over her shoulder and walked back to the chair that sat in front of her bed. I sat down and pulled my feet into it, wrapping my arms around my knees. I only intended to close my eyes for a minute or two, but before long I had passed out.

CHAPTER SIX
Interrupted Dreams

I HAD NOT dreamt in months, but on that night my dreams were vivid and unusual. I woke from a slumber, lying in an old porch hammock, buried in the warmth of an Egyptian cotton sheet. Looking east, I caught a spectacular view of the sunrise on the ocean. Rays of sun glistened on my face and arms as it kissed the horizon, staining the sky with hues of pink and orange and casting light across the water and land. The sun's reflection gave the appearance of fire on the waves and flakes of gold in the sand. I yawned and stretched my arms and legs as the rays warmed my exposed skin. A feeling of relaxation came over my thighs and shoulders as the fibers of my being uncoiled.

I lifted my legs from the hammock and sat up. My bare feet rested on old, white porch boards. The constant wear and tear of wind, sand, and salt water had left them warped and splintered. The white paint was peeling everywhere, but especially along a path from the stairs to the front door. I could feel the soft tickle of sand on my feet as I curled my toes back. I put my hands on my knees and stood up, relieving the pressure my weight put on the old, rusted hook that the hammock hung from. The support beams let out a sigh of relief as they squeaked back into place.

The porch formed an L-shape around the North and East ends of the home. The hammock hung on the east end, but close to the corner; near the stairs. I stepped down the stairs onto the sandy path. The warm granules of fine, white sand crept between my toes as my feet sunk into it. With every step I took, it felt like I was slipping backwards. The sand tickled the soles of my feet but was oddly relaxing, as a million grains of earth massaged my skin in a way human hands never could.

I stood for a moment and took a deep breath through my nose as I looked out onto the land. Green grass surrounded the home, but a sandy path led all the way to the water. The sweet briny mist made me think of a child's laughter and sand castles on a warm summer day. Wind had formed rolling dunes to the left and right of the trail. Tall grasses blew in the wind and purple-flowering vines gave proof of spring. Waves broke on the beach, pulling stranded life and seaweed back into the clear, blue water. Focusing on the sand, I saw a tiny, white crab scamper down the path in front of me. A rattle from inside the house pierced the soft roar of the waves. I looked back.

The house was beautiful. Its stucco exterior was almost the same color as the water, a cyan blue and the shutters were glossy white. The porch was the only part of the home that needed new paint, but it added character. A large, second-story balcony looked off to the east and was enclosed by white spindles. A room, almost completely encased in glass, lay behind the balcony. The house had many windows to allow light in and old bamboo blinds. The flowerbeds were filled with wildflowers and tall, wild grasses. Palm trees dotted the perimeter of the grass and corners of the home.

The sound I had heard was the front door opening. Brightly colored, stained glass windows surrounded the mahogany door, which had a huge starfish hanging on it. The hinges squeaked as it opened and a slightly older Katie than I knew stepped out. She was wearing white Capri's and a coral tank top adorned with tiny shells and sequins. Her hair was longer and kissed by the sun; it was messy and hung in her face, like she had just woken up. Her skin was tanner and she had put on just a few pounds. I walked to the porch and met her, as she smiled down at me. Handing me a cup of coffee, she hugged me tightly as she whispered in my ear "Morning handsome."

I kissed her on her cheek and took a sip of the strong, dark coffee as we sat down on the stairs. The aroma was rich and rejuvenating as I inhaled the warm steam through my nose; it was bold, with a cabernet-like wineyness on my tongue. "Thanks for the wake-me-up. Looks like I ended up passing out on the porch again; sorry. Feel like I always need to be vigilant. Thanks for the sheet!"

She looked over at me and her faint smile faded. Sliding her left arm onto my lap, she wrapped her fingers around mine. There was a certain comfort and security in the way her soft hands felt on my rough skin. She turned towards me and put her right hand on top of my knee, looked into my eyes and sighed as her lip quivered and her knee shook. The discerning expression on her face said what she couldn't. I hugged her "It's going to be ok Katie."

She broke down and began to sniffle. It hurt my heart to see her so scared for me, for us. I pulled her into me and put my forehead to hers as a tear fell from the corner of her eye and down her cheek. I kissed her forehead and she broke down into a soft cry. She squeezed my hand and whimpered "We'll have to leave again, wont we? Just say it! You're at the walls all day. I can see the fear in your eyes when you look at me. I can't lose you! I have lost too much!"

I closed my eyes and kissed her soft lips, not wanting her to see the emotion on my face. A shiver shot down my spine as I thought of losing her; my palms grew sweaty and a knot formed in my throat "Katie, look at me! You will never lose me!" I promised with an emotionally shaken voice. "I am down there every day to make sure that we are safe. I will fight to protect you, our family and this home." I looked out onto the land with a sweeping gesture of my hand "I will fight for all of this."

She curled up and pulled my hand into her lap, putting her head on my chest, "Jayden, there are so many things I thought I would never loose and have. I just want to swim in the water and walk on the beach without the fear that you won't come home. I'm tired of hiding behind the walls. I can't…"

The door opened behind us. She wiped her teary eyes on my shirt as I looked back. A little three or four year-old girl ran up and jumped in between us and wrapped her arms around me "Daddy, daddy, guess what?"

I looked up at her and laughed "What hunny?"

"Lijah turned the turtle into a puppy!" Her eyes gleaned with excitement as she laughed and jumped barefoot into the sand. She looked up to me with the same freckles and dimples as her mother, and a puppy dog face I could not resist "Daddy can we keep him? Can we, can we?"

"What? Oh no, not poor Murtle!" I exclaimed, as if it was a tragedy, with my eyes and mouth open wide. "How will he ever learn to live as a dog? I suppose we can keep him, but he will probably want fish for dinner and he'll want to live in your bathtub."

I couldn't help but chuckle as she stood there with a sad, concerned face. "Daddy, you can change him back can't you? I don't want him to live in my tub."

I nodded yes and laughed "Of course I can Jaylee!"

She giggled and ran up to me, wrapping her arms tightly around my neck "Love you daddy!" then looked over to Katie "Love you mommy!"

She sat down in front of us and Katie began to braid her long, light brown hair. Malachi quickly paced out of the house with the wet puppy in his arms "Crazy dog tried to jump in the tank and eat a fish." He had on blue jeans and a fitted, grey t-shirt that was soaked. He laughed as the dog barked and shook his wet coat all over us. His smile seemed genuine and unconcerned. He sat the puppy down and played with him in the grass. A white shell necklace bounced off of his chest as he lunged back and forth after the puppy.

Jaylee ran into the yard, jumping and running in circles as the dog chased after her. The loud pitch of her laughter was not enough to drown out the jet that flew overhead. A feeling of uneasiness grew as it circled back around and we noticed the red markings on the tail of the stealthy, silver craft; two crossed bones under a hatchet, the enemy's symbol. Malachi grabbed Jaylee and the dog and ran for the front door, but it was too late.

He let Jaylee down and handed her the puppy as three guards approached on horseback, wearing the crimson red uniforms of the opposition. Malachi stood his ground as he motioned for Jaylee to run inside. He didn't have to tell her though; she was smart enough to know what was going on. She ran inside screaming "Lijah, Lijah, Lijah!"

Katie looked at the guards and shouted from behind me "Just leave us be, we have done nothing for you to be here. There are horses in the barn and chickens in the coup. Take them and leave." She ran inside after Jaylee, bawling and pleading as the men hopped off their horses "Please, Please leave."

They laughed and spit at our feet as she walked inside. The largest of them took another step towards me, with a man on each side "We can trade Jayden, your life for hers. Or we can just kill you and have our way with her. She will make for great childbearing."

I hacked up the mucus from the back of my throat and spit in his face "Your filthy hands will not open that door knob before

I chop them off and use them to kill your own men. Then I will bring your dead corpse to your people and they will see that you are simply a man, not something to be worshiped or idolized!"

Malachi stood tightly by my side and put his arm around me as he whispered in my ear "We have prepared for this day brother. Our sacrifice will pave the way for our children's future. Do what you must. No questions, no hesitation."

We stood there staring at them as they drew their bows from their backs. I had no fear and I knew what I had to do. I waited until they drew their arrows back. They stared at us with no inhibition or sense of justice; happy to kill off another one of our people. Then they fired.

I put my hands up and closed my eyes, but immediately felt a tugging on my pants. Had Jaylee stepped between the guards and me? I quickly opened my eyes, jumping forward in the chair and looking all around me. I feel back and sighed with relief to see Caiohme and Chloe sleeping soundly in front of me. It was only a dream, just a dream. My heart was pounding in my chest and my skin was clammy. I put my hand on my eyes and rubbed them.

How could it have been a dream? It all seemed so real; a life with Katie, a family, all of the things I realized I couldn't live without during halftime of the football game. The emotion, the excitement, the fear pulsed through my body like it was me on that beach. I closed my eyes again, sure that I would open them and Katie would be by my side, but when I did I was still in Leotus. I was still in the place that threatened to take her from me.

I didn't know how long I had been asleep, but not long enough. My eyes were still tired and sore and my vision was blurry. My breathing slowed and I let my hands fall into my lap. My head fell to my shoulder and my eyes grew heavy. I tried to hold them open, flashes of dark, light, dark. I began to drift off again and my eyes closed. I yawned deeply, but didn't fall back asleep before I felt a tugging at my pants again. I opened my eyes and looked down. My legs were like springs as I jumped from the chair with a scream. Looking up at me, and waiving something in my face, was the creature from the Sequoia trunk. It jumped backward as I jumped out of the chair.

Caiohme rolled around in the bed and stretched as Chloe continued to talk in her sleep. I looked at the creature and then back at her. It continued to take steps backward, towards the door. I stood by the bed staring at it, waiting for it to lunge at me. I knew at any moment it might attack me, like the beasts in the darkness, waiting for its chance; I would not give it one. Caiohme pulled her head off of her pillow and barely opened her eyes "Jayden? Is that you?"

I looked back at the creature "Yah, it's me. Stay in your bed." I grabbed the lamp from the nightstand and took a step toward it. It was shorter than I earlier thought, no more than two feet tall. It had a scar under its right eye that stretched from the nostril to the outer corner of the eye. Its nose was tiny and pointed with its nostrils facing outward and it had thin pink lips, almost identical to a humans.

Caiohme sat up in bed, with the cover pulled up to her shoulders. She was more alert than before "Why are you here Jayden? What is going on?" she asked as she pulled the cover further up her body and drew closer to Chloe. Did she think I was there to hurt her, Chloe? Did she not remember inviting me?

I tried to stay calm and told a white lie to avoid startling her "You invited me last night. I drifted off and fell asleep in the chair until this large rat wandered across my feet. Don't worry though; I am taking care of it."

She screamed "Ewww, gross! Kill it, kill it!"

I raised the lamp in the air, prepared to throw it at the creature. It was shaking in the corner when it let out a shrill, rapid cry "No, no, no! Don't kill me. Master sent me. He sent me with the letter. He needs you. You are in danger, great danger!"

I dropped the lamp to my side. Even after all I had seen that day, a talking two-foot-tall rat still startled me. As I calmed down and studied him, the way he had backed into the corner, the tremors that rolled down his body, I noticed he was more scared of me than I of him. He did not mean me harm and I sat the lamp on the ground.

Caiohme threw the blanket off and got out of bed. "A talking rat huh? Since when do rats speak Jayden? What are you trying to hide?"

I stood their silently and laughed, throwing my hands toward the door "In Leotus I guess. Come and see for yourself. He does not seem to want any trouble."

She stomped around the edge of the bed, shaking her head as if there was not an ounce of truth to what I was saying. Then she saw it, grabbed my shirt and yanked me in front of her "Oh my gosh Jayden, what is it? Don't hurt it! It's shook. Can't you see he's shook?"

Then, the girl that cowered and shrilled in front of a little worm the day before walked right up to the creature. It held an envelope in the air and she took it from him "What is it, little guy?"

He was calmer without a raised lamp to threaten his being, but his speech was still skittish. His tone was high, but he spoke softly, like someone might be listening "Read it, read the letter. We leave today, at nightfall. My master has sent for you. He has told me of this day for many years and it has come. We haven't much time. "

A panicked cry came from the bed "Cai, Caiohme, Caiohme where are you?"

Caiohme handed me the letter and hurried over to the bed as Chloe began to cry. I held it between my hands and looked down at it. It was white in places, but most of its surface was covered with brown stains and dirt. I ran my fingers across the crumpled surface. It was soft and slightly moist to the touch. I brought it up to my face to examine the symbols across the front; it was a language I did not understand "ο αγαπημένος μου γιός." It smelt musty, like an unfinished basement or crawl space after a summer storm.

I was anxious, but scared to open it. What new surprises waited inside? What untold truths would be revealed? How many more lies would I have to face before I knew who I was? Would I ever know who I was? The envelope slipped out of my fingers and fell to the ground. For a moment I did not hear Chloe or Caiohme or the birds outside the window; all I heard was a sharp ping as the edge of the letter met the ground and then fell flat.

Everything was silent as I stood there starring at the letter. It felt like the whole world had stopped, but mine kept revolving. I bent my knees to pick up the envelope and they popped like a peanut shell being crushed on a dirty restaurant floor. I looked at the letter's wrinkled surface again, the foreign language a reminder of how little I knew of Leotus, of myself, of the whole situation. I reached my hand out and pulled the letter into my palm and all the energy of the room came rushing back; the soothing sound of Caiohme's voice, the giggle of a little girl, the soft song of a canary, a crickets chirp. Something was missing; the servant, the rat. Where had it gone?

My eyes quickly scanned the room: in the corner, under the bed, near the balcony. It wasn't until I became distracted by Caiohme's voice that I found him, up on the bed with the girls. Chloe was giggling as she combed through his matted hair with her fingers. He seemed to enjoy being petted; resting on Chloe's lap like a puppy getting his belly rubbed. He made a strange sound, a loud purr with occasional grunts. Chloe quickly fell in love with the strange creature and even Caiohme seemed to have a fondness for the mangy thing; I wasn't so sure. I didn't think he could cause us much harm, but what were his intentions? Who had sent him?

I walked over to the chair I had fallen asleep in and sat down, the letter in my hand. I ran my fingers over its edges, rotating it around and around. What danger could we face from inside the castle walls? Alcaeus was here, and Deseus, and Erebus. Surely, Alcaeus would protect us from any threat, but could he? He hadn't protected Ex.

Caiohme looked up to me and yawned "Just open it already! Maybe there is something important inside. Maybe it contains some truth, or in the least, it could shed some light on all the secrecy."

"Or, it could be just another lie, another disappointment!" I murmured, as I tore the corner and ran my finger against the top edge, splitting it open. I pulled the letter from inside and let the envelope fall to my lap. The pages were in remarkably better condition than the envelope, crisp and beige; they stuck together like dollars straight from the mint. Dad always encouraged the cashiers at our market to crinkle crisp bills up so that they didn't accidentally hand out two.

I ran my eyes over the black ink, not reading any word in particular. The calligraphy was unique, sharp points and curves, large arches. The lines were precisely spaced equal distances apart. Someone had put a lot of time into writing the words. I ran my fingers across the page and the ink stood off the stationary like brail. I read the first line in my head "My Beloved Son," but did not read any further before Chloe interrupted all the thoughts the salutation had implanted in my brain "Read it out loud, I want to hear the story too."

"It's not a story Chloe, it's just a letter. I'll tell you a story later." I did not want to read it aloud to her. I didn't know what its contents were. The words could have scarred her or it could have been a private matter.

Caiohme chimed in "Well, what if I want to hear it? Read it to us!"

"I don't want to scare her Caiohme." I said softly.

"I am sure it does not go into any gory detail and it can't be any worse than what she has already seen. Just read it." She looked down at the rat "Is it something she should hear too?"

He sat there for a moment and seemed to think about the right words. The movement of his tiny eyes, the creases in his forehead; it seemed like he was calculating the risk of it all. Then he looked up to me and nodded "The girl can hear."

I sighed and pulled the letter closer to my face. For a moment I read the first line over and over again in my head "My beloved son, my beloved son, my beloved son." Why had Alcaeus written me a letter and had it delivered in the middle of the night? How did he know to deliver it to Caiohme's room? Did he need the secrecy of nightfall, the lack of spoken word? Was it urgent? Or possibly, was the letter from my father in Havenbrook? Did he know of my predicament? Did he know I was in danger? Which father had the letter meant? The runaway train my thoughts were on quickly halted at Chloe's insistence "read it, read it, read it!"

I shook my head, rubbed my eyes, and began to read the letter aloud.

"My Beloved Son,

If my servant has delivered this letter to you then a period of urgency is upon us. Your life, others' lives, and your home are in danger. Many will lie to you and try to mislead you; it will be difficult to decipher friends from foes. You must trust my direction. I know your father, John Foster; he is a close friend of mine. He recited to you the virtues of a good man when you were a child; prudence, temperance, justice and fortitude. Every year, on your birthday, he would take you to the

hill that overlooked your land, and tell you "remember to have cour-
age not only in the face of danger, but also under pain. Remember
that justice is not only in law, but also in fairness and honesty. Use
your common sense and do only as much as need be done." He recited
this to you because he knew this day would come. Go to your room.
Under your bed you will find three loose boards, remove them. There
will be several vials along with various other objects; gather them all.
You must leave precisely at six thirty to make it to the safe house before
dark. Pack lightly and bring only those who you are sure you can trust.
The journey will be treacherous, but can be made in a short time if
all is well. My servant will escort you, he has the knowledge to get you
here safely, follow him. You will encounter beasts, many are friendly,
but some mean you harm. Delusions are common in the whispering
woods, keep your mind sharp and don't let fatigue set in. Lastly, be
courageous. I await your arrival."

There was no valediction, though the salutation told me the letter was from a man that called me son, a man that knew my father. The writer knew things about me, things I had never told anyone. I looked up to Caiohme and shared what I had silenced for so long "On my twelfth birthday my father took me up to the hill that overlooked our land. He told my mother it was to clean up debris that the spring storms had left, but when we got to the top he had me sit in the hammock with him. He told me things would happen in my life that I could not understand at that moment, but that I must learn the virtues of a good man and live by them. He recited them to me several times that day and made sure I understood them. If I strayed from the conversation he grew angry and stern, pounding the idea in my head over and over. Every year, on my birthday, we would have the same conversation; he never let me forget it."

I took a deep breath "Eventually, he had me recite the

virtues to him, explain them too him. He would ask me how I was using them in my life and how I could use them in the future. He warned me that soon a day would come that I would be on my own."

Looking back I did not take the warnings for what they were "I thought he meant when I graduated, went off to college, not now. He told me that I would struggle, but that if I lived by the virtues I stood as good a chance as any. I always laughed about it, joked with my friends about it. I never took him seriously and on my last birthday he didn't have the talk with me. I was thankful to not have to listen to it another year. Now it seems their might have been real value in it all. I never understood any of it until now. How could he have had possibly known that any of this would happen? " I let my forehead fall into my hands.

"You couldn't have known Jayden! You didn't know this day would come." Caiohme walked up to me and put her arm around my shoulder.

"I could have treated him better. It was one of the rare occasions he really took time to talk to me. It was…" a loud bang interrupted my sentence and then another. A door being slammed, something falling, another attack; the sound echoed in the hallway.

Chloe's shoulders jumped, startled by the volume of the noises "What was that?"

The rat was more startled than the rest of us. He jumped out of the bed and started pacing back and forth on the floor "We must go! We must go! We must go now Jayden!" Another loud bang sent us all to our feet!

"Hide me in a bag. I can't be seen; hurry, hurry!" he squealed as he paced the room. Caiohme grabbed the bag we had used to pack up the picnic earlier and dumped it on the bed. He quickly climbed inside and distorted his body to fit well below the top of the bag.

"Boom, boom" two more loud noises echoed in the hallway, much closer to Caiohme's room. I could hear footsteps from down the hallway, heavy on the floor. Chloe grabbed the blue blanket and stuffed it into the bag with the creature.

Caiohme wrapped her arm around Chloe "Good idea sis!"

"Let's get to my room." I insisted, as the footsteps grew closer.

Chloe grabbed the bag and we walked to the bedroom door. We listened for a moment and noticed the footsteps had stopped. I put my ear up to the door, nothing. I reached for the handle, but as I put my hand on it, it began to turn. I took a step backward, put my hands to the side and pushed Caiohme and Chloe behind me. The door slowly opened and in tip-toed Malachi, looking behind himself.

He was startled as he looked in our direction, jumping backward and throwing his fists up "Whoa dude, whoa! It's just us!" I divulged quickly.

He let out a big sigh of relief "Damn, you all scared me! What are you doing up so early?"

I had to think quickly; why were we up so early? I turned the questions back on him. "Oh, you know; couldn't get much sleep in such an unfamiliar place, decided to go get some breakfast and coffee. New town, new beds, loud noises! Say, you wouldn't know what any of those bangs were about would you? Where is Samarra? Why are you up? "

"Scarred of some shadows and loud chatter in the hall after what you have been through Jayden? Maybe you're right though, something strange is going on. The white coats are going room to room looking for something, someone. They have been aggressive; breaking things, twisting arms, questioning everyone. I knew nothing of it until I got back. Samarra and I have been up all night on the beach. She went to grab us breakfast and wanted to meet here to talk. I saw them searching room to room and tried to get inside before they saw me. The three of you should stay; there are things you should know! It seems like it could get ugly; wouldn't want you to be caught off guard!"

He stepped forward as he talked, scooting us deeper and deeper into the room. His words were uncertain, filled with stutters and pauses. I didn't feel like he was being honest with us and the less room there was between him and us, the more uncomfortable I felt. His dark eyes, his devious grin, why was he not more startled by the loud noises or the searches he spoke of? Why had the noises stopped when he got to the room? Why had Samarra not arrived yet?

"Well, we are pretty hungry. I think we are going to eat. Maybe we could talk about what you know after we get done?" I walked up to him and stood face to face until he stepped out of the way; then I walked out of the door. Caiohme and Chloe followed, totting our new friend.

He watched us walk out the door and down the hall "What's in the bag?"

Caiohme looked back as she walked "Just a blanket, we thought we might eat on the beach." She smiled and waved goodbye.

CHAPTER SEVEN

Growing Suspicion

KATIE, CHLOE, OUR new friend and I walked west quietly, toward Zephyrus hall. There was no need to draw attention to ourselves if the white coat story was true. Chloe handed the bag to Caiohme, with the creature buried inside, who handed it to me. We did not see any other wanderers until we had made it half way around the circle, where Sequoia trunks rose above the center court to the ceiling. Two young boys walked like zombies towards the dormitory, dragging their feet on the ground and rubbing their eyes. It was apparent the two had been awake all night. It was lucky fate that they were too tired to notice the rustling in the bag as we passed by them into the dormitory.

Caiohme and Chloe looked around the lobby as we walked back to my room, but didn't say anything until the door closed behind us. I threw the bag on the bed, forgetting what was inside.

"Jayden!" Caiohme gasped as she rushed over to the bed.

The creature rolled onto the bed, caught his bearings, and darted under the pillow "Wake me at dusk. I must stay hidden until then. The men must not find me." He seemed more scared than when I had the lamp raised above his head. Some familiarity with the loud noises must have startled him. I wanted to know what he knew about Leotus, but more than that, I wanted to know what was under my bed.

I lowered myself onto my knees and elbows and peered under the bed. I did not see a handle and could not tell if any boards were loose. I would have to crawl under. Chloe jumped onto the bed as I lay on my stomach; it rattled the floor just enough for me to see a couple boards bounce above the rest. They were loose; it couldn't just be coincidence. The words in the letter seemed to hold some truth.

Chloe comforted the creature as I crawled further under the bed "You don't have to be scared of anything when you are with us. Jayden and Caiohme will protect you. They are special!" I laughed. I couldn't even protect myself as the beasts beat me, how would I protect anyone else?

Dust and hair lay undisturbed on the floor. Whoever had removed the boards had not done so recently. I sneezed as I pulled myself up to the loose boards; they had clearly been cut away from the rest of the floor. My nails were not long enough to get between them. I hollered from under the bed "Caiohme, can you find me a knife or screwdriver or something to pry the boards back?"

"Um yah, any ideas where something like that might be?" Her voice was tired. None of us had gotten enough sleep.

I thought for a moment if I had seen anything lying around the room; on my desk, in the closet, in the bathroom; no, no, no. I had not even been in the bathroom. On my bed, the gift basket, there was a bottle opener in it "Yah, get me the bottle opener from my gift basket. It's near the footboard."

I waited patiently under the bed while she located the basket and rustled threw it. I tried to not breathe too heavily; dust always seemed to upset my allergies. I knew I would be sneezing for days. I tapped my fingers as I grew impatient. It was taking longer than it should have.

"Found it! Not fair, you got candy in your basket. Sour Patch Kids, my favorite!"

"About time" I laughed "You been eating my candy? Better stay out of that; I licked each piece earlier today in anticipation that Malachi might get into it."

She lowered herself to her knees, then her elbows, and crawled up next to me. With candy in one hand and the tool in the other she flaunted it in front of my face, pulling it back each time I reached for it and laughing "This what you're looking for? Huh? Huh?"

I lunged for it with the arm closest to her and she brought her hand behind her back. I was almost on top of her, reaching behind her, grabbing at the tool. The space was tight and I found myself starring at her as she kept it out of my reach. The way she smiled, her playful nature, it reminded me of Katie. I moved my left hand down her back and ran my other through her hair. I leaned in, kissed her lips and closed my eyes. For a moment I was back in Havenbrook, in the hammock on the hill. Caiohme was Katie and that was our first real kiss. Her hand fell on top of mine as our lips lingered. I pulled her head closer to mine and kissed her more passionately.

She smiled and handed me the tool as I pulled myself away from her. "So that is how you get your way, huh?" I questioned.

I laughed and took some candy from the bag that she had already opened. I popped a few pieces in my mouth and sucked on them. The sour juices moved to the sides of my tongue and my lips puckered; I scrunched my nose and my mouth salivated. I quickly chewed the candy up and the sweet, fruity taste overpowered the sour. I hated the sour taste, but once it was gone I always wanted more. "You're lucky you know! I never share my sour patch kids with anyone; not anyone."

She crawled out from under the bed "Better get used to it; I always get what I want." She laughed "Try to make it quick Jayden; I'm hungry."

I stuck the tip of the tool between the boards and wiggled it back and forth until I had forced it into the crack. On the first attempt I pulled the bottle opener up too quickly and the board came up and fell right back into place. I shoved the tool back between the boards and pulled it up slowly the second time, tilting it back as I pulled; first a crack, then a quarter inch, then a half inch. I stuck my finger under the board and dropped the tool. I reached my hand into the space and removed the board from the floor. I sat it aside, then the second, then the third board.

It was dark under my bed, but the morning sun crept beneath it just enough for me to see the rectangular wooden box. The box sat between two steel beams in a bed of saw dust, metal shavings and spider webs. It wasn't large, maybe as long and wide as a football. I reached through the webs, goose bumps shooting up my arm, and grabbed it. I hated spiders and was glad to see the corpse of a few that had long since been deceased. The box was very un-proportional; far heavier than it was large. I held it above the boards as I used my legs to pull myself from under the bed. No sense in leaving a trail of scratches that someone might see.

I rose to my feet. Chloe had passed out with her head below the pillow and Caiohme was sitting on the edge of the bed watching her sleep "The animal was too afraid to come out and Chloe didn't want him to feel alone. She's always been one to comfort; she is so compassionate, like our mother."

I smiled "Seems like the two of you have even more in common than I realized!"

I sat the box on my desk, pulled out the chair and sat down. The stains on the letter, the dust covering the lid, how long had the creature carried the message? Was it still relevant? Why had the man not come to take me from Leotus himself? I was nervous to open it. What were the vials he spoke of, what other objects were inside? What kind of journey did he expect us to make?

Caiohme walked over as I dusted the surface of the box. The color of the wood reminded me of a jewelry box my father had given my mother long ago, Patagonian Rosewood, deep reddish brown. The box was hinged in the back. I put my hands on the lid, with my thumbs on the front edge, and opened it up to a picture on top. Caiohme grabbed it before I saw it "Who are they?"

"I don't know; you didn't let me see it!" I held my right hand above my shoulder, waiting to see who was in the picture and rummaged through the box with my left. Three vials of dark blue fluid corked with wood, a pouch of silver coins, and a compass inside of a pewter case. Carved in the pewter were the astrological symbols for Mars and Venus, which represent man and woman, and a tree, which the symbols stood in front of.

I had been too distracted by the compass to notice that my fingers were coursing back and forth on the portrait. I pulled it down to my face and was stunned by what I saw. The photo was a black and white print of two men standing near the ocean, holding up their catch for the day. I couldn't tell how old it was, but my father was definitely the man on the left. The other man I did not recognize; I had never seen him with my father or in any pictures.

The man in the letter said that he knew my dad, but I was pessimistic as I read those words. If he knew my father, then did my father know of Leotus? Did my father know the significance of this man or was he simply someone he called friend? Why had Alcaeus not mentioned this? I turned around to Caiohme "I think we can trust the letter. The man with the biggest fish in this picture is my father, from Leotus. The two must have known each other and that is good enough for me."

Caiohme pulled the picture out of my hand and stared at it "That is strange; he looks oddly familiar to me, but I can't quite place it. I think…"

Knock, Knock, knock; she could not finish her sentence before a fist hit the door three times. I flinched wondering who might be at the door. We sat silently, hoping they would think we were asleep and leave. Three more knocks and then a light, feminine voice "Excuse me; may I come in? I have urgent new from Alcaeus."

Urgent news from Alcaeus; what could be so urgent as to wake someone that early in the morning? Maybe it had something to do with the loud bangs in the hallway. Maybe they were looking for the creature. Maybe Malachi was right and several white coats were standing outside our door. Whatever it was, I was sure if we did not let them in Alcaeus would come himself. The door handle rattled and there was another knock on the door "If you don't answer we will take the door down!"

I knew there wasn't time to think. I couldn't let them see the box or the creature that had come to warn us. I grabbed the box and dove under the bed. I put the box back into the dusty hole that had been its home for some time and moved the boards back into place. I responded with my best tired voice "What, huh? Just a minute please! I'll be right there."

I pulled myself out from under the bed and grabbed several blankets from the closet. I threw one on Chloe, making sure to cover the creature's feet, which were sticking out from under the pillow. I tossed one on Caiohme and wrapped the other around myself. I whispered in Caiohme's ear "Close your eyes and dream of me." She smiled.

"Jayden, is everything ok?" Her voice grew more impatient and irritated.

"Yah, give me just one more moment."

I pulled the blanket over my shoulders, hiding the dirty robe I had not changed from. I ran my fingers through my hair and walked to the door. I let my hand linger on the handle for a moment, afraid that I could not handle any more bad news or secrets. What if they wanted to come inside? What would they think of Caiohme and Chloe having stayed over? What if they saw that the boards had been tampered with? I looked back to the bed; I couldn't see under it from where I was standing. I twisted the knob and opened the door just a crack "Can I help you with something?"

A petite girl stood directly in front of the door, with a man dwarfing her on each side. When Malachi used the term "white coats" I assumed he meant the natives, but he had meant it more literally. They all dressed similar; black shoes and pants, a black button up shirt or blouse, and a white overcoat. Around their waist they wore a belt with handcuffs and a baton, but no other weapons. Each had a large metal cuff around their right wrist with a symbol engraved in it, an eyeball. Were they some sort of law enforcement or secret service? What significance did the symbol have? Could they be trusted or had the enemy made its way into the castle?

The girl tried to peer into the room, over my shoulders and around my body, but I only had the door open a crack and she was too short to see over me. Her blond hair was pulled straight back in a ponytail. Her light blue eyes looked curiously into mine as she grabbed a metal object from her pocket. It was a shiny, metal tube, about five inches long and hollow. She held it up to my face "Look directly into my eyes Jayden."

As I looked at her she brought the device up to my face and pointed it at my eyes. Without warning, a barrage of colorful light blinded me. It quickly scanned both eyes and she pulled it away before I could bring my hands up to shield them. I had to blink several times before I could see her face again; each time the room grew a little dimmer. She turned to the man on her left "Jayden Foster, it's him."

I had no time to react; they moved swiftly and decisively. Before I knew it she was pushing against me and into the room. She had no sense of personal space; her breast against my chest, her hands on my waist pushing me back. She was strong, but I could have held her back until the two large men pushed into the room behind her. I was in trouble. What would they do when they found the creature, when they knew that I had located the box? I closed the door and turned around "What is the idea behind all of this? You can't just barge in here like that!"

My words meant nothing to them as they went on with their business. The two men were like puppets and she was their master. They followed closely behind her until she started giving them commands "Check the girls, the closets and the bathroom."

The men were used to orders. Without hesitation or thought, they pulled the girls to standing positions and scanned their eyes, then released them before they could adjust. Caiohme was able to keep her footing, but Chloe tripped and fell to the ground. I rushed over to help her up and she wrapped her arms around my legs. One sounded off and then the other "Caiohme Clarkson" "Chloe Clarkson."

The woman scanned the room with the same probe she used to scan my eyes and the two men searched the closets and bathroom. The two-foot-wide ray of light swept through every corner of the room. They worked silently and quickly. I hoped they would leave as quickly as they came. The longer they stayed the less I trusted them; the aggressive way they handled the girls, the silence and the technology. There was barely electricity in Leotus; the most technological thing I had seen was the colors that danced on the walls. How did they have such advanced tools? Who had endowed them with such authority?

Chloe and I sat down on the bed as they gathered in a huddle and whispered about what they had found. Caiohme walked over and joined us; pulling the blanket closer to our backs. Had the creature's feet been showing? Had they spotted him? The girl turned around and looked back at us for a moment. Her eyes gleaned down at the floor and she took a step towards us. Chloe looked up at me "What do they want Jayden?"

"I don't know Chloe, but I promise to not let anything happen to you." I grabbed her tiny hand and wrapped my fingers around it. My hand was wet with the sweat of fear, but hers was steady and trusting.

I looked directly into our guest's blue eyes as she crouched down on the ground. Her composure was so rigid and her eyes so full of authority. I was sure she would pull the box from under the bed and zap us with some sort of laser or futuristic gadget. She put her hand under the bed, but rose without rustling the loose boards. Her hand was cupped around something as she looked at me with a smile. Had one of the vials fallen out as I rushed to hide it? Had she seen the picture?

She raised her hand and opened her palm. Between her thumb and pointer fingers was one of the red sour patch kids. "My favorite candy; haven't seen any of these for a while!" She popped the miniature man in her mouth and laughed. I sighed in relief, but all that ran through my mind was who eats candy off the floor?

She knelt down in front of us and the two men stood behind her "Alcaeus has requested your presence in one hour, in front of the life tree." The life tree, I had to think about it for a moment; then I remembered the tree Alcaeus had created from the wounds the beasts had left me with. It was mine, it was ours.

"Your eyes were scanned to make sure you had not been replaced with a manipulation of yourself. Our enemy is capable of replicating a person; their image, fingerprints, DNA, but there is something about the Iris they have not figured out. The room was scanned to search for a bug. They have created insects, the size of ants, capable of audio and visual recording, made of an alloy that cannot be crushed or destroyed by heat. The only defense we have found is to scramble their memory chips."

I looked at her with curiosity. The implications of such creations sounded dangerous, but the technology sounded amazing. It was like nothing we had in Havenbrook. As far as I knew, such technologies were still beyond the scope of possibility in our world. The woman stood up and turned around as she prepared to leave, but I still did not understand what had spurred their investigation "Why did you suspect they had come after me, that they had been spying on me?"

She turned around and looked at me with frightened eyes and puckered lips. Had she been instructed not to tell me? Had something horrible happened? She was silent for a moment. I was sure she wouldn't tell me anything as she turned to the door, but as she walked away a few words floated from her lips "Last night there were several disappearances! Samarra cannot be found, a manipulation was left in her place."

It did not hit me all at once, but as she strutted out of the room I pieced together what she had said. Samarra, a manipulation; how was it possible? She was strong, polite, kind. She had been taught by Alcaeus, alongside Malachi. Malachi? A light came on and the small flicker of suspicion that fluttered in the back of my brain overcame me like a wildfire racing through the dry prairie.

I stood up and paced the floor as I pieced it together in my head. I did not have to assign blame out loud though; someone was on the same page as I. The creature slid from under the pillow and muttered the words that I hadn't "It was Malachi!"

The words flowed out of his mouth like an accusation, not a question. He was sure; so was I. I paced, thinking out loud

"The way he had treated me in the room, his hatred for Leotus. He did not want to be here, he did not want this fight. His obedience in front of Alcaeus at the dinner festival must have been a ploy to gain his trust, our trust. His kindness to Samarra was a way to get her alone; it allowed him to be near her, to study her habits, her weaknesses. She trusted him." I had looked past all of it; I could have again had it not been for the noises in the night, the way he looked behind himself as he crept into Katie's room, making sure no one had seen him. He turned the blame on us, questioning our actions to take suspicion off his own, telling us some phony story of her whereabouts to throw us off his trail. The only weird thing going on that night was what he had done. He hoped they would be distracted by the other disappearances, not take notice that she was a manipulation.

It was too late now; I knew what he had done, but did they? Did they know that they were searching for a traitor, for Erebus' son, for Malachi? Alcaeus was right; one of our own had betrayed us and no one had taken notice. It was in that moment that I realized the density of the situation. Who would listen as I blamed the son of a powerful creationist? How much time was there? When would Malachi come to replace Caiohme, Chloe, myself? The creature was right; we were in danger and we needed to escape as quickly as we could. Only the shadow of nightfall could provide the vale we needed to get a fair head start.

CHAPTER EIGHT
Viral Hallucinations

THE HOUR FOLLOWING my room invasion was nerve racking.
I found myself searching the room for alloy insects as I got ready
for the day. Several times I was sure I had come across one of
the spies, only to end up with bug guts on my socks. I flinched
at every pair of footsteps I heard in the dormitory and found
myself looking over my shoulder in my own room. I wasn't the
same person I had been in Havenbrook; all sense of safety had
deserted me.

Caiohme insisted on going back to her room and getting
ready, meeting in the center court, but I begged her that we not
separate again. I searched my closet and ended up changing into
one of the only outfits that wasn't a blue robe; dark denim jeans
that were a bit snug and a dark gray polo that was tight in the
arms and chest, but came down over my belt. I quickly brushed
my teeth and ran a comb through my curls. I looked horrible.
The dark rings under my eyes were a deeper purple than they
had ever been. I was too anxious and nervous for a nap, but
completely fatigued.

I came out of the bathroom and found Chloe and Caiohme

near the door, waiting impatiently to leave. I looked under the bed; the boards were still in place, I would come back for the box before we left Leotus. Caiohme had the large picnic bag in her hand and I assumed the creature was inside. I threw on a pair of brown moccasins and met them at the door. I interlaced my fingers in Caiohme's and looked her in the eyes "They didn't sneak in and replace you with a manipulation did they?"

"Let's hurry and get to the girls dorm. Chloe is getting grumpy, she's shagged, and I think we could all use something to eat. It sounds like it could be another long day." She didn't laugh and I didn't blame her. Any excitement or sense of adventure that Leotus had inspired the day before had been overcome by mental and physical exhaustion and a sense of hopelessness. Even Chloe, who was normally full of energy and questions, walked out of the room dragging her feet.

The hallways were busier, but we still only passed a few people. Most seemed energetic and careless; they had no idea what was going on, no one had told them. It wasn't right for them to be pulled from their homes, put in danger and not even told of the circumstance. Who was I to tell them though? To be honest, my only concern was getting Caiohme, Chloe and myself out of Leotus without being noticed. How would I do it though? I didn't know the layout of the land or where we were going. I didn't know who we could trust or how to fend off those we couldn't. What if our guide was killed, what if we got lost? We would need food, gear, weapons.

We entered the girl's dormitory and it was empty, aside from a few girls that were leaving as we walked in. Where was everyone? It was almost eight in the morning. An eerie silence filled the air and I wondered how many disappearances there had been. I stood guard outside Chloe's door as Caiohme went with her to grab a few things. Caiohme quickly returned with an emotional Chloe "Her roommate is gone; the bed is made and it looks like no one slept in it."

I did not want Chloe to worry; she was too young to have those things on her mind. "Maybe they are all eating breakfast or Alcaeus invited them to meet in front of the life tree too. Maybe housekeeping made the beds already. It could be anything Chloe."

Caiohme put on an unconvincing smile "Yah, I guess you're right."

Chloe looked up at me and shook her head "You're not right. I had a dream; Leotus was burning and they were all gone. It was just us, a few of us, and Malachi, and the bad men. It was real. This is real."

I squatted down and looked in her eyes; was this why she had been so silent all morning? Every ounce of her believed what she was saying and nothing I could say was going to change that. Maybe her dream had seemed as real as mine; the intensity of every feeling and emotion rushing through her body like adrenaline. I took her hand "It was just a dream Chloe; I had a very similar one. If any part of it was real though, I promise that I won't let anything happen to you."

She smiled, hugged me, and whispered in my ear "I know. You're the one who saves us!" I knew that if such a thing happened I couldn't save us, but I would save her or die trying. I didn't say anything; instead, I let her hold onto whatever piece of security the dream had given her. She was young and Leotus was no place for her. Why had Alcaeus brought her? What could he possibly expect her to contribute?

I sat on Caiohme's bed as Chloe and she changed in the bathroom. I thought about what Chloe had said and the visions and prophesy of Alcaeus' father. They both had seen me as a leader in this revolution, as a victor. I wondered how Chloe could have possibly known of the conversation between Alcaeus and me. Had she heard the story from others in Leotus and dreamt about it or was the dream her own? Was she some type of visionary or prophet? Surely not I thought, but anything was possible in Leotus.

Caiohme's room was untouched since we left it last; the contents of the picnic bag scattered across the bed. Samarra's blankets were crisp and free of wrinkles. The room was quiet, too quiet. In the silence I saw it out of the corner of my eye, an ant sitting on my shoulder. Given my prior experiences I would have assumed it was just another bug to squish, full of guts, but it did not move. The ant simply sat on my sleeve, listening, watching. For a moment I swore I could hear the signals it was sending to the enemy, to Malachi.

I reached for my shoulder to grab the ant and it jumped backward. This was no ant; ants don't jump I thought. It moved slowly and I was able to pinch it between my fingers. Its metal nippers pierced my skin again and again, like a lancet in the tip of my finger. I screamed and Caiohme came running out "What's wrong Jayden? You ok?"

"The ants are in your room. I found one on me." The words raced out of my mouth and my tone was filled with panic.

At first it didn't register, but then Caiohme realized what I was saying "We need to get out of here, they're probably all over us!" she squealed as she raced to grab Chloe from the bathroom.

Then I heard it, screams coming from outside the room; first a boy, then a girl, then many more. Over and over and over they screamed. I did the only thing I thought might work. I grabbed one of the bottles from our picnic, unscrewed it, ripped the ant from my finger and dropped it into the liquid. I hoped it might destroy the circuits, like it had so many of my cell phones, but I didn't get to see the result before the hallucinations started.

The poison coursed through my veins. The hallucinations were mild at first: distorted faces, blurred colors, the feeling of each bead of sweat dripping from my pores. The screaming was so loud I thought it might burst my ear drum. The heat consumed me; flames rolled over my skin, charring to the depths of my bones. I rolled across the ground, but it only fed the fire. Voices, Katie's voice, Chloe's voice "I told you it would burn," filled my head. Screams, painful screams echoed all around me. Noise, noise, loud noise. My ear drums exploded. Blood flowed out of my ears, my eyes, blood everywhere. All of my horses were dead. My mom, my dad, Katie, they were all dead. Dead, but screaming as the flames consumed them. "No," I screamed, "NO!"

I didn't know how long it lasted, minutes, hours, but when I woke I wasn't lying in Caiohme's room anymore. My body was paralyzed in a cot, covered with ice. The sun was high in the sky; three years in boy scouts told me it was probably twelve-thirty or one. I had been out at least three hours. I tried to raise my head, but my muscles were so sore that I fell back into the slushy ice. Finally, I found the strength to raise my head from the cot and I was astonished by what I saw.

There were rows and rows of cots, seven deep and at least twenty wide. Most cots were filled with people, child and adult, but a few laid empty, the ice tinged with blood. Nurses briskly paced from cot to cot with probes, wires, tools and machines. Deathly screams pierced the still air. Screams like I had never heard on the football field, cries of agonizing pain. Some convulsed, some rolled around restlessly mumbling the words of their nightmares. Some lay silently, motionless. The strong smell of antiseptic wafted through the air.

I pulled my hand from the ice; it was swollen, red and purple up to my shoulder. Tubes ran out of my arm and fingers, allowing a yellow discharge to drain. An IV, in my right arm, delivered clear liquid into my veins. Then I saw them, a hundred yards to the right of me, the dead. All of them tossed into a pile; green gowns, white gowns, children, adults, as if no one person meant anything. This attack was no coincidence, it had been planned. Was Malachi capable of murder, capable of orchestrating such an event, or was it arranged for my escape? My stomach cringed at the thought that I could be responsible and I vomited over the side of the cot.

Caiohme, Chloe, had they suffered the same delusions, the poison? Was it the disaster Chloe had dreamed of? I used what little strength I had to pull myself to a sitting position. To the left, the right, the girls were nowhere near me. I couldn't force myself to survey the dead. They weren't dead I told myself, they would have fought.

The nurses were busy taking care of those in pain and none had noticed I was awake. I screamed "Nurse, nurse!" Two nurses came running over frantically, but one became distracted by a man that had fallen out of bed and was digging at the earth with his hands. He flung dirt in all directions "The bombs, the bombs are coming. We must get underground!" It took three nurses and a doctor to restrain the flailing man and an injection to finally calm him into a stupor. I was too busy watching them drag him back into his cot to notice that the nurse was by my side, examining my hand.

She put her hand on my head "You're warm; the poison has not left your system completely and your hand is infected. The virus they used for the attack is short lived when the body temperature is kept low. Lie down and give it a little more time. Your fever may not break if you exert yourself too much. The virus thrives in hot environments, multiplying and producing hormones that manipulate the temperature control center in your brain, causing fever and an even more favorable environment."

"They? Do we know who carried out the attack?" I asked. She looked at me with a blank stare, as if I should have already known the answer.

"The Farrians are responsible! No one had to tell us, every-one already knows Jayden." Her voice was belittling and slightly irritated. Had Alcaeus not warned them of the traitor he feared was among us? Had she not correlated our arrival with the attack? I wanted to shoot back with a quick reply, tell her who I suspected, but I held my tongue.

She put a hand on my back and the other on my forehead and tried to lower me into the icy bath. "No!" I screamed as I swat-ted her hand from my forehead. She jumped back, not expect-ing such a strong reaction from the sick. Looking at me and then to the other cots, I could tell she was frustrated and wanted to get back to more pressing needs "Look, I'm sorry, I'll let you get back to them. It's just, Caiohme, Chloe, have you seen them?"

She smiled "Is that what you are worried about? They're fine. They insisted on looking after you, but Malachi assured them…"

I swung my legs from the cot and ripped the IV from my arm, interrupting her "Malachi what? Where are they?" A sud-den rush of adrenaline shot through my veins. Ripping the nee-dle from my vein caused a light stream of blood to trickle down my forearm and the sudden movement made me light headed. The site of my own blood added to the nausea. I could stand the site of anyone else's blood, but going to the doctor to have my own blood drawn always made me queasy.

She put her hand on my knee, as if that would stop me from standing "Jayden, what's wrong? Why are you so upset?" Why was I so upset? What could Malachi do to them in front of all these people? A lot of things, I thought. Bring on the darkness, turn them into a flock of colorful birds, unleash an army of ven-omous ants, send them missing like he had Samarra. She could never understand though. No one suspected him, no one but me, me and the creature.

I slammed my palm onto my knee and shouted "Where are they?"

This quickly drew the attention of several nurses and roused the man next to me from his drug induced slumber. He sat up for a moment and starred at me, then rambled off a strange rhyme with increasing urgency and tone.

"A house in the woods,

a pond and a creek,

a man with one eye,

and the trees that can speak,

the sky will turn red,

the forest pitch black,

a hole in the ground,

the only way back."

As the last flailing word left his tongue, he gasped for one last breath of life and fell back into his icy bath. His body laid still and lifeless. His arms hung limp over the side of the cot and his open eyes stared directly at me. The nurse soon confirmed what I already knew; he was dead. Dead like so many others.

I turned back to the nurse. Tears ran down her flushed face like a gentle stream. She was quiet and tried to keep her composure, but I could see the pain in her eyes. Had she known this man? I wrapped my arm around her shoulder and pulled her into me "I'm sorry!"

She wiped her face and put on a fake smile "I'll be ok. He was a good friend. I just thought..." she paused to take in a deep breathe "I just thought we would be able to see him through this. It was selfish; to care so much for him with so many others in pain and near death."

I grabbed her chin and pulled her face directly into my gaze

"No, it was human! To give him anything less than everything you are capable of would be selfish. To give that to everyone would be impossible. We can only hope they too have as good a friend as he did."

The fake smile on her face morphed into something more real as her lips separated and the lines in the corners of her eyes grew deep. Perhaps all she needed was someone to support her. Perhaps that's what we all needed. She put her hand on my shoulder "Malachi escorted them to the square to train with Alcaeus, Carmine and Adrianna. I know it's hard to trust someone else with their safety, but Malachi is a strong leader and a good man. He was to escort them to the square, then set off into the woods. He vowed to find the men responsible for the attack and to search for Samarra and his father."

She stood up and looked down on me as I wondered what he wanted with the woods. Did he somehow know we planned to escape to them that night? Was he going to meet with the Farrians? Would they plan the next attack or talk about the outcome of the first? The nurse must have seen something in me; the nervous tapping of my fingers on my leg, the distraught look on my face or the worried tear that fell down my cheek as I thought of the girl's safety. She put her hand to my head and whispered "Go after them if you must! Your fever is beginning to break. I will cause a distraction to buy you time."

As she walked away I felt she was someone I could trust, that a bond had been formed. It saddened me to think of the next attack, plague, army of hallucinogenic ants, bombs, or fire that Malachi might bring. Sadness turned to rage as I thought of Alcaeus teaching Caiohme and Chloe silly tricks while his people suffered and died. I questioned his leadership and character. What type of man was he to stand in the background during such trying times? Did the loss mean nothing to him? His was not the type of courage my father had taught me; he was not a man of virtue.

I knew I had to find the girls. If Malachi was a traitor and Alcaeus could not protect his people, then who would protect Caiohme and Chloe? I would! If Leotus wanted a real leader I would give them one. I may not have been able to make birds out of beasts and trees out of pain, but I was courageous. I may not have been able to stand up to the beasts, but I could stand up and be a voice for the dead and the sick. I could be more than a creationist; I could be a leader of words, a voice of reason.

A shrill scream from a cot far from mine indicated the distraction had begun "Ants! Ants! They are crawling all over this man! Help us, please!"

Every nurse, doctor and able bodied person ran to the victim to lend whatever help they could, creating a small window of time for me to escape. I grabbed the side of the cot with my good hand and rolled myself onto the ground. My bad hand erupted in pain as I landed on it; like falling into a patch of stickers, each thorny spike burrowing deep into my flesh.

I used my good hand to pull myself to my knees and then my feet. The ground was water beneath me and I was a piece of driftwood; everything was constantly shifting. My knees wobbled under my weight and my head was foggy. I assumed the bright orange snake in front of me was a hallucination until its scaly skin brushed across my ankle. I jumped into the air and must have floated for ten minutes before I fell back to earth with a thud. It took a moment to get my bearings after throwing up, but I knew I didn't have much time. I took off running.

With each step my brain rattled inside of my skull. My name rang out from all directions "Jayden, Jayden, Jayden." I clamped my hands down hard over my ears. Were the screams a consequence of the nurses discovering I had left my cot or a growing manifestation of the voices inside my head? Perhaps it was something worse; the beasts coming back for me. My feet grew tired and heavy. Each step was a challenge, like running against the river's current. Everything I passed starred at me; the trees, a ravaged three headed beast, even the ant had returned to my shoulder to haunt me. The windows overtook the homes and grew into dark caverns, hollow and ready to consume me. As I approached the homes, I realized that the square was near.

I allowed my pace to slow to a slog. Sweat and poison streamed out of my pores and stung my eyes as it dripped from my wet hair. The poison coursed through my veins less swiftly as I walked. The haze that clouded my thoughts burned away and my load lightened. Each step became more perceptible and I noticed, for the first time, that I was barefoot. The soles of my feet stung and blood crept from open sores. Each blade of grass was a sharp tack, strategically placed to cause me harm. All but one tube had fallen out of my hand and yellow ooze dripped from my fingers. The swelling had dropped considerably as the poison poured out.

My mind cleared and I recognized the homes; colorful gardens, rustic red walls, wood thatched roofs. A child's laughter came from behind the next row; it had to be Chloe I thought! Waves of color erupted above the rooftops, like fireworks in the July sky, and explosions shook the homes. There were no signs of struggle or a fight, until a shrill cry rippled through the still air. Without a second to think, my body jolted around and I took off running.

I broke through the brush and into the clearing to see Caiohme standing face to face with a flaming dragon. Its scales were an armor suit of dark, metallic black and its wings, a crimson red sail ready to take flight. The beast towered twenty feet above her head, but her eyes met his as he blew steam from his nostrils. Each gentle flap of his wings sent a gust of wind through her hair, but she never took her eyes off his. She was fierce; not the scared girl I had met the day before.

I was frozen, my eyes fixated on the beast that could end her life, until I heard Alcaeus' voice ring out from behind it "Don't let it intimidate you Caiohme. Mount it or kill it now!"

I took a step forward and a twig snapped under my feet. Without hesitation, the dragon's head snapped around and I fell into his gaze. His deep crimson eyes were thirsty for blood. Before I could turn and run he lunged forward, his tale flailing in the air, a steady pant of steam coming from his nose. A burst of flames swept past my right side, singeing the hair on my arm. Caiohme ran up on the beast and her eyes caught mine "Run Jayden!"

I couldn't run. My feet were like lead and the ground was quicksand, consuming them. Besides, I promised to never leave Caiohme and Chloe again. My heart raced as part of me hoped the dragon was another hallucination, but he was real. Caiohme wrapped herself around his tale and jumped to his back when he flailed it in the air. An unfamiliar voice called out "Rein him in now Caiohme!" as the dragon approached me. It was Carmine, yelling from far back in the square with his hands cupped around his mouth.

Everything happened in slow motion. My knees broke to the ground as his feet shook it violently, his claws and teeth thrashing towards me, his eyes dead set on his prey. I watched Caiohme make her way up his back, to his neck, and I threw my arms in front me as he lashed his claws inches from my face. His scaly head came close enough for me to see the black spots on the back of his tongue and the grooves in his teeth. Then, before he could crush my skull with his jaw, he was gone; on a rapid ascent to the clouds with Caiohme on his back. The girl I had sworn to myself to protect was on an express ride to the heavens and there was nothing I could do about it.

I froze for a moment, in shock, and didn't even notice Chloe walk up to me. When I did, I picked her up and we looked to the stars together. We watched silently, optimistically, with a tight grasp on each other as Carmine joined us, then Adrianna and Alcaeus. We all stood, huddled together for a few minutes as the dark clouds began to move in. When a raindrop hit my nose I began to lose hope. Hope that she would return, that she would make the journey with me that night. Chloe must have been able to see it in my expression, because she burst out with the same optimism she had displayed through everything "Don't cry Jayden, she has to make it back! I saw her in my dream. You picked her up and kissed her after we won!"

Everyone laughed and I smiled "I think I would like that Chloe!"

CHAPTER NINE

A Brewing Storm

THE CLOUDS ROLLED in, building atop one another, and the sky turned gray. What started as a spit of rain soon turned into a full-on monsoon. We took cover under one of the giant trees, but no amount of gesturing could keep Chloe from standing in a puddle and waiting for Caiohme to return from the heavens.

The storm wasn't like those back home, that you could watch rolling in from miles away; it seemed to develop and intensify right above us. The rain met the earth with force, splattering mud and stirring the insects from the grass. A clap of thunder shook the ground and sent Chloe running to my leg. Lightning lit up the giant anvil approaching from the ocean and struck the ground a hundred yards in front of us. We all jumped and Chloe covered her eyes and turned her face into my stomach. The lightning intensified with another strike, then another seventy-five yards away, and another. We weren't safe and neither was Caiohme. If she had tamed the dragon, the only chance she had of surviving the electric storm was to get above the anvil.

The storm grew more rapidly, lighting up the sky again and again. We all huddled around the tree trunk, peering out on the storm until a bolt struck a tree twenty feet from us. Alcaeus moved quickly, pushing on the tree that provided our shelter with both hands. White light radiated from under his palms. "Protect us!" he demanded.

I wanted to curse him for playing games while his people died, for protecting such a small group when his whole community needed him. I wanted to ask him how he could let the dragon take Caiohme away. I was so angry, but my only concern in that moment was Chloe; she was scared and I needed to be there for her.

A brilliantly white light shot up the tree, illuminating every vein of every leaf. Its branches creaked like old wooden porch steps as they swung to life. First one big branch, then another, fell to the ground and dug in around us, like the weeping branches of a Willow. I dropped to my knees and pulled Chloe into my chest. In no time, hundreds of branches were falling on top of one another and intertwining themselves. The flashes of light grew dim as a cavern formed around us. Leaves and branches created a barrier, almost insulating us from the roar of the thunder. Even the rain had a hard time penetrating the shelter. What the shelter couldn't do was help us forget about our friend and sister, left to fight for her life in the storm. We sat, listening to the storm and glancing through a hole in the limbs.

I got up and shifted several branches and peeked into the square; that's when I saw it. Illuminated by a flash of lighting, a red blur spun to the ground like a comet breaking through the atmosphere. I put my hands in the gap and pulled the branches further apart. "Caiohme!" I screamed as the dragon made impact with the ground, skidding across the deserted pavement and into the fountain.

Someone grabbed my legs as I squeezed my head and then my chest through the branches. I could hear Chloe screaming from inside "Let me go, let me go! He needs my help!" as I kicked my legs free.

I fell, face first into the ground. Muddy water shot up my nose and the last tube was ripped from my hand as I grabbed the branches to break my fall. My elbow hit a rock and pain shot up my shoulder as I drug myself to my knees. I grabbed my arm with a grimace and wondered why they would have ever called it the funny bone. The poison had made me tired and weak, but I ran faster than I had ever run to her aid. I looked back as I ran; they were all watching me from a larger hole in the cavern. Chloe fought to free herself from Carmine's grip, but her cries were muffled by the heavy rain.

Rain drops pinged off the ground and flowed in a steady stream to a pool of water that had developed near the wreckage. Each raindrop reminded me of the ant bite as it bounced off my skin with force. I looked down; my hand was only slightly swollen and the rain had washed away the puss. The ground was littered with scales, bits and pieces of flesh, and a trail of blood that led up to the beast from twenty feet out. I slowed myself as I approached from behind the dragon, not wanting to startle the beast. His tale still moved and light puffs of steam came from his snout.

As I got closer I noticed the dragon's injuries were worse than I thought. Deep gouges in his armor allowed blood to tinge the pool of water red. His lungs still took in air, but his breaths were shallow and intermittent. One wing lay on top of the other and the skeleton had broken through his thick crimson skin. I didn't see Caiohme. Had she fallen off in the storm? No, I wouldn't believe it; she had to be lying in front of him. I walked into the bloody water and put my hand on his back "its ok boy, its ok!" His scales were smooth and strong, like a turtle's shell. He lifted his head a few feet off the ground, but as quickly as it rose it splashed back into the water. His breathing became strong and quick only for a moment, then it ceased. The dragon was dead and Caiohme wasn't there.

A lightning strike illuminated the bloody pool of water and I saw my reflection. It should have been me, I thought. I stared down at myself as another strike flashed across the dark sky; I hated myself. Why did I let her save me? I should have been the one saving her. Thunder shook the ground and a high pitched scream rang out from behind me; I turned around. Chloe was running toward me. The lightning provided glimpses of a face filled with fear as her tiny feet splattered muddy water into the air. I ran to meet her. There was no need for Chloe to see the dragon, to wonder if Caiohme had suffered the same fate. He had fallen from the heavens like a dying star.

I expected her to run to my arms, but she ran past me "Run Jayden, run!"

I didn't know what she meant but I chased after her as she splashed into the pool of water and around the dragon. When I caught up to her she had her arm on the dragon's wing and was trying to push it up. Thud, ThUD, THUD; hail the size of golf balls began to slam into the homes in the distance. She mounted her legs and pushed harder "Help me! We need to get under the wing with Caiohme before it gets here!"

I didn't think we would be safe under the wing once the hail reached us, but I had to let her see that Caiohme was not there. If I didn't give her that opportunity she would always resent me. I moved her to the side and wrapped both hands under the broken wing. Chloe was on her knees looking underneath, rain dripping from her hair, when the hail began to fall on the pavement. Some hail shattered into thousands of pieces as it hit the ground and some bounced off the pavement like ping pong balls. We were out of time.

The first stone to smack my back stung like a football helmet between my shoulder blades. I didn't notice the next few pieces of hail, because as I pushed the wing above my head the other wing unrolled to reveal an unconscious, but unharmed, Caiohme. Chloe was right; she was alive! Chloe ran underneath the wing and jumped on top of Caiohme who opened her eyes, shaken and confused, but alive. I walked underneath the wing and lowered it slowly on top of us just as the stones began to fall with more intensity. I snuggled up beside the girls and grabbed Caiohme's hand; the dragon's thick, leathery skin sheltered us from the storm.

The hail lasted only a few minutes, but it was about twenty or thirty minutes before the storm let up enough for us to leave our shelter. Chloe and I spent the time explaining the series of events to Caiohme, who seemed to be suffering from some sort of amnesia. By the time we had gone over it twice Caiohme began to remember what had occurred. She told us that the dragon had taken her over the Farrian city when the storm rolled in. When the lightning and hail got bad, he wrapped her in his wing and sacrificed himself to make the descent into Leotus.

"How far was it? What was it like?" I asked.

"On a dragon's back it didn't take any time, but it is deep in the woods, near some small mountains. I didn't see it long, but it was far different than Leotus or Dalkey. The buildings are tall, metallic, and clustered together. Sky bridges connect them to one another. Tunnels are built into the mountains and trains come and go from there to the city. The whole thing glistens in the sun like a big mirror. I didn't see any people, parks, lakes or farms; it's all cement and metal, surrounded by woods. It wasn't any place to call home. I don't think we should ever go there." She got quiet as the rain let up.

We all pushed the wing off of us and Chloe grabbed Caiohme's hand "Sis, we have to go. We have to go tonight! The fire will be here soon." The look on her face was serious and I knew she was right, just like she had been about Caiohme and the storm.

When we stepped out into the drizzle the ground was covered with branches and leaves that had been stripped from the trees and bushes. The beautiful gardens had been shredded and colorful pedals were scattered amongst the giant leaves. Wooden shingles and glass windows were cracked and broken and a few holes had been punched in the stucco walls. The hail had been even stronger than I thought; though the damage was relatively minor, it was widespread.

The ground shook and caused my attention to shift from the beautiful homes to the cavern where Alcaeus, Carmine and Adrianna emerged unscathed. The tree limbs pulled themselves from the dirt and reached for the emerging sun; broken, muddy and nearly leafless, but having done their job. The branches shook free of the mud in the light breeze, like a dog right out of the lake shakes his coat. Carmine and Adrianna immediately ran to us as Alcaeus stood and assessed the damage, cupping his hand around his mouth "Are you ok?" Each word was long and drawn out, as if he was still shouting against the deafening thunder and hail.

I threw my thumb up in the air to signal that we were fine. He stopped and talked with the few residents that emerged from their homes as Carmine and Adrianna consoled us. Adrianna bent down and looked over Chloe as Carmine apologized "Sorry Caiohme, I had no idea he would act like that; it wasn't in his character. I tried to hold Chloe as long as I could, but she knew something was wrong and I couldn't stop her."

Caiohme laughed as if she had endured something minor "If he was the playful dragon then I'd hate to meet his vengeful friends. Really though, he saved my life." She then looked to me "It's a good thing you let her go, she saved Jayden from quite the hail storm. It seems she has a knack for seeing things."

Carmine laughed "A knack? She was brought here because she is one of our most powerful prophets, only second to Casteen in Fariah." His lips seemed to seal after he said it and an expression grew on his face that told me he shouldn't have volunteered as much as he did. He smiled "Let's keep that between friends and yes, the dragons I train for war are much more aggressive and talented."

I wanted to tell him just what kind of prophet she was. I wanted to tell him about the note, the rat, and our plans to escape that night. I wanted to invite him and Adrianna along. I wondered what he would make of Chloe's dream and the impending fire that had put us on edge. The more I thought about it, the more I questioned the dragons and whether Carmine could be trusted. Could he be on Malachi's side? Was it possible that his dragons could be the cause for fire in Leotus? I looked him in the eyes "Can you control your dragons or is it possible that they could turn on you and destroy all the things we are trying to save?"

He thought about it a moment and smirked, but his reply was too omniscient "Their fire could turn an enemy town into an inferno, so intense it could destroy everything. It would pave the path for a new start on life. Nothing is ever one hundred percent Jayden, but I believe they will serve their purpose."

Chloe turned her head towards me with big eyes, a chest full of air, and her little fidgeting fingers. Her expression said what she couldn't in front of him. His words raced through my mind like the bright, cascading flames that raced through the corn fields after harvest, "so intense it could destroy everything" Malachi, Carmine, Adrianna, Alcaeus, who could we trust enough to bring with us? No one, it had to be just us three I decided.

The clouds had broken and the sun shined down on my face. It brought about an image of Caiohme, Chloe and myself burning on the beaches of Leotus; the fire consuming us. We had to get back to the castle and prepare for our journey that night.

When Alcaeus rejoined us, the square began to swell with men carrying rakes and saws, totting wheelbarrows filled with shingles and supplies. The response was rapid and I wondered if the victims of the ant attack had begun to recover, if the aid was no longer needed at the castle. I wondered if they were able to shelter the injured before the storm struck. I grabbed Caiohme's and Chloe's hands "Let's get back to the castle."

Alcaeus stepped up beside me "We will see you after dinner for level two training. We will need to catch up on what you missed today. Caiohme can teach you, she caught on well. We will all meet back in the square at seven; it will be cleared by then. Get some food and have your hand looked at." His words came out as an order, not a question, firm and direct. I no longer felt like a guest, but a soldier in training.

"I'll be there." It was the only answer I could give him. I knew it meant they'd come looking for us sooner than I had hoped, but anything else would have drawn suspicion. We would have to make a quick start. All I could think about was the stables; if I could find them we could cut the journey in half.

Most of our travel back to the castle was silent, unable to talk about our plans in front of the others. As we approached the castle I grew confused. The cots had been cleared, the dead taken away; no machines or nurses remained. Had it all been a hallucination or had they been able to clear the area in the short time I had been gone? How had they disposed of the dead?

I looked down at my feet as I walked, trying to separate reality from hallucination. The ant on my shoulder, the fire in my bones, my loved ones and horses burning, the man digging to escape the bombs, the nurses, the dead, the poem, the ice; what of it was real? Crunch, crunch, crunch; the cold rippled through the bottoms of my scarred feet as I walked over the melting ice. The ice, it had been real.

It made me sick to think of how many had died and how swiftly they were swept away. I became lost in my own thoughts, a jumble of right and wrong. Do you try to save those on the verge of death or do you prepare others to save what you can, to save what is left? The faces of people I didn't know raced from lobe to lobe haunting my conscious; children on fire, women, pregnant women, the man with his warning! All of their faces burnt in my mind. I unknowingly jumped in front of Alcaeus as he walked and violently shook his shoulders hoping to pass the pictures to him "Why were you not with your people as they died? Are your war games, the training, that much more important? Why did you not try to save them? What kind of leader are you? How many will you bury today?"

I fell to my knees, shaking and gasping for breath and digging my hands into the wet ground. How many graves would the people of Leotus dig today? Was death the only way to leave this nightmare I was walking in? I wanted nothing more to be back in Havenbrook; no blood on my hands, no people to save. I wanted to hold Katie, to ride my horses, to have some of Ms. Mayberry's pie and to tell my parents all the things I didn't say enough.

"Today I will bury my best friend! Tomorrow I will bury my son, your brother. If I cannot teach you, than soon I will bury an entire country. There was nothing I could do for the dead, but teach you to fight for their families and for all those we lost. What sacrifices have you made Jayden? What sacrifices will you make?" His voice was filled with grief as he looked down on me and spoke with a strong heart; his words chosen more carefully than mine, and spoken with more knowledge than mine.

I realized he was right, I had been selfish, cowering to save myself, running to save Caiohme. Not once had I thought about what I needed to do to save anyone else. I simply put all the blame on him, expecting that he could do it all. I looked up to apologize, but he, Carmine, and Adrianna had disappeared into the castle doors. Caiohme reached for my hand "Get up, this is not the time for pity or anger. We only have a few hours."

Once inside the castle the three of us stopped at a coffee shop for a very late breakfast that Chloe coined "disgusting" and Caiohme said was "mediocre at best." I understood it wasn't biscuits and gravy or scrambled eggs and chocolate milk, but the strong black coffee and chewy whole grain bagel hit the spot for me. I finished everything on my plate and the remnants on theirs too. Chloe looked at me with either disgust or awe; I couldn't quite decipher what her gaping jaw meant. Caiohme just rolled her eyes and laughed "pig."

The coffee shop was a quiet little hole in the wall with dim lighting and the soothing melody of light instrumentals. The warm tones of yellow and orange were inviting and the seating was plush and comfortable. The colorful flower arrangements in the center of each table caused my mind to drift again to memories of Havenbrook; high school dances, Mother's Day, Valentine's Day with Katie. There were so many times I stopped by Ms. Pearl's flower shop on Main Street, Pedals, to pick up flowers.

Ms. Pearl was a frail older woman that had run the shop her entire life. She donated any spare time and unsold flowers to the old folk's home in town. She had seen most of her friends and family pass, but the store kept her busy and it was something to hand down to her granddaughter, whom had inherited her name already. I couldn't help think of my own grandmother every time I went into the shop. She had passed away from breast cancer when I was only seven and the two had the same sweet demeanor, laugh and light blue eyes. On occasion,

I would help her bring flowers down to the home; it was something that made me feel good about myself, a feeling I missed.

A burst of young, playful children forced me back to reality. Joking and laughing, they were able to escape the harsh reality of everything going on around them so easily. A short memory for all the evil in the world and a constant optimism for the future seemed to be inherent in all of them. I watched them, wishing I could steal a little piece of happiness from each. Caiohme and Chloe discussed heading back to the dormitory, to pack each of us an extra set of clothing and a light blanket. I suggested that they get a short nap while they were able, but both seemed too anxious for sleep. I spent the hours before dinner gathering supplies from the center court and meeting a few interesting people.

My first stop was the archery shop, where I had seen the bows in the window the night before. Once inside, I realized there was a lot more to the store than bows. Knives, fishing gear and tackle, climbing gear, traps and snares, first aid, lanterns and water sanitation tablets all lined the shelves. My intention was to stop in for only a few supplies, but I came out with a lot more.

CHAPTER TEN

Gathering Support

I WALKED INTO the archery shop and wandered around the tables for a while before I noticed his dull gray eyes on me. The grizzly man behind the counter kept a constant watch, but glanced away every time I caught his stare. He was the type of man I imagined totting an ax through the forest, hacking away at towering pine trees. His shoulders and arms were strong and his belly protruded deep into his overalls. His brown hair was speckled with gray and looked like it hadn't been combed or cut for months. His lips were chapped and cracked and his cheeks were rosy.

His stare was belittling and intimidating and became uncomfortable quickly. I was on guard though, ready for him to launch his own attack on me, on Leotus. Anyone was capable of harm in my eyes. I grabbed the things I needed, a small serrated knife, some sanitation tablets, a couple thin ropes, and some nuts and dried fruit, and walked up to the counter. I was greeted the same way he had greeted the gentlemen before me "Hi, how are we doing today? Do you need any tackle or insect repellent?" His voice was gruff and deep.

"Sure, throw some insect repellent in the bag too. Alcaeus said that anything I need can be put on his tab until further notice." It was a bold face lie, but I figured he owed me for the last fourteen years I spent without my brother, for the secrets, for everything. Besides, I had no other form of payment thanks to my brisk arrival in Leotus.

The man stroked his beard and looked down at me with knowing eyes; he could tell that I was lying. He grabbed a clear bottle of liquid from a shelf behind the counter and shook it in front of my face "You're going to need a whole lot more than insect repellent for the beasts you will encounter in the whispering woods. I have something for you. Come with me." He opened the door behind the register and stepped inside.

It wasn't a question of whether or not I wanted to follow him, it was an expectation that I would. It was a command I was not ready to follow. I didn't know if he knew of our plans or was just anticipating a trip into the woods, but it made me uneasy to think that our secret might have leaked. I spent several moments starring into his muddy eyes and trying to peer over him, into the dark room. What did he have for me? Why should I trust him anymore than the beasts, the stern Leonoid woman, the man in the center court, or Malachi?

He reached inside the pocket on the front of his overalls and stepped towards the counter, revealing a pewter compass with the same tree and astrological engravings as mine "I am on the same side as you! Now come with me, time is ticking away."

Had he anticipated my worries or was he inside of my head? I wasn't aware I had chosen a side. The only side I cared to be on was the one that brought the girls and I back home. I starred up at him "What side is that?"

"The side where you come out of this thing alive and lead our people to peace" he mumbled. "The side the young girl has also seen." he said louder.

The compass, his knowledge of Chloe's dream, it was enough for me to follow him the second time he turned his back to me and walked into the dark room. The compass was linked to a picture of my father and Chloe to Caiohme; if I could not trust that, I couldn't trust anything.

It wasn't a room, but a narrow corridor, three of four feet wide and descending. The walls and floor were composed of rigid stones with flat surfaces and it had the same musty smell as the hole in the tree. Lighting was spaced ten feet apart across the ceiling and the bulbs were dim and flickering. The left side of the wall was piled floor to ceiling with boxes of merchandise and an arsenal of guns, ammunition, and knives. I got a strange feeling that I was walking into an ambush, like I had taken a wrong turn in a scary movie and everyone was screaming for me to turn around.

Past the merchandise, cobwebs, and a few rat-like rodents with quills, about forty feet back, we came to a small room, no bigger than six by six feet. The walls were filled with pictures of the castle and surrounding land, maps of the topography and a detailed architectural layout of the entire castle. Lights ran around the perimeter of the room, illuminating the walls. There was a desk with a small lamp, ink pens, more drawings and pads of paper.

My attention shifted to him as he began to rip maps and drawings from the wall in front of us. The speed with which he dismantled it all told me that our time was short. In the middle of the wall was a maroon stone, larger than all the rest. He put his hands against the stone and pushed on it with all his weight. It collapsed into the hollow wall behind it and shattered into pieces on the ground. He reached his arm deep into the hole, up to the cuff of his shoulder, and tugged a gray duffel bag from the small opening.

He brought the bag over to the desk and set it on top of the drawings. Upon closer examination, it was really a blue bag covered in crumbled mortar and dust. He pulled the zipper open, having to jerk it several times to remove the tiny pebbles that had accumulated between the teeth. Once it was open he scooted to the side "The contents of this bag will prove invaluable on your journey. Forget anything else you have gathered Jayden, it will only slow you down."

"Will you come with us tonight? We could use a strong hand that knows the land." The words came out of my mouth moments before I remembered the commands of the letter "bring only those who you are sure you can trust." I didn't rescind the offer; instead, I stood waiting for an answer. He was the type of man I wanted with me if I was to face the beasts again.

He let the offer consume him for a moment and then met my eyes with a smile "It would be my pleasure Jayden." He extended his hand which was strong and large enough to crush my skull "They call me Patches!"

For a giant, his hand shook mine with an unusually modest grip. His callouses were like sandpaper against my skin and his fingers extended up to my wrists. "It's nice to meet you Patches. We haven't much time; you should get your affairs in order. I only hope we can trust you as a companion and protector in Whisper Woods."

He released my hand, unclasped his overalls and raised his shirt, revealing three discolored patches of hairless skin. One patch stretched down the center of his abdomen, one across both pectoral muscles, and the third was a jagged patch across his right bicep. Between the patches was the remainder of his hairy torso, riddled with scars. He let his shirt fall "Patches of pig skin; it was the only suitable replacement our medic could find in the forest to cover the wounds. I received them defending our people against a Leucrocota; whose voice mimicked a child's to sneak into our camp. He nearly sank his fangs into my heart before Alcaeus put an arrow through his left eye. I have proven my allegiance. I will protect you Jayden; not because I am a noble man, but because I know that you will save our people."

I thanked him for his companionship and confidence as I reached my hand into the duffel bag. He explained each item as I placed them individually on the desk. Most notable, a garment woven of an alloy created by scientist in Fariah and brought to Leotus by deserters. The alloy was extremely tensile and the lightest known by Leonoids to exist, but strong enough to prevent most weapons from penetrating through it. There was also a dagger capable of secreting lethal doses of Lucula, a metal rod that opened only in my hands to shoot hallucinogenic tracking darts, a vial of liquid capable of restarting the heart and one of the devices used to determine if a person was a manipulation and to scan for enemy technology.

I tossed the items back in the duffle bag, zipped it up, and handed it to Patches "Thank you for the gifts. Can you bring them with you when you come tonight?"

A picture on the wall had caught my attention as he took the bag from my hands "I'll bring it tonight, along with a travel pack and water." I walked up to the picture and put my finger right on top of the stables full of stallions and then looked to Patches "Alcaeus' stable?"

He nodded his head "Your stables."

"We will need to make it there as fast as possible. Can you lead us?" I said, tapping the picture on the wall.

He smiled and nodded his head "I know this land like the back of my hand. I can get us there and I know a shortcut from the beach; it's a ten minute run through an abandoned mining tunnel."

It was all great news. I had found a travel companion that knew the land and where the horses were, how to survive in the

Whisper Woods and with knowledge of weapons and hunting. I couldn't have asked for more from the man that possessed the same compass as I. I shook his hand "Thank you!" and walked up the corridor.

Before I reached the door, I looked back with one last fleeting thought "One more thing Patches. You can't tell anyone; your closets friends, your children, not even your wife."

He nodded in agreement "My lips are sealed friend."

There were a few angry customers when I walked out the door, but I felt Patches could keep them in order. I grabbed another cup of coffee and a chocolate muffin from the café the girls and I had eaten at just a short while before, which I found to be named Java Jabber. Then I made my way to the offices were Ex had died. Filled with inhibition and not knowing who I could trust, there were still others I decided I wanted on our side. There were people who had made an impression on me; the nurse who tended to me in my hallucinations, the two boys that greeted me in the dormitory and Deseus. I may not have known them well, but I knew the girls and I could not make the journey alone.

I didn't find the nurse in the offices, but after offering a short description to the secretary, "auburn hair, short, green eyes, kind," she was able to tell me that her name was Lillian. An idle nurse volunteered more information. Lillian had left for break ten minutes earlier and tended to enjoy her lunch in the sub shop with her husband Leysner. I thanked her and she obliged me "Anything for you Jayden." They would not be so kind if they knew the fate I planned to leave them too. I felt bad knowing I could not bring more good people, that they would be incinerated in enemy fire.

I found the couple, in an upscale sandwich shop, enjoying turkey on fresh baked pita bread and sweet sun tea. She was surprised to see me still awake and in good spirit and I was surprised to find that Leysner was much older than she. Gray streaked through his dark, curly hair and wrinkles filled his forehead. His skin was light brown and dark freckles dotted the bridge of his nose. In small talk, I found out that he was one of three doctors in Leotus and that Lillian and he had met while she was training in the ER with his staff. Leysner told me "All the blood made Lilly nauseous" and "That is why she works in pediatrics now." She laughed and detested his statements, saying "I simply love to work with children." We all agreed that it was a great position, with the recent influx of many new youth in Leotus. I could tell it would be hard to draw the two of them away from their work, especially on the eve of a disaster, but I knew they could be of great use to our group as well.

I asked them to lean in and listen carefully as I quickly confided in them about the letter, Chloe's dream, and the journey that lay ahead. The news rattled them and it came out that they had a ten year old son. Neither was anxious to leave Leotus and both agreed that they couldn't without their son. Even after convincing them that he was welcome too, they decided it would be best to stay and save whomever they could. I could not disagree with the logic and I asked them to keep the conversation private. I was not too worried that they would say anything; I had not given them a time or location, only brief details. I left them to their lunch after promising that I would return to Leotus when things were more clear and safe, but neither seemed to have much of an appetite left.

I headed back to the dorm to check on Caiohme and Chloe and change before dinner. On my way to the dormitory, I ran into Cordell, the older of the two boys I had met the previous evening. He was hunched in the corner of the stairwell, shaking and sniffling. When I sat down by him and asked what was wrong he explained that the ants had attacked both him and Henry, but that Henry was not able to beat the fever; he was dead.

Seeing the bodies had been enough, but putting a face to one of them sent a shock of sadness and anger down my chest and abdomen. I felt it coming up, leaned over, and vomited up the chocolate muffin. The bitter taste in my mouth was the perfect adjective for how I felt, but I needed to be the strong one for Cordell. I took his hand and he broke down into tears; he seemed in no condition to be alone. He pleaded, like Alcaeus had for Ex, to take his brother's place. I couldn't risk telling him about the trip until we were on the beach, but I invited him to join the girls and me for dinner. He accepted, happy to not be alone.

We stopped by Cordell and Henry's room first, but he said he couldn't bear to go in again and see his brother's clothes scattered about the floor. The site had brought him to his knees in the stairwell moments before. I stepped inside the room until he could no longer see me, and fell against the wall. I took a deep breath, ran my fingers through my hair, and closed my eyes. I saw Henry's face and then Chloe's. I couldn't stand being in a place where young life was so easily sacrificed. What if it had been Chloe or Caiohme? I knew we were doing the right thing leaving. I grabbed a robe from the closet and walked out the door "Here you are Cordell."

I handed it to him as we walked to my room "Thanks Jayden. You could feel Henry in the room, couldn't you?"

I couldn't say it, but I did feel a presence. There was heaviness to the air in the room. It was like the urge you get to look over your shoulder when you're alone in the dark. I could feel his eyes on me, wanting to warn me of the person responsible for his death. All that was too much though, so I gave Cordell something better to think about "I think he came back to make sure you made it through, but he is in a better place now. Also, you don't have to thank me for anything. It was the least I could do."

He sighed "You're probably right. Thank you!" I couldn't help but laugh at the fact that he remembered his manners even during the hardest times.

I wished that I could bring Cordell's brother back, like Alcaeus had saved me from the cusp of death. Who was I to be saved when so many around me were suffering and dying? Would I be the one that would lead the Leonoids, bring them peace? I didn't think so; it was time for Alcaeus to look elsewhere. The only thing I planned to lead was my friends, out of dangers way. Speaking of danger, I hoped Malachi wasn't in the room as I turned the handle to my door.

"You're lucky to share a room with Malachi! Does he teach you anything?" Cordell asked. I seemed to be at odds with the whole community over Malachi, but I had no time to explain "Haven't seen him a lot since we arrived!"

He sat down alongside the mess of things on my bed "I heard he is out hunting for his dad and Samarra. I hope that he finds them before things get worse."

Whether Malachi was out hunting for family or planning his next attack it was clear he had not been back to the room since our first encounter. The football he had created was still lying on his bed. I grabbed a blue robe from my closet and pulled it over my head, then went under the bed and retrieved the box. Cordell's curious eyes poked below the bed as I lifted the box from the hole in the floor "What are you doing? What's in the box?"

I scooted out from underneath the bed and laid the box on the sheets. I opened it up and handed him the picture of the two men fishing "The man on the left is my father in Havenbrook, the town I am from. These things were left here for me by the man on the right. Tonight, you and I and some friends will take a journey and these things will be important. You must tell no one what you have seen Cordell."

His mind was much like mine, constantly churning and full of questions "Where will we be going? Why must I keep it a secret?"

I couldn't risk putting the items in a bag that someone might come across, so I stuck them all in the pockets of the pants I still had on under my gown "We are going somewhere safe, but if we tell the wrong person it may put the group in jeopardy. That is all I can tell you right now. We must go meet the girls for dinner."

Cordell and I made our way out of the boy's dormitory and through the desolate hallway, half way around the circle, and into Notus hall. I hoped the absence of noise meant we were running late for dinner, rather than the silence of another attack. Seeing a few stragglers rushing out of the girl's dormitory was certainly a reassuring sign. I recognized one of them as the girl who had asked me if she could help me find something the first time I arrived in the girl's dorm. Somewhere in Leotus she had found someone to fill her blond hair with streaks of purple. I smiled at her in passing "Hi!" She blushed as she smiled back. The group of girls she was with giggled at the idea that I was saying hi to them.

Heavy eyelids must have become too much for the girls to fight. We found Caiohme passed out in the chair and Chloe passed out in bed with the creature hiding under Caiohme's pillows. They were both as soundly asleep as they were when I had my first encounter with the letter bearing servant. Three small backpacks were packed and waiting by the bedside for our departure; two pink and one orange. What great colors for camouflage, I thought sarcastically. Clearly, they had never hidden from anything in the woods.

I moved Caiohme's hair from her face and rubbed her

shoulder until she peacefully woke from her slumber "It's time for dinner."

She rubbed her eyes "I must have fallen asleep. What have you been up to all this time?"

"I have been making friends!" I smiled and rolled my eyes toward Cordell "This is Cordell."

"Hi Cordell!" Caiohme put her hands on the arm rest and pushed herself up from the chair, grabbing her back and groaning as she stretched. She was clearly sorer than when we found her wrapped up in the dragon wing. Rest had allowed the muscles to stiffen up.

"Hi" Cordell whispered in a very timid tone.

I let Caiohme wake Chloe, thinking she would prefer to see her sister's face first. Little did I know that she would be disrupting a violent nightmare. When Caiohme shook Chloe's shoulder "Chloe, Chloe, wake up Hun," she burst forward, flaring her fists in Caiohme's face and screaming "Let him go, let him go. It's killing him. He'll die."

When Caiohme managed to calm Chloe down, the young visionary looked over to me "Why did you invite him? It's not safe for him." Cordell? Patches? Who, I wondered.

Then Caiohme looked up "Who did you invite?"

I looked at Caiohme, but set my eyes on Chloe "There is no time to discuss who I have confided in. It was just a dream, we will all be safe. Now let's get to dinner. Come on Cordell." I turned my back on them and walked up to the door. The letter was mine, it was addressed to me, and who I trusted enough to bring was my decision; it wasn't up for discussion.

As I twisted the door knob Caiohme's defiant voice rang out angrily "It's not just your decision you know. It should have been all of ours."

It gave Chloe the confidence to rattle what else was on her mind as well "You changed everything! It's all different now."

Whether or not I had made the right decision, it was done. I knew I was wrong, I knew what Chloe was capable of, but it was already done. Cordell and I walked out of the room and into the stairwell. They silently followed several feet behind us all the way to the dining room. It was the first time since I had met them that I felt something come between us. I knew the journey would be more dangerous if we weren't all on the same side, so I turned around "I'm sorry. I should have mentioned it, but there were a few people I couldn't leave. It didn't cross my mind until I stumbled upon them. I'm sorry!"

The apology did nothing to ease the grudge, as they both looked at me with blank stares and said nothing. The similarities between the two were even more evident in that state, with their puckered lips and angry eyes. I hoped dinner would provide them time to forgive me, but the evening only got worse when I opened the dining room doors and saw him sitting there alone.

Cordell pointed his finger in the direction "Look Jayden, he's back! I wonder if he found them. Let's go ask."

I grabbed the back of Cordell's robe as he tried to walk away from us, but didn't say a word. He was right; Malachi was back. He was back just in time for the looming disaster to begin, and with no sign of Samarra or his father. Alone, the way he wished to be left.

CHAPTER ELEVEN

Leaving Leotus

DISGUST, RAGE, ANGER, traitor, liar, murderer; those were the words and feelings that catapulted me into a hateful state when I walked into that cafeteria and saw Malachi sitting there. Fear was not among my feelings for him; only a subconscious twitch that rippled across my skin when his eyes met mine. I didn't look away. I held the stare until it was broken by a passerby who bumped me, not showing any weakness.

The room was not set up as it had been the night before. Rectangular tables had been pushed together into rows and people sat where they pleased. Crystal had been replaced by plastic cups and colorful ceramic plates. There were no guest speakers, theatrics or skating servers. Instead, we found a large self-service buffet and a table full of iced down, bottled beverages. The descent of the locals told me the presentation wasn't a common occurrence, but little did they know it wasn't a common time.

A Leonoid woman in her mid-thirties broke through my thoughtless observations and I noticed I still had a hold of Cordell's robe. "Casual tonight, Alcaeus must be up to something!" she exclaimed.

"I hope they're planning another party" chimed the young girl by her side.

I released Cordell; who was staring at me impatiently. The girls had stepped into the diminishing line and I was sure he was hungry too. I walked up to take my place, wondering if any of the locals suspected another attack. Did Malachi have any friends to warn? Did the creationists know that an enemy lurked? Had anyone else dreamt of the fire or had other visions? After all, Chloe and Patches had already seen the attack; who else could be running into the woods?

My worries were drowned out by the scent of grilled red meat, fish and fresh fruit that overpowered my senses. My stomach growled; I was hungry after losing my breakfast in the stairwell and there was certainly an abundance of food. I loaded two plates with chicken coated in pineapple-orange sauce, lamb stew on a bed of wild rice, three cheese potato skins, steamed spring vegetables, and a medley of fresh fruit that encompassed a hue of bright colors. I grabbed a couple glass bottles of water, even though the inhibiting properties of Lucula juice sounded like a nice reprieve, and followed Cordell to a table the girls had chosen.

It must have been too much for us not to sit by Malachi; he slammed his glass bottle against the table and let his chair fall behind him as he stood up. He starred at our table, his eyes fixed on me, as he marched our way. He stammered right up to the empty spot beside me, gripped the table tightly, and bent down to my ear "Now is no time for others to see that we have our differences; it could drive the community apart and make us vulnerable. We need to talk, now. There are things you need to know."

I shook my head and rolled my eyes "I have nothing to say to you Malachi. I assume you planned on never talking to me again after the events of today; soon you won't have to. Anything you want to say to me you can say in front of my friends or it can wait until training tonight."

He slammed his fist on the table and stormed out of the cafeteria without making much more of a scene except to say "You think you have it all figured out, but you don't know anything. Don't blame me when things don't end as you expect them to."

I knew I didn't know much, but it was all the more reason not to trust him. I had no intention of going to training, let alone talking to him, but I couldn't stand to listen to him anymore. Why did he want an ally then, when all he wanted earlier was to be left alone? Why did he need me by his side when everyone admired him already? To me he was a snake, hissing his lies in my ear, manipulating me with his gaze; the sound of his voice like a wet whisper, agitating me to the point of aggression with each word. It reminded me of an old hag of a teacher I had in grade school. She would smoke her cigarettes and drink her coffee, then get right in my face and bark orders about everything I had done wrong. The stench of her breath, the moisture in my ear, it took everything to not turn around and bite her face; then she'd never get that close to me again.

The dispute between Malachi and I only made things at our table more strained. Cordell was confused; he couldn't understand why things had grown so tense between Malachi and I. Caiohme and Chloe were just satisfied to see someone else angry with me. I had gone from friend to foe in only a few hours. I wondered how the girl who had forgiven me for leaving her in the darkness could be that angry over a much milder dispute.

I'm confident we would have spent the rest of our meal in silence had it not been for the roar of a loud engine, so close to our heads that it shook the building that sheltered us. I looked to the clock on the wall, 5:30. Had the attack already begun or was the aircraft our own technology, stowed away for such a circumstance? The Leonoids must have never experienced anything like the thrust of plane engines; they all looked around nervously and gossiped about what could have caused the tremor. Whether it was our planes or enemy planes, spy planes or bomber planes, I had no intention of being caught in the middle of it. I didn't need to tell the girls what I thought might be happening or even suggest we get our things and leave. Chloe was on her feet, Caiohme's fingers tightly intertwined in her own, before I even said "Let's go!"

The loud noise, the fear in Chloe's eyes, the sternness in my voice; something had shaken Cordell into an unresponsive state. His posture was firm, like a statue, but his eyes were open and his breathing was heavy. I shook his shoulders to rouse him from the panic "Cordell, Cordell, CORDELL!" My voice grew stronger with each passing moment.

A second loud roar signaled that our time was getting short as others began to panic. I had two choices; leave Cordell to burn or carry him and risk our own safety. In that thought, the whole room went up in flames and everyone caught fire. Some fell to the floor, resigned to burn, and some ran back and forth, frantically batting at the flames and knocking over buffet trays and glass bottles. Screams filled the room, death's last hollow pitch, as a smoky cloud of burning flesh consumed me. In the heavy smoke, Cordell's burning body, half skeleton and half flesh, jumped into view and grabbed my shoulders. I gasped and snapped back to reality with Caiohme shaking my shoulders "Jayden, Jayden!"

There were no flames or burning skeletons, only the bustle of people leaving the cafeteria Dinner trays hit the wall of a plastic trash can as Chloe's gentle voice assured Cordell "You are going to be all right."

I turned around and saw Chloe holding Cordell's hand and helping him to his feet. Her caring nature had enabled her to do what I couldn't, rouse him from the panic. He still seemed groggy, with wobbly knees and a foggy mind for what had happened to him. I offered my shoulder to help support him and looked up to the clock, 5:40, and then to Caiohme "Your call; leave him or bring him? He doesn't know enough to tell anyone anything."

She didn't answer the question directly. She only rolled her eyes and smiled "You're something else Jayden. Chloe and I will go and get the bags and meet you by the Life Tree. I don't think he can make it up the stairs. Come on Chloe!"

I let Cordell sit down a few moments to catch his barring's as the girls made their way into the hall. I watched young boys, girls, mothers and fathers all make their way out of the cafeteria and I wondered how many would grow up and play football or dance, fall in love, grow old. I watched each one walk into the hall, wondering what they could contribute to the world. When a man came up to wipe down the table we were still sitting at, it was time to go. We patiently made our way through the crowded hall, where the younger children had perched to chat, and into the center court, where White Coats stood guard at every exit. Each Coat had a hollow, metallic tube in his hand and a stern look on his face. I had to think of a way for us to get out the doors? Why had Caiohme not come back to warn me of their presence? Had they arrived in the minutes since I last saw her?

A group of teenage boys walking in front of us tried to walk out the same doors I had planned to use. A guard quickly stepped in front of the door "Sorry boys, it's a level three alert. No one is going outside!"

The guard's voice was kind, but unwavering as the boys questioned him. "Why can't we just go outside?" "Yah, why are we being held inside?" "Why are we under alert anyways? I'm not scared of the beasts." "When can we leave?"

His response to every question was firm and scripted "We

are under a level three alert. Please back away from the door. You will be notified when your exit is permitted. Thank you."

I knew of a few other ways outside, but I was certain that guards would be at every door. A distraction might provide a window for escape, but if I was pegged I might not make it to the rendezvous point on time. I couldn't think of any honest excuses to leave the castle walls, so I did the only thing I could; I lied.

First I turned to Cordell, who still wobbled like he had consumed a bottle of Lucula juice, but was able to understand my commands "Listen; if we are going to get out of here I need you to play along. Don't question anything I say."

He shook his head "Yah, ok." Not an enthusiastic or persuasive agreement, but it would have to do.

I grabbed his arm and pulled him up to the guards "Alcaeus ordered that we be permitted outside to retrieve medicine for an elderly man from the square. Poor fella is nearly in diabetic coma and won't make it too much longer without his medicine."

The two of them stood in front of the door staring at us for a moment, looking into my eyes and watching Cordell bite his nails. I thought Cordell might crack and I almost offered more information about our ordered mission, before the smaller guard stepped aside. A sigh of relief almost slipped my lips before the larger guard stuck his arm out in front of us "I don't mean to question you Jayden, but surely it won't take the both of you to retrieve this medicine?"

I looked to Cordell and back to the guard. I leaned in, cupped my hand around my mouth and whispered "The kid had a panic attack when his brother was killed by the ants. He swore that he saw his ghost in the room. I was the first one there to comfort him. Ever since, I can't let go of his arm without him going into a new attack. He'll just fall to the ground, shake and vomit. Trust me; it's not the kind of scene you want in times like these."

The guard looked at Cordell, who was rubbing his eyes and sniffling at the mention of his brother, and removed his arm from our path "Keep an eye on him and get back quickly. The next wave will be leaving soon."

I felt bad as I wondered how many of Cordell's tears were caused by what I had said; all of them, I assumed. I hadn't expected him to question why the two of us needed to go together and it was the first excuse that popped in my head. I felt horrible.

We stepped into the warm sun and I wondered what the guard had meant when he said "The next wave will be leaving soon." The next wave of troops, planes, ships? What had catapulted us to a level three alert? What was a level three alert? We hadn't been told anything about an alert system.

The air was as calm as the moment we arrived in Leotus. There were no planes, or dragons, or spies. There were no piles of corpses or ice filled cots. The stars shined brightly in the heavens and the fireflies glowed in the lanterns. The prairie grass flowed and the trees swayed. When I listened carefully I could even hear the soft roar of the waves breaking on the beach. In that moment, Leotus reminded me of Havenbrook, with a peace that men rarely take the time to enjoy. My time in Leotus told me the still wouldn't last long though.

Sure enough, as we took cover behind a large tree in close proximity to the Life Tree, a wave of planes emerged from the east side of the castle. There would have never been enough time for us to get to the square and back. They weren't like any craft I had seen before. An ovular body, void of material in the center, met and came to a sharp point at the cockpit and rear. A wing extended from each side of the cockpit, outward and upward to nearly the center of the plane. A long, sharp edged, piece of metal extended from one wing to the other, forming a triangle with an engine in each corner.

One plane rolled out from behind the corner, then a second then a third. The planes lined up in a row, briefly paused and took off straight from the ground in unison. The thrust was so strong that it shook the trees. They made a quick U-turn, flying over our heads and out onto the ocean, ripping leaves and branches from above us. What could they possibly be targeting over the open waters?

I followed the planes until they disappeared into the horizon and looked over to Cordell who was very alert and on his feet. He paced back and forth in the shade of the tree with his hands over his face. I stood up, walked over to him and put my hand on his shoulder "You ok man? What's going through your head?"

He nudged my hand off his shoulder and shouted "These people, this place; do you even know where we are? Do you have any idea what this is all about? How do you expect to find somewhere safe? We can run, but they will find us out there too. It'd be better had I just died with Henry. He was all I had! Our parents died in a car accident when I was just six. I just, I just, I don't want to go. Just leave me here."

He stomped off near the life tree and fell to his knees in the grass. I wanted to say something, but how could I argue with his logic. He lost his parents, his brother, and was stuck in a weird place, in the middle of a war being fought over things I didn't even fully grasp. I walked over to him and put my hand on his head "You have us and I won't make this trip without you."

I sat in the grass beside Cordell and starred at the Life Tree, *"it will grow as this young man grows and its story will be the story of our people."* If the Leonoids were to see the Life Tree then it wouldn't have provided them with much hope, but I did see myself in its tired, drooping branches and its withering leaves.

I was beginning to worry as the sun sank deeper in the

western sky. We had been outside ten to fifteen minutes and there was no sign of the girls. Had they seen the guards and turned around or been captured trying to escape? It was close to 6:20, our rendezvous time. I knew soon I had to decide whether to go on without them or return to the castle; I vowed to not leave without the girls. I couldn't walk away knowing they might not make it out.

As the moments turned into minutes my eyelids grew heavy in the warm sun. I talked of home and football with Cordell, both to keep myself awake and his mind occupied with things less serious. I learned that he was from England, but we shared the same favorite football team, the Dallas Cowboys. In the gap between our conversations it began, the high pitched screams of another attack from inside the castle. We both jumped to our feet and turned around to see that several individuals had escaped the castle doors.

Running towards us, hands full of pink and orange bags, were Caiohme, Chloe and an older gentleman I did not recognize. What I thought were cries from a hundred feet back, turned out to be uncontrollable laughter. The man tried hard to put on a stone face, but even he could not help but grin a few times. Barely audible below the laughter, Chloe offered a feeble warning "Run, run."

As they ran up on us; Caiohme grabbed me by the arm, Chloe grabbed Cordell, and the poor gentlemen was left totting the creature the entire bumpy run down to the beach. Between the heavy breathing and intermittent laughter it was impossible to get any words out along the way, so we ran. We ran like we might be able to escape Leotus if we moved our feet fast enough, like our warm beds waited in the distance. Thing is, when we got to the bottom of the dunes all that lay below our feet was sand and water; no Patches and no secret tunnel. We could have only been moments late.

The old man dropped the bag in exhaustion, apparently forgetting that something living was inside, and plopped down in the sand. He sighed; the soft ground offering some comfort to his worn joints. His arms and calves were strong, but I imagine old age had taken a toll on his endurance. The creature rolled out and gave the old man an angry stare as he shook the sand from his matted hair. He then turned in a full circle, observing his surroundings and babbling some sort of calculations.

Caiohme released my arm and strolled beside me as I searched the area for signs that Patches had been there "You should have seen their faces when the floor split open and Weed Walkers of every color started crawling out. It was just the distraction we needed."

I laughed, happy that we were talking again, but confused "How did you manage that and who is he?" I tilted my head in the direction of the old man, whose head was bobbing in the warm sun.

"I really can't take any of the credit for the worms; the whole thing was Chloe's idea. I just put a few of the tricks Alcaeus taught me to good use. When the guards left their post to find out what was going on, we snuck out. The old man saw us leaving and I figured I shouldn't leave him behind with that knowledge, so I nudged him along. He is just one of the chefs from the kitchen; said his name was Kaylon."

I laughed "You'll have to teach me a few tricks. As for him; I'm sure he could throw us something together for breakfast. We'll make good use of him."

The echo of two loud explosions rang out on the beach and drew our attention to the open water, where an unusually large wave rose above the rest. It was nearly five feet when It crashed against the beach, but its roar couldn't drown out his burly voice "Well come on already. We haven't got all day."

I laughed at the scramble that ensued when Patches

emerged from a tunnel in the sand. Chloe ran up and hid behind Caiohme and the creature back peddled, like he had after rousing me from my sleep. Cordell was starring off into the water and only flinched at the sure volume of his voice. The old man wasn't bothered one bit; it seemed the warm sun had been too much for his heavy eyes. A few moments later, a second large wave pushed sand and saltwater into the cook's mouth and nose. He jumped up, ran straight into Patches and fell onto his butt. I thought he might scream when he looked up and saw Patches towering above him, but he smiled "Patches, it's nice to see you old friend."

Patches offered his hand and helped him to his feet "Kaylon! You decided to take a swim I see. Probably ought to get inside that tunnel; we don't have long before someone notices us all missing." He pointed to a mound of sand in the dunes, which had been moved away from the top of an old, wooden entry door. The door was still propped open from Patches emergence.

Scraggs and Cordell met up with the girls and I; then the five us met Patches and Kaylon at the tunnel. I told them who Patches was and explained my plan for making it through the woods "His name is Patches and he works in the center court selling hunting gear. He knows the layout of the land and says this tunnel will get us to the stables quickly. We can get where we need to faster and encounter less danger on horseback. I think that we can trust him as we have one another. He had some of the same visions as you Chloe and he carries a compass with the same engravings as mine. It is enough for me; I hope that it is for all of you as well."

As we came up on the tunnel I noticed Scraggs rambling under his breath. I stopped in my tracks, right in front of him, and squatted down to speak while Patches lowered Cordell into the tunnel "What's wrong Scraggs?"

His eyes twitched from side to side, making sure no one was

listening, and his fingers tapped nervously on his leg. He drew his mouth in close to my ear and the words spilled out like a run-away freight train "Jayden's in danger. These people, this tunnel, it isn't safe. Master said only those you trust; we can't trust any of them. I am supposed to lead the way. This is not the way." He put his shaking hands to his forehead and pressed on his temples, his brain clearly overloading with thoughts "We'll die, we'll all die!"

I turned to see Patches lowering Chloe into the tunnel, her wide eyes set square on mine. Her meager confidence in his arms was because of my trust in his character. If I was wrong, I wasn't just putting myself in danger, but all of them. How had I grown to trust my new friends so easily; Patches, Cordell, even Scraggs? I couldn't find an answer to my own question, but I felt secure around them all. I looked back at Scraggs "We can't trust Cordell? We can't trust that young girl that has followed me since our first moments in Leotus? They were brought here just the same as I. How are you to know who we can or can't trust?"

He looked into my eyes and put his hand on my knee "Trust invites deceit. Don't trust anyone and we might live."

"I'm going down into that tunnel with my friends; you can come with us or turn back around. I made a promise not to leave them again and I won't. Once we are at the stables and we have the horses, then we can find a way back to the path you are to lead us down." I stood up and turned my back to him.

"Then you condemn me to death too," he mumbled as I walked up to Patches.

Patches cheerful manor did a lot more for my demeanor than Scraggs pessimistic rambling. The giant's smile was as warm and contagious as a child's; it calmed me. He handed me the blue duffel bag, still covered in dust, and another camouflage bag "Some nuts and jerky. I was beginning to wonder if you'd make it past the diversion."

"The diversion?" I asked.

"Yes. I told Alcaeus that I believed an attack was imminent; that he needed to issue an alert and keep the guards inside. I encouraged him to launch the planes out over the ocean. I needed to buy us enough time to make it to the forest, but I fear our time may be running out. Down you go!"

He offered me his hand and lowered my feet to a rail, about half a body length below. I squatted, grabbed the rail in my hands, braced my feet against the wall and lowered myself to another rail and then the ground. I looked up; the base of the tunnel had to be ten feet below the surface. I saw Patches face and then Scraggs came over the hole in his hands "Look out below!"

Plunk, he fell into my arms with a gasp. He didn't even give me a chance to let him down; he simply took handfuls of my robe and propelled himself to the ground. He was so light that his descent didn't put much strain on me. Once he was on his feet, he quickly wandered off and examined the tunnel.

The tunnel made me feel claustrophobic. It was only about seven feet tall and just wide enough for me to spread my arms and touch both walls. Two men could fit through tightly side by side, unless one was Patches size. The dirt and stone walls were crumbling, but steel beams held the big chunks of earth together. The only lighting at that moment was sun light from the surface.

Patches size fifteen shoes stepped down onto the ledge just as a scream rang out from above the ground "Wait! Don't leave; don't leave without us!"

I didn't recognize his voice and apparently Patches didn't recognize him either; he hastily dropped from the first ledge to the ground and grabbed the metal latch that was attached to the wooden door. The voice shouted as Patches pulled the wooden door shut and secured it to the wall with a chain "Jayden wait!"

With the closing of the door, the tunnel grew dark until Patches turned on a lamp that was strapped to his forehead. As the others waited for my lead, I wondered if someone else had seen Caiohme sneak out. Had one of the guards come looking for us? Had someone else had a vision and come to join us? Had Alcaeus sent a creationist to bring us back? Was it Deseus?

Patches grabbed my shoulder "Let's leave before more of them show up and block the exit."

He was right, but as the man hit the door and called out my name again "Jayden," a faint familiarity for his voice crossed my mind. The dialect he used to pronounce my name jumped around in my brain until an ember of familiarity grew into a flame of sureness. It was the nurse's husband, Leysner. I unhooked the chain. "Leysner? Leysner, is that you?" I hollered.

The wooden door opened to the bright evening sun and sand fell into my eyes when I looked up. I brushed it from my lashes and saw the outline of a man radiated by the sun. As two other figures leaned over the tunnel, they drowned out the sunlight and I was able to see their frightened faces. Leysner, Lilly and their son stood above me. I waived them down and Patches stepped up next to me to help. His voice was as hurried as his movements "Send the boy down first, we must move quickly!"

The boy was red from holding his breathe by the time his feet hit the floor. His muscles were tense and his eyes were set on the ground. He was slightly younger than Cordell, but about the same height. His hair was short and filled with tight brown curls and his skin was very light brown. I squatted next to him as Patches helped Lilly and Leysner to the ground and held my hand out "My name is Jayden, what is your name?"

He looked up for just a moment "Isaiah." and then looked back to the ground.

I grabbed the compass from my pocket "Isaiah; what a name! I have something that I want you to hold onto for me ok?"

I held out the compass by the chain and he looked at it for a moment and then took it in his palm. He ran his fingers over the design on the surface gently, but tightened his fist around it as the wooden door plunked down and frightened him. He looked up at me and held his gaze for a moment before opening his palm and looking down at the compass again "What is it?"

I had no idea what the compass was for, but I wanted to give him a sense of significance in the whole ordeal so I made a story up "It was given to me by a very wise old man. It will lead us to a place where all people can live together peacefully. I need you to hold onto it for me and make sure you keep it safe. For now, put it in your pocket and let's follow Patches out to the horses."

Patches squeezed in front of me and handed me one of the headbands with a light attached. Within moments we were jogging through the narrow tunnel, Patches in the lead and myself in the rear. In between was the assortment of people I had come to trust, their families and a misfit; Leysner, Lilly, Isaiah, Cordell, Caiohme, Chloe, Scraggs and Kaylon. They were not the youngest or most fit group, but the people I would depend on when danger reared its head.

The tunnel was a cool relief from the warm sun and water dripped from the earth, accumulating in muddy puddles on the ground. Nonetheless, as we ran perspiration formed on my head and dripped into my eyes. At times it seemed like the group was so close together that there wasn't enough oxygen for us all. I thought of all the scary movies I'd seen, being buried alive or trapped in an underground cave, and I was sure I might suffocate.

Several times, Kaylon stopped to walk and I had to fall back and nudge him along to keep up with the group. The old man couldn't jog more than a couple minutes before becoming winded. Chloe and Cordell almost tripped over a rocky ledge sticking up from the ground, but caught themselves on Patches back. He barely noticed, but stuck his arms out to be sure they were able to stay on their feet. Patches shirt was soaked and sweat pored like a waterfall from his hair onto his back. Lilly, Leysner, and Isaiah seemed to be the most fit, as they kept pace with the group and avoided obstacles.

Minutes underground seemed like hours before we began an ascent towards a metal door. The ground must have descended slowly the whole jog, because the ascent was fairly steep. By the time we reached the door everyone was breathing heavy and perspiring. Patches put his ear up to the door, which was latched from the inside "I can't hear anything, y'all stay put and I'll make sure it's safe."

I pushed through the others until I was by his side "I should go too, in case someone is out there." I realized how silly it sounded after I said it. What protection could I offer a man of his stature and experience?

He looked down at me, putting his giant hand on my shoulder and smiled "You stay here and make sure these people remain calm. Latch the door behind me and wait for three quick knocks to open the door."

He jiggled the rusty latch free and pulled the door handle. Rays of sunlight flooded the tunnel and my pupils constricted to the point of blindness. My legs grew restless and I wanted to run into the sun. Maybe I'd end up on the football field, under the Friday night lights, with my friends and family cheering for me. Maybe Havenbrook was waiting for me to step back onto the field and lead our team to another victory.

Boom! I knew something had gone wrong when several loud shouts echoed through the tunnel and the door slammed shut. I grabbed the handle, as my pupils adjusted to the dark, and felt around for the latch. It took all my strength and both hands to keep the door closed against pulling resistance from the other side. I leaned back, with both hands on the handle, but slowly rays of light began to creep inside and fingers appeared in the opening. Then, with a bloody mist and a deep scream, the door slammed shut, the resistance was gone, and four mangled fingers lay on the ground.

I latched the door and fell against the wall to my right, swallowing the lump that was rising in my esophagus. I stared at the fingers lying on the ground, hoping that they weren't Patches, and then to my friends who were becoming accustomed to blood. Caiohme and Chloe were sprawled out against the right wall, cuddled together with Scraggs in Chloe's lap. Leysner and Lilly were leaning against the left wall with Isaiah between them. Kaylon's eyes were closed, as he sat on the ground Indian-Style with his head resting on Leysner. They all seemed afraid, but not one of them had a tear in their eyes. I thought the incident might go unspoken of until Cordell's voice rose up from my right side "I told you they would find us!"

He was right; someone had come for us and by the looks of things they weren't here to bring us back to the castle. Several seconds of silence ensued, broken by three distinct knocks; boom, boom, boom. Each knock echoed down the tunnel, startling Kaylon and bringing the others to their feet. I reached for the latch and Scraggs grabbed my leg "Jayden, don't!"

I hesitated for a moment, my fingers running up and down the latch. What if it wasn't Patches? What if they had tortured him for the knowledge of our code? What if they had a gun to his head? What if? What if? What if? I was tired of questioning my intuition, I knew it was Patches. I pulled up the latch and pushed the door open to sunlight that flooded the tunnel again.

I stepped out onto soft ground as my vision began to return. Sun light illuminated several bodies scattered across the ground and a large figure walking away from us. As my pupils dilated I noticed stables and beautiful black horses. A backdrop of dense woods emerged from the blur.

Patches was standing near the gate to the stables with a gash across his forehead. Blood dripped onto his chest as he motioned for us to come that way "Hurry, we haven't got much time before more soldiers arrive."

I stood for a moment, looking down at the dead while the others meandered towards Patches. The three soldiers wore the same armor that was hidden in the castle for me. They were tall and strong and didn't wear anything to make me think they were Leonoids. Were they Farrians, I wondered? Why were they at the stables? Did they know we were coming? Had someone warned them? None of it really mattered. The soldiers were dead and we were about to set out on an adventure into the one place we were told not to go, deep into the Whisper Woods.

The tree line was ominously dark and murky and I couldn't see past the first few rows of moss-covered trees. Vines hung silently from the branches as a dark fog billowed out from the base of the woods. There were no chirping insects or singing birds, curious eyes, croaking frogs, or monkeys swinging from tree to tree. There was only silence; the forest was still enough that I could hear the horses gnawing on the tall grass and their tails swaying from side to side.

Horses had always been my escape and they seemed just as peaceful and free in Leotus as they ever had at home. They were black beasts that gave meaning to the word horsepower. They stood calm and ready for adventure, with my friends on their backs. Caiohme and Chloe shared one, as did Cordell and Isaiah. Kaylon, Leysner and Lilly each had their own, and Patches met me with the reigns of the largest two. He handed over control of the strongest horse and helped mount me on top with Scraggs. Patches took to the back of his own horse and we all turned our attention to the woods.

Behind us was a place we had seen friends and family die. In a few days we had witnessed the darkness, beast attacks, hallucinogenic ant bites, storms, and traitors. We had been lied to, deceived and kept in the dark. We could have stayed and faced the inferno, but we turned our backs, trusting our intuition and the message of a man we had never met. I looked to my left, into Caiohme's eyes, but raised my voice for everyone to hear "My dad always told me to have courage and my coach always said to walk onto the field without fear. I soon learned that it was courage that allowed us to be bold and brave in the face of fear. I believe we will endure many challenges and difficult times, but nothing we cannot overcome together. We are a team and this is our field. If we have the courage to defend one another then we do not need to fear those who mean us harm. You are my friends and I am glad to have you with me."

I grabbed the horse's main and squeezed him tightly with my legs "yah, yah, yah, run boy!" Patches grabbed hold of my waist as we bolted toward the forest with the others following from behind. We galloped into Whisper Woods as the sun began to set.

CHAPTER TWELVE
The Traitor

AS WE TROTTED into the forest, the horse's hooves broke through the dense, dirty fog just long enough to see the thick brush on the forest floor; then the fog enveloped their leg's as quickly as it had broken. The whole mass of fog rolled off a large swamp, a few hundred feet to the right of us. Trees rose from the water and formed a canopy, allowing only the dimmest light to reach the ground. Vines and a small creek, fed by the swamp, made travel treacherous. There was no telling what lay beneath the gray precipitate.

Scraggs was supposed to be our guide, but he seemed to be at a loss for words. Perhaps he was still angry with me for bringing the others along or maybe the route I chose had left him a little disoriented. He did seem to be paying attention to each step, looking for something familiar, calculating; he was always calculating.

Several times, the horses stepped into holes and stumbled over obstacles, almost losing their footing. It was a relief as we moved deeper into the woods and the fog began to diminish. Calm overwhelmed the tension that had been building all day.

The horses nudged each other, Caiohme and Chloe giggled and even Kaylon seemed jubilant and awake. A deep silence allowed me to drift off into the empty spaces between the girl's laughter before I was startled by the high pitch of Scraggs alert "There, there, over there!"

The abrupt alert caused everyone to huddle together and Patches to pull the bow from his shoulder into his hands. He was ready to fire and we were all ready to run, but nothing sinister presented itself. I leaned closer into Scraggs ear, speaking as not to be heard, "What is it Scraggs? What do you see?"

"Over there. It's the creek I followed to get to Leotus, it will lead us home."

We all let out a sigh of relief and Patches flung his bow back over his shoulder. I had expected to see a wild beast or an army of Farrian soldiers. The sight of flowing water, of something familiar, was a welcome reprieve from the fear I had felt for days.

As the horse's hooves met the edge of the stony creek, they stopped to take a drink. I reminisced of my childhood at Chisholm Creek, splashing around in the water, throwing handfuls of it at Katie. We were young, seven or eight, and had nothing to live for but the long summer days. She was in a pair of frayed jean shorts, cut off from jeans she had outgrown that winter, and a swim suit top. Her hair was bleached by the sun and her skin bronzed from the hours we spent outside every day. I must have looked like a goof with my baggy swimming trunks and wet curls hanging in my eyes. As I kicked water up at her, I never would have imagined how much she would grow to mean to me.

I looked up as my horse began to trot at the pace quicker than those in front of him. I had fallen to the back of the drove, but quickly made my way to the front under Scraggs' insistence. We followed a path ridden with landmarks that Scraggs remembered: a fallen tree, a bend in the stream, a crumbled foundation, a grouping of large boulders. We followed his lead for hours; in and out of fog, through thick brush, across the creek and around boulders that grew larger as we rode.

Flowers and tropical shrubs speckled the forest floor, but only where the sun was able to peak through the dense canopy. The large leaves and heavy brush trapped the moisture and made for a hot, humid ride. Sweat accumulated on my back and chest and dripped from my hair. Unlike other forests, I could hear my horse breathe, each twig that snapped below his hoof and the whistle of the wind grazing the leaves. There was no life, aside from the occasional tree frog and a few snakes. I did not hear the buzz of the bees, or the song of the birds. There were no ants marching down the branches or deer chasing tail. There was only silence, deep silence.

The silence morphed into shrill cries and unfamiliar noises as the sun began to kiss the horizon. Our group tightened as rattles, hisses, coos and deathly cries pierced our eardrums. Beyond the noise, below the pitch of the insects, I could hear something that I kept to myself. I could hear Katie's voice, warning me to turn around, telling me to come back home. I could hear the pain in each word as she begged me to save her, but these were the tricks we were warned about in Whisper Woods. As we approached a clearing, a spot were the moon could be seen rising in the sky, a spot we all decided would be a good place to get some rest, it happened.

As swift as the silence had broken, as the breeze moved across the land, the beast pounced into the clearing and was gone. I saw him out of the corner of my eye, a black flash of lightening. His movement was so precise and deliberate that I cannot describe much about his features, except to say that he ran on four legs and was as black as midnight. His coat of hair was slick and the night was his camouflage. Just like that, the first in our convoy was dead.

Leysner saw it first, then Patches. The rest of the group followed as they ran to Kaylon's aid. His bloody face fell in my direction and I sat there starring into his empty eyes. It was too late; there was nothing they could do to revive him. It was a reminder how quickly things could change in Leotus. The silence had given way as the beasts we were warned of had come out to stalk their prey. None of us were safe, not in Leotus and not in the woods. The empty expression on his face reminded me of the relief that death offered from this land and for the first time I wished for my own.

Leysner and Patches drug his lifeless body to the edge of the woods as Caiohme and Lilly shielded the young from the bloody slaughter. Scraggs tried to distract Cordell, Isaiah and Chloe by taking their hands and telling them a story of ancient times, but I could see in his eyes that he blamed me. I blamed myself; it was a journey I should have made on my own. It was my letter, it was my father in the picture, and now others were dead because I had chosen to bring them along. I closed my eyes, but all I could see was the gash the beast had left in Kaylon's throat.

The vivid images left me in a semi-comatose state, in an enigma walking amongst the dead. A graveyard full of those who had passed and those whose death I feared most left me unaware of my surroundings. Henry escorted me, ant bites covering his body, leading me past a tomb of those who had perished in the attack. Stepping up to a freshly dug grave, we peered into an open casket ready to be lowered six feet into the earth; one more time I saw Kaylon's dead body, his neck stitched shut and ready for viewing. Then Henry led me to another grave, piled high with beautiful flowers. I fell to my knees as he mentioned her name, "Caiohme." I turned to shake him, to demand that he release me from the vivid lies, but he was gone, descending into the tomb of the dead, vanishing from my reality.

When I opened my eyes, I starred not into the bloody face of sacrifice, but into bright orange and red flames. The fire danced below the night sky, like young children so full of life. The flame crackled and with each burst of energy sparks shot into the air, reminding me of the firefly's that lit the streets of a more peaceful Leotus. Piles of burning wood lay in a circle around the clearing, but the flames in the middle jumped the highest, illuminating makeshift shelters.

As I became more alert, I noticed Caiohme and Chloe snuggled up to me on the soft earth. Our bodies were sheltered by material tented over us, supported by broken tree limbs. My head stuck out from the shelter and through the clearing I could see the brightest stars, the ones the fire's light had not drowned out. As I followed them across the sky, to the horizon, I saw Patches pacing back and forth around the perimeter.

I slipped out from under Caiohme's arm and crawled out from under the shelter. The air was still and everyone but Patches and I had found their way to sleep. Glowing eyes lurked in the woods and the chirping of insects and howling of wild beasts echoed in my ear. I didn't make it two feet before the twig that snapped under my weight caused Patches to pivot my direction, bow drawn in his hands. He recognized me and lowered his weapon as the fire illuminated his dirty hands and face. He had been busy sheltering us, protecting us. His eyes looked tired. Soot and dirt covered his rosy cheeks and his smile had faded.

As I approached him he put his arm around me and sighed "I didn't serve my purpose today. I could not save my friend." He sighed and took in a deep breath, his nostrils flaring like a dragon's "I've known Kaylon since he was an elite soldier, sworn to protect the creationists. When his wife and children were killed by the Farrians, he snapped. I don't think he knew what to do next, so he hid away in his home, plotting his revenge. I didn't even know he was working again until I saw him cleaning up in the kitchen; he wouldn't say a word to me. His expression was so empty. I thought their deaths had beaten him until I saw him today with you, but now he's dead."

I wrapped my arm around his back and looked up to the heavens, pointing to the brightest star "You know, sometimes the brightest stars die in an explosion of chaos. Their gone, but we can still see their light here on earth for hundreds of years. It's like great people; they may be gone, but we can still see their light in all the things they accomplished over their lives. In the lives they changed, the people they affected, they live on, just like the stars light. Just remember Patches, he lives on in you."

A grin grew on his face and he wrapped his arms around me, squeezing me tightly "thank you Jayden."

I gasped for air as he pushed it out of my lungs with his strong arms around me "Well don't kill me yet. I haven't had my chance to shine." I laughed.

The conversation had made me more optimistic about leading my friends to safety. I had been a leader my whole life and I was sure I could be a leader in Leotus too. I looked up into Patches' tired eyes "Why don't you lay down and take a nap, get some rest before the sun rises. I can watch the perimeter while you sleep."

He patted my shoulder and laughed "I can't leave you alone Jayden, not after what happened to Kaylon."

I reassured him "I have armor in my bag and weapons to protect the camp. If I am in danger you are twenty feet away; sleep Patches."

He looked down at me and gripped both my shoulders "You are brave Jayden. I believe in you and I believe you will live up to the prophecies. Listen to Chloe, but always trust your own instinct. The future is always evolving; no one can tell you what it holds for certain. Goodnight friend."

With that, he walked back to the group of makeshift shelters and lay down under the stars. I grabbed the stained duffel bag from the ground, near my shelter, and unzipped it. I unfolded the lightweight armor and slid it over my head and arms. I secured the dagger and dart gun to my waist with a belt that Patches must have packed in the bag. I left the manipulation scanner inside and zipped it back up. I dropped the bag to the ground and walked back out to the perimeter.

I sat down on the ground, looking out to the woods and wondering what the next day would hold. Would there be more death or would we find peace and answers? Would we make it to the man who wrote the letter? Would my father be there? Would there be a way back home, back to Havenbrook, to Katie?

I must have been deep in thought; I did not notice Caiohme approaching from behind until her soft voice startled me. She quietly sat down next to me "You're doing a great job being the lookout!" she giggled.

She clasped her fingers in mine and laid her head on my shoulder; we both looked out on the woods together. I said nothing for a moment, taking the pause to enjoy her company as I let my head rest on hers. I lifted my head slightly and kissed the top of hers "All I want right now is for these woods to be my woods. I want to swim in the creek and lay in the hammock. I want to be able to look up to the stars without worrying what terrors the next day will bring. I want a soda and some marshmallows to roast over these flames. I want to see my friends, my family. I want for none of these bad things to have happened. I want to forget all of this, but I don't want to forget you. It's sad that tragedy brought us together and allowed me to feel complete for the first time in my life. What's worse, I would take none of this back if it meant not meeting you."

I wrapped my free hand around her shoulder, opposite me, and pulled her close. I put my hand on her jaw and kissed her head. I let my lips meet her soft skin and linger on her forehead. Her skin had a hint of salt as I licked my lips and kissed her again on the cheek and nose. She dropped my hand and wrapped her arms around my shoulders as my lips met hers. I grabbed her chin and kissed her softly and then again harder.

My heart beat strongly and my stomach lifted as my chest met hers on the soft ground. I kissed her neck and collarbone as she ran her hands up the suit of armor. I sat back on my ankles and pulled the alloy over my head, taking it and the robe off. As her nails ran down my bare chest, a bright flash of light caused me to jump to my feet. I quickly pulled my robe and armor back on as the repetitive flashes of white light made me nauseous. Red and orange flames filled the horizon in the distance, in Leotus.

As the fire grew in expanse, an explosion rocked my ear drums and shook the ground. Black smoke billowed up from the immense amount of light that was being created. The rippling earth woke the others and they joined us side by side, speechless. We stood there like children at their first Independence Day show, frightened, but curiously in awe. We huddled together like a family, arms wrapped around one another.

I was torn by opposing feelings as the stars disappeared behind a veil of smoke. Part of me felt relief; a strong since of gratitude for the man that had written the note, for the creature that had delivered it and toward the girl that prophesied the fire, Chloe. I was grateful to be alive, to have the opportunity to save my friends, to make it back to Havenbrook. On the other hand, my heart ached and I swore I could hear the cries of the young girl who thought Alcaeus had something up his sleeve, of venders in the center court, of Flora as her vines withered, and the last pleas of Alcaeus as his people fell. It saddened me to know that a place which was so simple and peaceful, could suffer from the same demons as mankind. The pasture would burn, the flowering vines would wither, and the white sand would be covered in soot. All that would be left would be the bones and ash of a people that only wished for peace.

There was no time to pity what was already done; evil lurked in Whisper Woods, waiting for the most opportune time to strike. What more opportunity could we have provided, distracted by the fire, our backs to the woods? Who knew what the fire would send our way or how quickly the flames would spread. We didn't know if Malachi was on our trail, or when the Farrians would come searching us out. I was ready to rally the others, to gather our things and hop on horseback, when all hell broke loose.

Right as I was about to encourage our departure, Patches readied his bow and swung around one-hundred-eighty degrees in single smooth motion. It seemed as if time slowed down as I watched the arrow leave his bow. The pointed tip sliced through the calm air with a whistle and penetrated the chest of a black beast as it leapt into the air, towards us. Suddenly, my senses caught up with reality and I could hear the barking howl of a pack of beasts headed our way. As Patches readied another arrow, I pulled out my dagger, but his tone was firm "Run Jayden! Lead them to safety now!"

I did not hesitate. I ran up to Chloe and swept her off her feet with one arm. With the other I grabbed Caiohme's hand and ran toward the horses that were sleeping near the shelters. She pulled her hand away from mine to swipe Scraggs off the ground. I hollered back at the others who had fallen behind "Run Isaiah, run Cordell."

I grabbed the handles of the blue duffel bag as I ran past it, nearly tripping on my own feet, but maintaining my balance. As we reached the horses, I heard the cry of another beast as an

arrow pierced his black coat, but I did not look back. I saddled
Chloe on the horse's back and then helped Scraggs, Caiohme
and Cordell. Leysner helped Lilly and Isaiah onto one horse and
took another for himself. I grabbed the horse's main and pulled
myself onto its back, joining Chloe. The chaotic howls of many
beasts seemed to fade into the deafening roar of one large beast
as they approached. Before I kicked my heels into the side of the
horse, I could not help but look back to my friend, to Patches.

I could not hear anything Patches screamed to me over the
hollow howl, but I knew what he was saying as he gestured for
me to leave. I kicked my heels into the side of the horse and we
began to gallop away. As I lead the charge, I turned around to
see a black beast five times the size of those that surrounded it,
break out into the clearing. The beast stopped for a moment to
meet the gaze of Patches, as he stood strong with his bow.

The beast's eyes were dark and hollow, without a soul. His
black fur accentuated his canines, making them appear as white
as a cloudy sky. His nostrils flared in and out with each breath
and his jaw shook with rage. His ears were stiff and his hair
stood on end. The muscles in his legs were strong, but he looked
like he had not eaten for weeks. His ribs were defined and his
gut was empty. As my horse met the edge of the woods one of
the last things I remember was seeing the beast charge Patches.

What happened in those next moments isn't very clear, but I
remember that as I began to open my eyes I found myself lying
in a puddle of muddy water with my left cheek down. The light
was bright as it hit my pupils and the back of my head was sore.
I tried to shield the light with my hand, but I couldn't move it;
it was as heavy as a lead weight. There was certainly a female's
voice coming from behind me, but I could not discern what was
being said. It was muffled and the words seemed to scramble
inside my head, but there was something familiar about it.

I tried again to open my eyes, but as my vision cleared I

became aware that something awful had occurred. Lying next to me, starring into my eyes was Chloe. Her face was motionless as blood streamed from her brow, down her nose and into the puddle of water. There was no gash on her forehead, but her hair was matted with clumps of dried blood that had attracted flying insects. I wanted to cry or scream, holler out for Caiohme, but I did not want the enemy to see that I was alive. I wouldn't be able to help anyone if they realized I survived.

I waited until I could no longer hear the rambling of the woman's voice and then used what little strength I had to lift my head. As quickly as I was able to get my face out of the murky water and see the others lying around me unconscious, she approached me in her black veil. I knew her voice as she threatened me "You should have stayed in Leotus and died with your father, you should have kept your eyes closed."

She leaned over me with a metal rod clutched tight in her fist. Her eyes were hollow like the beast's and her fist shook with anger. Her tone was as calm as the night I had met her, but there was hateful rage in her voice. She had not disappeared, she was not a victim. She was on Malachi's side. As she raised the rod above her head, I looked into her eyes and screamed "No, Samarra! Traitor!" just before the cold, metal rod struck the side of my head.

CHAPTER THIRTEEN

The Prison Bust

I WOKE UP to the metallic smell of blood that still trickled down the side of my face and a pounding on the right side of my head that throbbed with each beat of my heart. I could feel dried blood on my cheek and there were large clumps tangled in my hair. The gash was still open, from above my right ear to my forehead, and painful to the touch. Flies pestered in the wound, but I was too sore to swat them away.

My mind was foggy. I didn't know where Samarra had taken me or what had become of my friends. The cold cement floor and my damp clothing drew the heat from my body and made me shiver. Metal bars stretched across the front of the cell and confined me to the dark, wet prison. Water dripped from the cement ceiling above me and pinged off the floor like rain drops on dry ground. The prison was dim, but when I lifted my chin off the ground I was able to see that my cell was one of many.

I reached my arms out and gripped the wet, rusty bars with both hands, giving them a brownish-red pigment. I took a deep breath, closed my eyes and bit my lip, as I pulled myself forward. My back was so sore that I thought my arms might separate at the shoulder. I remembered the times I would go heavy on bench days and would not be able to raise my arms above my shoulders to wash my hair. I let out a heavy breath and moaned as I drug my broken body across the ground. I lifted my chin onto a bar that ran across the base of the cell and looked out into the darkness.

Light from the heavens shined through an opening in the high ceiling, which was guarded by some sort of wire mesh. The light grew dimmer as it reached the bottom of the tall tower and illuminated a rusty, spiral staircase. Platforms provided an entry point to each level of cells. I counted each floor as I scanned for other prisoners: one, two, three, four, five, six, seven, eight, nine; nine, circular levels of cells and not another soul to be seen.

Maybe I couldn't see the prisoners on the first floor, in the dim light, or maybe I was alone after all. Alone to be tortured and killed. I didn't want to get the wrong person's attention, but I also didn't want to die in a prison cell by myself, so I screamed soft at first, but then louder and louder "Help! Help me some-one, anyone! Help! Helpp! Helllpppp!"

I thought I heard a soft moan, but it quickly faded and I continued to scream "Anyone! Is there anyone else out there? Please, help me!"

Then I heard the moan again, louder, and I was certain I wasn't alone. The moan turned into a soft cry; a cry that was too close, too familiar. As I turned my head, I realized I hadn't taken the time to look behind me, to look in my own cell. Lined up against the wall were five motionless bodies in white gowns. White hoods were drawn over their heads, and Scraggs lay cuddled between them. Awake, and crawling towards me, was Chloe. She was alive!

I used the bars to pull myself into a sitting position, and then fell against them as Chloe crawled into my lap. She had a large goose egg above her left eyebrow, and matted blood in her hair. Her whole face was dirty, but her right cheek had mud caked on. The dirt made the white of her eyes as bright as ever and I could see her childish optimism in the way they shined. Her head fell onto my shoulder and she wrapped her arms around my chest as she lay in my lap. I couldn't hold back the tears that fell down my cheek as I rejoiced to see my friend alive. I wrapped my arms around her tightly and kissed her head.

Seeing her alive, her vigor, filled me with energy. If she was alive, who else was alive under those hoods? I was anxious to crawl over to the five drooped bodies that lined the wall, but Chloe's grip was tight around my chest as her body shook. I looked down into her eyes and saw her biting the skin around her nails and for once, I had to reassure the always reassuring Chloe "Chloe, it is going to be all right. We are going to get out of here. We are going to be ok."

She looked up into my eyes with a fear I had not seen in her, wrapped her arms around my neck, and pulled her mouth close to my ear. With a shallow and shaky voice she began to whisper "She is here. She is somewhere in the tower. Samarra is here! I can't see it though; I can't see what happens next."

I tried to stay calm, but I knew she had a knack for foreseeing the future and I doubted my body could handle any more harm. I didn't know how to escape, or where we would go if we were able to, but I knew it was time for me to be the strong and optimistic one. I looked her in the eyes and brushed her matted hair behind her ear. I counted each one of her faint freckles as I smiled at her "Chloe, you remind me a lot of a girl I have known ever since I was a little boy. You are funny, outgoing, courageous and beautiful. I need to see that in you now more than ever. Be strong and I promise I will not let anything happen to you. Now rise to your feet, we have to wake the others and get out of here."

She hugged me and I knew she believed we could overcome

our circumstance. She stopped shaking and rose to her feet. She offered me her hand, but I used the bars to pull myself up. It made me slightly dizzy to stand and I could see specks of light flying toward me. The longer I stood with my eyes open the more alert I became. I heard the moans and cries of other prisoners. My vision became increasingly clear, and while my head still hurt, it did not throb with each beat of my heart any longer. I took a moment to take a couple deep breaths and realized I was badly in need of a bath and some hygiene products, but that was the least of my worries at the time. I licked my lips, they were chapped and painful, and I was sure I was dehydrated.

Chloe had already woken Scraggs as I rose and approached the others. He was confused at first, much like myself, but was soon pacing the floor and ranting like normal. He cleaned his dirty fur much like a cat, licking himself and combing his hair with his yellow nails. He momentarily looked up to me with a glare that said everything he wanted to; he had been right about bringing the others and now we would all die, I had doomed him. He quickly went back to pacing without a word, knocking on the walls and inspecting the hinges on the bars.

I stood for a moment, afraid to pull back the hoods of the other five, afraid that they might not have survived. I knew Patches was not among them, none were his size. I did not want to think of the fate I had left him to, of the black beast. The image of it pouncing on him played over and over in my mind. I saw his dark eyes staring at me and the way he yearned for a meal. I stood there, trying to find my way out of those thoughts, until Chloe did what I had not been able to and pulled the first hood off.

I fell to my knees as she revealed Caiohme's face, no blood, no bruises. Chloe's eyes lit up and tears began to stream down her cheeks again. Her dimples grew deep as she wrapped her arms around Caiohme's neck and kissed her. With that simple touch of love, Caiohme lifted her head and opened her eyes. Her mind seemed foggy as she looked up to her sister "Chloe?"

Chloe was overcome with joy as she squeezed her tightly "Caiohme, you're alive! You're alive! I love you! I love you so much!"

I stared down at her chest for a moment and watched it move up and down with each shallow breath; she was alive! I took her hand and softly kissed it as she began to come around and realized what had occurred. She looked to the ground and then up at the two of us "Has she come back? What does she want from us?"

Chloe knew the answer better than I and she went on to whisper softly to Caiohme "She has not come back yet, but she is in the tower, I have seen her. We must leave soon. Help us with the others."

As it became more apparent that Caiohme was going to be fine, my eyes shifted to the remaining four bodies. I was overcome by tears to see that their chest's too moved up and down with each breath, some shallower than others. I released Caiohme's hand and moved down the row, removing each hood: Cordell, Isaiah, Lilly and Leysner. Though we were prisoners, we were alive and there was reason for hope.

With a little bit of time and rustling they all opened their eyes, all of them but Leysner. His chest rose, and his heart pumped blood, but he was in some sort of stupor. Lilly and Isaiah did not realize what was going on yet, as I rubbed his chest and whispered words of encouragement "Come on Leysner. Wake up, snap out of it. Leysner? Leysner?"

As the others became more alert they crowded around Leysner and I. Lilly tried to shield Isaiah from the comatose state his father was in, but her tears told another story. He crawled into his father's lap and put his forehead up to the side of his father's ear. Tears fell from Isaiah's eyes onto his father's robe, as his shaky voice stuttered to find the words. Lilly put her hands on Isaiah's shoulders as he began to speak in a tone that was both angry and helplessly sad "Don't you leave me. Don't you leave mom. Wake up Dad! Fight!"

The tears began to stream out with more consistency as he sniffed his runny nose. His voice grew shakier and Lilly tried to hug him, to pull him away, but he grabbed his father's head and pulled his face in tightly, smashing his nose against his skull. The anger left him as he began to plea "Dad, please! Please wake up! I need you, we need you! I love you! Please dad!"

Isaiah let his chin fall to his chest, as he clung to his father's robe. For a moment, it seemed like time had stopped it was so silent. I put one hand on Leysner and the other on Isaiah's back and I forgot I was a prisoner as I prayed out loud "Lord, please don't take this man from us, this father, this husband. Give him another day with his son, his wife. Help him to fight. Help us all to fight! Lord, I ask you, spare Leysner!"

For the next few breaths I thought we had failed, that we would have to find a way out of that cell without Leysner. Then, like the storms clouds creep out onto the empty prairie, I felt his hand meet my leg. Without warning, he suddenly jerked back to life and grabbed Isaiah's arm firmly. His head flung backwards and all I could see was the whites of his eyes as he jumped to his feet. Both of his hands firmly gripped Isaiah's shoulders, shaking him. Lilly jumped up and tried to rip Isaiah from his tight grip and screamed "Leysner, let him go! What are you doing? Let him go now!"

The whole group of us jumped up and tried to help her pull Isaiah from his grip, but it was firm. There was yelling, cursing and shouting, but it was all a jumbled roar of noise and chaos until Leysner finally flung him across the cell and into the metal bars. Cordell and Chloe fell to the ground beside him, but were quickly able to get back on their feet. Lilly ran to Isaiah's aid as he lay on the cement, looking up to his father with wet eyes and puckered lips. All I could see in Isaiah's face was the hurt of not knowing what he had done wrong.

I looked into Leysner's eyes, ready to tackle him into the wall, as I pushed Cordell, Chloe and Caiohme behind me. He wasn't himself. I could only see the whites of his eyes and his body convulsed. Waves rippled down his arms and torso. Had the blows to the head been too much for him to overcome? Was he dying? I stepped forward to grab him, to help him to the ground, before I was overcome by fear.

As I grabbed him, his skin, his robe, it all began to crack like the earth does without rain. Then, like a windshield struck by hail, his body shattered and fell to the ground, and Samarra stepped out from the shell that was once a human being. She had a smile that stretched her face and her laugh implied a humorous joke, but no one else laughed. I took a step back from her as she stepped toward me. I continued to step back and she continued to step toward me, until I was against the wall and she was inches from me. Stuck in a corner, I did what I hadn't had the bravery to do before; I pushed her away from me.

She laughed as she fell to the ground and her elbows hit the cement. The others huddled in the corner together and I knew it was time for me to do what I had promised, fight to save them or die trying. I grabbed the dagger from under my robe and lunged at her, but just as I nicked her skin I was suddenly on the outside of the bars looking in. She laughed as I grabbed the bars and rattled them "Run and save yourself Jayden, or stand here and watch as I kill each one of your friends. I can change every-thing you've ever known. I can create a whole new hell for you. I can slit each one of their throats and then go and kill Katie too! I can destroy Havenbrook and everything you live for, or you can come and fight for us. You can fight for the Farrians Jayden and I will spare your friends and the existence you know as life; your choice."

Without a second to spare, she was on her feet and Chloe was in her arms. The particles of life that had been Leysner's body came together to form a sharp blade in her hands and her brown eyes met mine "What will it be Jayden?"

Before I could answer Caiohme threw her arms out and the knife fell to the ground like a hundred grains of colorful sand. She looked Samarra in the eyes as Chloe slipped her grip "Screw you," and then charged her into the cement.

Caiohme hit her once across the left cheek bone with her right hand and then knocked her head the other direction with her left fist. Before she could land another punch, Samarra grabbed her arm, flipped her over, and climbed on top of her. Then Samarra threw her arms back and trapped the others in a cage while she put her hands around Caiohmes neck "Now you're going to die slowly and everyone is going to watch. Then I will hunt your mom down and kill her while your sister watches. Lastly, I will torture and kill Chloe as she watches us wipe the earth clean of your kind."

I rattled the bars as Caiohme gasped for breath and I realized I couldn't do it, I could not watch her die. Chloe struggled to escape the bars and screamed as tears fell down her face "Let her go! Let her go Samarra! You're killing her; stop!"

I became desperate, willing to do anything to save her, to spare Chloe of the experience. I couldn't lose the girl I had such a special bond with, that I had connected so deeply with. I didn't know quite what it would mean for me, but I cried out the only deal I ever made with her "Let her live, spare them all, and I will fight for the Farrians!"

Samarra laughed as Caiohme's face lost its color and she choked for air. She kept her hands tight around her neck "You will fight for us even if I kill them all. You will fight as long as there is someone left to fight for and right now the Farrians have Katie. Her life is in your hands."

I fell to my knees and wept as Caiohme's arm fell motionless and Samarra released her grip. I looked on helplessly as Chloe rattled the bars and cried so hard that she was coughing. Chloe's face was red and she was having difficulty breathing. Lilly tried to hold her, to console her, but how do you comfort someone in that situation? I thought of Katie too and what the Farrians might do to her. Would the beasts ravage her like they had me? Would she be tortured, killed?

I didn't know what direction to go in that moment. I knew I couldn't get up and run, that I couldn't leave Chloe, that I couldn't give up. It was difficult to think that I felt bad for Samarra when she went missing. I looked onto her face as she stood. Her smirk, her threats, the look in her eyes, it all made me want to take her life in the same way she had my friends, but I didn't have too. He came.

The back wall of the prison imploded and the sunlight shined in, almost blinding me, like it had when Alcaeus came to rescue me from the darkness. The bars that held us captive disappeared in a metallic shimmer. Before I realized what had happened, he swooped in on the dragons back, jumped to the ground and drove a spear through Samarra's heart. He grabbed his chest as he fell to his knees. Using what strength he had left, he pulled my duffel bag from his shoulder, grabbed the vial from inside and poured its contents down Caiohme's throat. We all looked on as she gasped for breath and jerked into a sitting position. The blood pulsed through her body as he fell to the ground. Malachi had saved us.

I looked down on Malachi as Caiohme and Chloe exchanged hugs and loving words. I was shocked, confused and scarred. The man I held as my top enemy had just saved my life, the life of my friends and possibly others. Somewhere inside himself, he found the strength to put a spear through the heart of the only person he seemed to care for and he was clearly in pain. His face was red and beads of sweat accumulated on his dark skin. His pupils were dilated and he sank his teeth into his lower lip as he grasped his chest with his right hand. His respirations were rapid and shallow. He moaned as he released his chest and motioned for me to come closer.

I leaned in closely, over Malachi's chest. Listening was the least I could do after the sacrifice he had made for us. His breathing was labored and his breaths were diminished. He spoke in short, broken sentences, but with speed and urgency "Get to Alcaeus. Leotus has fallen. Good people will die. You were never meant to be here. Get to the house in the woods; to the one eyed man. Carmine will lead you. The servant will lead you. He will know what to do."

I lost my concentration and turned around as the dragons began to cause a commotion. They shuffled around and grew antsy as Carmine began to load the others onto their backs. He boosted Lilly, Cordell and Isaiah onto the large, black dragon that was perched on the cement ledge. Caiohme helped Chloe and Scraggs onto the small, red dragon that was crouched in the prison cell and then climbed onto its back. Each was similar to the dragon I had seen in the square: armor scales, tough leather wings with a skeleton frame and a pointed tail.

Malachi stopped talking for a moment and leaned over; we both looked around the dragon and out the hole in the wall. In the distance, was a swirling cloud of darkness, like that which had overtaken us when the beast came for me. Red and orange flames illuminated the trees and leapt high into the sky. The fire burned with intensity like I had never seen, the heat radiating into the darkness. My thoughts got lost in the flames before Malachi began to speak again "Alcaeus is his master. Alcaeus wrote the note. He knew the war was coming too soon, that you weren't ready!" he said pointing to Scraggs.

He took a shallow breath and continued "He sent you to the forest to keep you safe. The man in the woods is a friend of your father's and a friend of Alcaeus. He knew you had to survive for hope to survive. The man in the picture is the man in the woods. Go to him. You, Caiohme, Chloe, you must drink the vials when you get there; then you will understand. Soon you will be ready. You must go now!"

He looked up to me and his eyes met mine "Samarra didn't lie; they have Katie. Fight for her. Remember the virtues: prudence, temperance, justice and fortitude. Thank you for reminding me of them, for changing my heart. The humans will write of you as a God or you will vanish in flames as a coward. Be brave. I believe the prophecy. I believe you can beat my father. Now go!"

I didn't know what to say as Carmine gave me a hand, helping me up from the ground. I looked down on Malachi, injured and in pain, and I had just one question "Why are you helping us?"

He let out a deep sigh and moaned in pain as he reached into his pant pocket. He pulled out a photograph and handed it to me. It was a young girl, with skin as dark as his and curly black hair. Her smile stretched the length of her face and her teeth were pearly white. He looked at me, trying to contain the tears that accumulated in his eyes "My sister, Aricela. I hated Alcaeus for taking me away from her, but failed to see all he wants is to save her. I have followed my father too long. I have done many bad things. It's time for me to do something right. She does not deserve to die. Fight for her Jayden, fight for them all!"

I looked at the picture for a moment, until a loud explosion shook the prison walls. Carmine grabbed my shoulder and took the picture from my hand "It's time to go Jayden"

As I climbed onto the dragon's back I glanced down to Malachi one last time. I saw the emotion on his face as his lips quivered. For the first time he did not seem unreachable; he seemed, human. Carmine pulled a vial from his pocket and poured it into Malachi's mouth as he bent down to hug him. They exchanged a few gentle words, too quiet for me to hear, and Carmine placed the photo back in Malachi's palm. Malachi brought the photo up to his chest and looked up to me as Carmine boarded the black dragon with Lilly, Isaiah and Cordell. He did not send me off with words, but with a simple gesture he had failed to give me the first time we met, a smile.

With that simple goodbye, Carmine gave his command "hold on tight everyone." The black dragon, with Carmine and my friends on its back, appeared to nosedive off the ledge. It seemed like minutes before the dragon swooped back up to eye level, the wind from its wings blowing across my face and through my matted hair, but it had only been mere seconds.

As I watched the dragon soar into the deep blue sky, I failed to notice that our dragon had approached the ledge and we were looking down onto the metallic buildings of the Farrian city. The scenery was much like Caiohme had explained it, but it was apparent that the Leotus forces had put up a fight. Many metallic buildings stood, but others had been obliterated into smoking piles of cement and steel. The rail lines had been destroyed in many locations between the mountain side and buildings, making transport impossible. The streets were still as desolate as she had explained, even as new buildings caught fire and occasional explosions rocked the streets. There were no ground troops or tanks to be seen, so I assumed the attacks must have been by air or other means.

I didn't understand why the Farrians had destroyed the land and built the type of city they hated the human race so much for building. Why had they inflicted the type of war that they opposed humans for fighting? As I observed the city, I kept close watch over the dragons movements and noticed as it began to lean forward and elevate its back side, sending me several feet higher, looking down onto the cement streets. I hesitated for a moment, fearing a plunge to my death, ready to yell anything to stall our fall, but it was too late.

Before I could suck in enough air to scream or jump off its back, the dragon draped us in its wings and twisted head first off the ledge. I hugged the girls, pulling them in close to me, as our descent increased in speed. Without the wind against us it almost felt as if I was floating, like the sky was fighting to pull me back into the heavens. Draped in darkness, beneath the dragon's smooth, leather wings, I don't know how close we came to the ground. What I do know is, before we hit, he opened his wings and they trapped the air like a parachute. I felt the same relief that a skydiver does when his pack opens at 125 miles an hour; an exhilarating rush of adrenaline.

The abrupt conclusion to our fall pushed us tightly against the dragons back as his wings lifted us above the burning buildings. Each powerful flap brought us higher, but the turbulence rattled me enough to bring out a new fear of falling to my demise. We held onto each other tightly, but onto the rein even tighter. Our ascent continued until we were hundreds of feet above the tallest building and the black dragon came into view. The air was thin and it was hard to breath, but the ride became less tumultuous as we stopped climbing higher into the sky and began to glide with the wind currents.

As we came up on the side of the black dragon, I could see our friends. Lilly and Isaiah were both shaken, but I was not sure if that was due to the ride or what they had witnessed inside the prison cell. Both were factors I was sure, but who knew if they even realized what was going on. Cordell was calm, nearly absent. As we came within feet of the right side of the other dragon's wing, Carmine released his rein and put a thumb up in the air, I suppose to tell me that everything was all right as we glided hundreds of feet above the fire and rubble. Looking past the woods, to the fire in the distance, I wondered if Carmine even knew what had become of Leotus!

For the first time I focused on the words Malachi had said "...you can beat my father." I realized I had been wrong to judge him, to question his character. He too had left family and friends behind in an existence that he was ripped from. At some point, he had dealt with the fact that he was a child of the God's, not of the flesh that had raised him. Worse, his father was the reason that we had been taken from our homes and cast into a ragging war. Malachi and I were more alike than I had ever thought possible and I hoped I would see him again.

CHAPTER FOURTEEN

Blue Truth

IN CASE YOU never get to experience a ride on the back of a dragon, you should know that their speed is unmatched by any bird in the sky. The strength in their wings is beastly and makes for a turbulent ride, but when they stretch their wing span out and glide through the blue sky, the trip is as peaceful as a top-down-ride on the open interstate. It can be quite breezy at several hundred miles an hour, but their large bodies block most of the wind and the fire in their heart radiates warmth off their back.

In no time at all we were beyond the plumes of smoke and the metallic buildings, which reflected the sun so well that I felt the slight warmth of sunburn on my exposed skin. One fire behind us and another ahead; the smell in the air reminded me of when the farmers in Kansas would burn their fields after harvest. Spring fires brought new life; these fires only seemed to bring death. Samarra lay breathless in the Farrian prison and Malachi was left to an undecided fate. The way he fell when he killed her made me wonder just how connected Caiohme and I could truly be.

The green tree-tops of Whisper Woods were below us as we flew toward the city that we had set out to flee. Rarely were there breaks in the dense canopy, but as we flew over them flowers and fruit bushes crowded one another reaching for the morning sun. The sun's rays broke through the smoke and glistened on the horizon, letting us know that another day was upon us, another opportunity to find something worth living for. All I could think of as I looked toward the sun, kissing the water as it met the sky, was all the time we waste as humans. The sunrises we don't get up early enough to see, the stars we don't stay out to watch, the blooming flowers in spring, the smell of the crisp mountain air, the golden wave of wheat, children as they grow, our animals as they beg for our attention, and all those I love you's that we take for granted. I knew that if I ever made it home I would take the time to really live.

As I glanced into the sun, something my mother told me to never do, I failed to realize that we had begun to circle above a dense canopy. I began to wonder what was wrong. Were we lost or had Carmine seen something that caught his eye? Were there enemy troops nearby or were we simply close to the house in the woods? The dragons drew closer to the treetops without moving their wings, simply falling from higher altitudes gracefully, like cotton falls from the tree on a still summer day. I thought that the dragons might have simply been landing for a rest on the canopy, before it began to disappear. Like a hologram, the image got blurry, flickered a few times, and then was gone. Lying below us was the house in the woods.

As we hovered several feet above the ground a strange feeling grew inside of me, until it consumed my thoughts. I raced through the images in my mind, but could not place the feeling. Caiohme confirmed what I felt "this place, it's so familiar," as we completed the next sentence together "it's like I have been here before."

My eyes met hers as she turned towards me and something inside me flickered; her and me running through that clearing together as small children. She wore a pink floral dress and reminded me of Chloe. She laughed as I chased her and the leaves fell from the trees all around us. A man watched cautiously from the painted white porch, monitoring the woods in all the directions he could see. Finally I caught her and threw my arms around her, falling onto the ground. The vision ended as the dragon thumped into the hard ground.

I shook my head and smiled, realizing I had been staring at her as the images consumed me. Her giggle filled my stomach with butterflies and I had the sudden urge to kiss her. The passion for her filled the empty spaces inside of me, growing like a vine. Instead of making a scene, I grabbed her hand and helped her down from the dragon's back as it knelt to let us off. I bit my tongue, not sharing what I had seen, but wondering if she had any memories of the two of us. I released Caiohme's hand and grabbed an exhausted Chloe from the dragon's back and helped her to her feet.

I was not sure if the day dream was real or just my brain's construction of a story to satisfy my longing for answers. What I did know was that I felt a familiarity, a safety, which I had not felt in days. The home had aged significantly, but it was the same porch the man had so carefully watched us from. Many of the large glass windows were cracked or boarded over. Shutters dangled from their original position or were missing entirely. The glossy white paint that coated the porch was dull and chipping and vines invaded the cracks in the boards. Shingles were missing and the roof sagged over the porch, ready to cave in. Even in this condition, a pleasant sign still hung over the rusty-red door "Family Makes a House a Home!"

If the yard was once safe to run and play in, it certainly wasn't anymore. An assortment of sharp, rusted scrap metal and glass shards dotted the open land; some stuck up from the ground and some were hidden amongst the tall grasses and shrubbery. There were no roads leading away from the house or a clearing in the woods, making me wonder how one traveled to and from town. I picked up Chloe and followed Carmine toward the house. The front door opened and a man stepped out from the shadow to greet us, the man from my dream, or was it?

He was not nearly as young and his skin was wrinkled and speckled with age spots. Time had robbed him of his right leg and eye. He was equipped with a prosthetic; some sort of mechanical contraption made of levers and hinges, but walked with a limp. His hair was gray, short and extended into a five o'clock shadow. Black bags hung from under his eyes and his teeth weren't nearly as white or straight as the people in Leotus. All said, the only comparison to the man in my vision was his gender, but deep inside my brain the fog began to clear and I knew it was him.

He walked toward us swiftly, for a man with only one good leg, and I let Chloe down to greet him. The only expression on his face was a faint crooked smile as he approached us and embraced me tightly, wrapping his arms around my neck. His head rested firmly against mine as he spoke softly "Jayden, it's good to see you again."

He then turned to Caiohme and embraced her equally as strong "You've grown into a beautiful, young woman since I last saw you. I know under that soft complexion is a strong woman though; a fighter."

He smiled as he knelt down next to Chloe, favoring his good leg and resting his palms on each knee. He reached in to brush the hair from her face, but she stepped back from him with a shyness I had not seen in her. He laughed hard from his gut "That's not the Chloe that I remember. You used to climb on me like a jungle gym and dangle from my arms. You'd run your fingers through my hair, though it was longer then, and fall asleep on my lap. I seem to remember you having a fondness for the baby chicks that hung around my house, especially the one you called Waddles!"

Caiohme chuckled and looked down at Chloe "She still has a thing for ducks; bathes with a little rubber one every night."

We all laughed as Chloe looked up to Caiohme with squinted eyes "Do not!"

The mystery man, who had greeted us all with so much familiarity rose to his feet again, put his two pointer fingers in his mouth, and let out a loud whistle. To everyone's surprise a momma duck came running from around the side of the house with five chicks following her, all flapping their wings and quacking. He looked down to Chloe once more "May I present to you Waddles and her five babies."

After holding back for about ten seconds, the cute little ducks were too much for Chloe or Caiohme to overcome. The comfort of an animal, the example of new life in bad times, it was a blessing after what we had experienced. Like watching a flower bloom or the birth of a new child; new life has the ability to wash away old and hurtful realities. New life reminds us that there is a tomorrow and that there are better days ahead.

In the commotion I had forgotten about Isaiah, Cordell and Lilly and the loved one they had lost, until I turned around and saw them huddled together on the ground, near the dragon. Scraggs stood his ground beside them, as if to guard them from whatever evil might try to bring them more harm. He did not try to console them, or pace back and forth; he simply stood there, watching the woods.

Carmine broke the momentary silence, reminding us of where we were and what the circumstance was "People are dying, our home is being destroyed, and Leotus is falling! We must get to Alcaeus now! They must drink the vials!"

The old man looked at me with grazing eyes and a raised brow, and then to Carmine "What, they have not had the elixir? They must think I'm a crazy old fool. No wonder they acted how they have, they don't know me from any of you. Why did they not have the elixir when they arrived in Leotus Carmine?"

He shook his head as he looked down to his feet "A lot has happened, but there isn't time for explanations or excuses. The time just wasn't right. Alcaeus wasn't ready for them to know. It was not my place to have a different opinion."

The old man kicked a rock across the ground and looked toward the smoke rising from the fires in Leotus "It is no one's place to stand against the will of Alcaeus, but these are different times. Fire may scour our lands, scorching our buildings and killing our sons, but the ash always brings new life. That hope, that new life, it begins with these children. It is time that they finally know the truth. It is time that they know just who they are. For time is withering the branches of his tree, and if we do not act soon, they too will be devoured by the flames."

He looked into my eyes, more seriously than before, more desperate "Pull the vials from your pockets Jayden; one for Caiohme, one for Chloe, and one yourself. Drink them, before time takes from you what it has from me!"

I reached beneath my robe and into my pockets and let the cold glass linger in my hand for a moment. The neck of each vial slipped between my fingers and I gripped them tightly. The truth, everything I had wanted to know until the opportunity presented itself, was stored in those vials. An answer to all the secrets, deceptions and lies was in my hands. Once the opportunity presented itself, I questioned what I really wanted to know. Aren't some things better kept quiet, unknown? Aren't there times when the truth only creates more questions or causes for more grief and pain?

The life I wanted, all the truth I needed, was back in Havenbrook. I had parents that loved me, a girl that I cherished, a team and community that supported me. I wanted Ms. Mayfield's pie or a glass of sweet tea, Saturday morning breakfast with my mom and to work with my friends at our market. I wanted to throw the football, splash around in Chisholm Creek and kiss Katie's forehead as we lie in the hammock on the hill. Those were the things that defined me, the moments that life is made of, my real truth.

Then I thought of the brother that Cordell had lost, the father that Isaiah had seen perish in front of his eyes and all the people that were fighting in Leotus because they believed we could save them. I thought of Patches and how he had stayed behind to fight the beast so that I could live to win the war. They all had their memories, but there were moments they would never get to live again, truths that they would never experience again. As much as I wanted to be selfish, I knew that I owed it to the Leonoids to find out what truths those bottles held and to fight for what they had left. I hoped that we might preserve some of those truths that make up a life.

I looked down at the vials in my hand, as everyone's eyes turned to me. The light blue solution seemed to move in the sunlight, spinning like the clouds in the sky. It never crossed my mind that the solution might be poison; it was the people that had saved us encouraging us to consume it. The world seemed to revolve around me as everyone walked in my direction. Scraggs left his post, followed closely by Lilly, Isaiah and Cordell. Caiohme and Chloe dropped what they were doing with the animals and approached me, the ducks waddling behind them. The old man had regressed to his porch, but he and Carmine observed from there. Even the dragons turned their heads our way.

I popped the tops off of the vials and handed one to Caiohme and one to Chloe. Their eyes got lost in the blue solution and I wondered if they had the same worries as me. The ground shook as something exploded in close proximity, interrupting the calm silence. I knew that if we were going to make a difference we couldn't wait any longer. In a somewhat sarcastic manner, I held my vial out towards the girls and grinned "cheers!"

Their vials met mine and then our lips. I quickly guzzled the solution down, barely taking time to notice the way its sweet tones lingered on the back of my tongue. The taste reminded me of the blooms from our neighbors Honeysuckle bush, which we would suck on in the spring. I closed my eyes, ready to be barraged by images of Leotus, of the truth, but nothing came as I let the vial fall to my waist and slip from my hand. I opened my eyes to Caiohme staring at me, perhaps wondering if I had seen anything. Before we had time to question the liquids effectiveness it began. Chloe began to shake and then her muscles became flaccid and she fell to the ground. The shaking only lasted a moment and then she was still, deathly still. Before I had the time to fall to my knees and check on her, my eyelids fell and the visions began.

The visions began as short episodes that weren't even coherent; bright glimpses of color, flashes of light, speech that was jumbled or too soft to hear. The flashes began to fade together and the blurry colors became more defined, until the unrecognizable images were like videos of my childhood. What I learned that day I would never take back, but it changed everything. I learned my purpose in that blue vial; I remembered what I was created for.

The first complete vision was a continuation of the one I

had begun on the dragon's back. After Caiohme escaped my arms, she got up and ran as fast as her little legs would carry her, giggling and squealing like little girls do. I ran after her, almost catching her before she fell into his arms. I looked up into his face, his eyes glistening with a joy I had rarely seen. You see, it wasn't the old man's arms she fell in to, it was my father's. Every year, he would hug her and kiss her and tickle her like she was his own.

Eventually Chloe began to come to the house in the woods as well. My father would treat her no different than the rest of us. He seemed to love them the same way he loved me, instilling in them the same values he had raised me with. He was not our birth father, but he was the man the Leonoids had entrusted with my upbringing, our training. One of the rare humans that was able to see into our world, he was special.

I learned that the man in the woods had a name, Desiah, and that he was my father's best friend. When we were not training, my father and Desiah would take us down to the ocean to fish, play in the sand and paddle out past the tall waves. They would take us to the edge of the Farrian city to look down on our enemy from the mountain tops. They would play with us in the leaves and the rain and build sand castles with us on the beach. Every trip to Leotus was an adventure. I learned that the best memories with my father were the ones that they had hidden from me.

Every fishing trip, birthday, every outing that my father and I ever made was in Leotus. Alcaeus, Deseus and Erebus would meet us in the woods and teach us how to turn something as simple as dirt into the most beautiful flower or bird. They would teach us to control the wind, bend the trees, and draw fountains of water from beneath the earth. They taught us to heal the wounded and to nourish the body. They taught us how to read thoughts, change memories and manipulate emotion. They taught us how to draw weapons from the air and to destroy our enemies by breaking apart their very composition. They taught us how to walk between Leotus and the places we called home. They taught us everything that a creationist needed to know.

Several times the other children would come to visit us in the woods and work with us. I didn't know it before, but I had met Malachi, Samarra, Adrianna and Carmine. I had met them and many other children. Some days we would play war in the woods, using dirt balls and water pistols like normal children, but other days we would practice our skills against one another. We would dress up as Farrians and Leonoids and practice survival techniques and mind games. We knew each other like books, one of the downfalls of being able to see a man's thoughts.

When we were alone, Alcaeus would sit with me and remind me that I was special and that I had special gifts. He would talk about how one day I would control the beasts that roamed those woods, like I had learned to control the wind. He would meditate with me and encourage me to look within myself and find out who I was. He promised that once I found myself, I would find the ability to use those gifts that were unique to me. Every day I would search my soul and sit outside the house in the woods and practice, and every day I would fail. Then one day, something happened that turned something deep inside of me on and I found myself.

Dad and I had come to the woods for what was supposed to be a relaxing weekend, a late 10th birthday celebration for Caiohme. It was a small gathering, my father and Desiah, several of the children, and a few families from Leotus. We were all playing in the field and the adults were sitting on the porch enjoying fresh lemonade, when several men approached from the woods. At that point, we had always been told to hide at the perimeter if we saw anyone we didn't know. We all scattered and hid in different places, except Chloe, who ran behind the house to save the ducks.

Talking soon turned into screaming and shouting. Their voices were angry, but I could not tell what they were saying. Then, one of the men pulled a gun from under his jacket and shot Desiah in the leg. When my father tried to intervene and grab the gun from his hands it went off again, hitting Desiah in the eye. In the commotion, one of the men slipped behind the house and grabbed Chloe. The Farrian drug her from her hiding spot and out to the other two men, screaming in my dad's ear and shaking her. I don't know whether it was fear for myself or for my friends, but in that moment I found the strength to summon the beasts.

I closed my eyes and found a pack of wolves in the woods. Then, it was almost like I was able to jump in to one of their bodies and lead the others to the men. As they got close I was not sure whether I was looking out of the beast's eyes or my own. They ran with a speed I had never seen and pounced onto the three unsuspecting men before they could even turn around. They dug into their faces and necks, biting them again and again, and then drug them off into the woods to finish what they had started.

I don't know whether it was my aggression or animal instinct that caused the wolves to be so vicious, but part of me was thankful to see the men dead. It was not time that had robbed Desiah of his eye and leg, it was the Farrians. They had been tipped that I was there with my father and they had come for me. I learned that day how important I was to the Leonoids and of the pledge that so many had taken to protect me. I learned that I was a child of the Gods!

Over the next several visits, I practiced again and again with the beasts. I found it hard to use my gift when I was not angry or afraid. Making a squirrel chase its own tail or a duck peck at my father's leg was easy, but controlling a beast like a Leucrocota was something I was never able to do. I grew angrier with each failed attempt, even as I became more powerful, controlling lions, rhinos and tigers. Finally, one day I decided that the Leucrocota were untamable and that the only way inside of their head was on their own accord; they were beasts with a brain.

There was so much that I discovered, but it was clear trip after trip what I valued most. The girls became more important than anything else I knew. Caiohme understood me like no one else could, more than my father, more than even Katie. I would come back to Leotus, to the woods, more and more often to see her. Those days and nights with her were the only moments I felt complete. She grew from a playmate, to my best friend, to a girl that I loved. They would warn us not to come, that the woods had become too dangerous, but the distance was too much, the time apart too long.

It was not until that moment that I realized just what Malachi had sacrificed. I recognized that there was a special bond between the pairs, but I had forgotten how incomplete I was when she was not around. He had given part of his soul, his memories, his truth, so that I could live. For the first time, I knew that he must have really believed in me; even more than I believed in myself.

The last vision tied it all together. Toward the end of my thirteenth year, my father brought Caiohme, Chloe and myself out to the woods to meet Alcaeus. We traveled on horseback, from the house in the woods to a cliff that overlooked the most horrible thing I had ever seen. Below us was a Farrian death camp. It was a place where they sent those who did not believe in their human extermination plan. They tossed them into mass graves without thinking twice: women, children and men. That was the Farrian's prerogative. That was how serious they were to start over with a new creation, a future without humans.

I wanted to unleash a herd of elephants to stampede through the camp and kill the guards, but Alcaeus was in my head even before the thought was. He urged me to not be the same kind of men that they were. He insisted there were talks under way to end the genocide. I did not know then that I had a brother, let alone that he was the one in talks with the evil men. I cried that day in front of them all as I watched innocent mothers and fathers lose their lives to protect my friends in Havenbrook.

We all sat around the fire when we got back to the house in the woods and Alcaeus and Deseus reminded us that it had become too dangerous for us to be in Leotus. They told us that a war was possible and that someday they might need for us to fight for the humans, for our friends and family, for Leotus. They talked of the need to protect us and promised to look over us and allow for our return as soon as it was safe. There were tears shed and arguments made. I did not know how I would make it without seeing the girls I had grown so close to, but they assured me that the time would be short.

At the end of the night, after marshmallows had been roasted and hugs given, Alcaeus pulled three blue vials from his white robe. He twisted the tops off of them and handed them to Caiohme, Chloe and myself. He insisted that we drink them, that it was time to forget about Leotus, the house in the woods and our friends, until it was time for us to come home again. He told us that the memories would remain, trapped deep inside of us, in that 90% of our brain that we don't use. He told us that one day he would come for us and that we would know what it meant to be the children of the Gods again. We did as we were told, because like Desiah said, it wasn't our place to stand against the will of Alcaeus.

Since that day I hadn't remembered all the adventures I

had with my father and my friends in Leotus. I didn't remember the countless hours I spent training or all the times I had met Malachi and the other children. I didn't remember Chloe or even Caiohme, a girl I was passionately attached to. I didn't remember the man in the woods and all the others that had vowed to protect me, that believed in me. I didn't know what I was fighting for, what I was capable of, until I drank that little blue vial again.

When I woke my vision returned slowly, fuzzy at first, until I could make out the face of each individual that formed a circle around me. Caiohme and Chloe joined them, making it to their feet before I had even opened my eyes. The memories were now vivid in my mind, as if I had made them only days before, but a more recent memory stood out. Until that point I had forgotten about the man in the cot that had a rhyme for me: "A house in the woods, a pond and a creek, a man with one eye, and the trees that can speak, the sky will turn red, the forest pitch black, a hole in the ground, the only way back."

I reached my hand out for help off the ground, and I was overcome by who stepped forward to offer theirs. He was busted up with a bloody lip, a black eye and tattered clothing. His arm was in a sling. His large biceps were bruised and his legs were scabbed with several lacerations. His right hand was bandaged and his knuckles were purple, but it was my pleasure to put my hand in his. It took much of his remaining strength to pull me to my feet and toward his body. He towered above me and wrapped his arms around my shoulders as I looked up to him; a tear fell from his cheek onto my forehead. I tightly wrapped my arms as far as they would go around his chest "Patches, you're alive!"

He laughed, as he smiled and looked down on me "Just another patch on my back Jayden. I was happy to see that you made it here as well! Now we must make all these sacrifices worth it. I am at your disposal."

Carmine's voice echoed from behind me "Jayden, Jayden we need to go now!"

I didn't understand his urgency in the moment, until I turned around. Embers must have sparked a new fire and it was approaching quickly. The forest was black with smoke and the flames raced up the evergreen trees. The smog had begun to creep out from the tree line and into the clearing; it quickly filled the canopy. Within moments the roar of jet engines could be heard in the distance, but were not visible through the clearing. I hoped that the hologram was still disguising our presence.

I looked over to Caiohme who looked fearless now and wondered what memories she was able to conjure up "We need to get to the tunnel now and get back to Leotus." I shouted.

Carmine chimed back with a descending tone "What tunnel? We need to go by dragon back; they will get us there much more quickly."

Then, I heard a voice I had heard so many times in Havenbrook coming from behind me "The tunnels that we built for this day; the tunnels that we built when Alcaeus told us of his father's prophecies."

I turned around and threw my arms around my father, happy to finally have a piece of Havenbrook there with me. He smiled as the others approached him for hugs and handshakes. It wasn't long before he got right down to business, being the leader the Leonoids had charged him with being. He left no time for pleasantries or stories from back home as the fire crept to the edge of the woods and surrounded the house. One last Leotus landmark stood in the path of the flames. Suit and smoke filled the air and made it difficult to breathe and the heavens were no longer visible through the opening in the canopy.

My father took the lead like I had seen him do so many times at the market "Carmine, take Lilly, Isaiah and Cordell to safety and meet us in Leotus. Desiah, lead the others to the tunnel in the basement. Patches, use the compass to get to Leotus, Alcaeus has fallen prisoner to Erebus. Jayden will catch up with you in the tunnel. Jayden, come with me."

The others followed his orders quickly and without question, clearly used to that level of command. Without the vial I would have never understood my father's presence that day, but in that moment I knew what he meant to the Leonoids. He was a familiar face, a friend, and someone they could trust. He drew closer to me and put his arm around my shoulder as the others followed behind Carmine and Desiah "I see that Patches provided you with the duffel bag. You have the compass, the weapons?"

I had experienced so much in the last moments and days that it took me a few seconds to recall exactly what it was he was talking about. When it finally clicked, I went running toward the dragon's just as Carmine finished loading them for takeoff "Isaiah, Isaiah the compass, I need the compass!"

As I approached the dragon, Isaiah reached into his pocket and pulled the compass out by its chain. He looked down at it for a moment, running his finger over and over the symbols on the surface, and then gently placed it in my palm. He leaned over, wrapped his arms around my neck, and whispered in my ear "Beat him for all those people that died in the fire, for Malachi. Beat him for me. Beat him so that we can go home to our friends. Beat him for my dad. Goodbye Jayden."

I wrapped the chain around my hand and grasped the compass tightly in my palm. I looked up at him and smiled as he straightened himself on the dragon's back and Carmine took the reins in his hands "This is not goodbye Isaiah. I will see you soon friend. I'll see you soon!"

I turned around and began to walk toward my father, as the dragons began to flap their powerful wings and pull away from the ground. Each flap brought a gust of wind that rushed through my hair and threatened to knock me off my feet, but I maintained my composure in the turbulence. I turned my head to wave goodbye and I was jealous of the dragon's majesty. What a wonderful gift, to be able to spread your wings and leave all the troubles of this earth for a time. It's wonderful to have the fresh air against your face as you fly closer to the heavens. Flying away is an ignorant bliss, high above the arguments, heartache and bloodshed that plagued Leotus.

Before I could turn back around, my father was by my side. His demeanor had turned much more melancholy than moments earlier. His eyebrows drooped and I noticed the black bags under his eyes. The white glow of his teeth was no longer visible and his laugh lines faded back into his pale complexion. He put one hand on each of my shoulders and looked me straight in the eyes "Son, I love you! There aren't enough moments to explain everything you have learned the last few days or to apologize for who I have been asked to be. The Farrians have written one end to today's battle, but know that you can write another; it has been seen. They have Katie and they stand on the cusp of our world ready to erase human existence. Today is the day I have prepared you for and you are ready. Your power is unmatched and you have freewill, but I ask you to make a decision for the greater good. Follow your heart and remember the virtues and tomorrow we will wake to a beautiful sunrise. No matter what happens, no matter what they say, you have always been my son. Don't forget my love for you. Now get down to the tunnel and follow your compass to the others. I will see you soon."

I wrapped my arms around his neck and pulled him closer to me than I had in a long time. I no longer remembered the games he had missed, or the late hours that he worked. What I remembered was a father that had given his life to prepare me for that day and who had loved me unconditionally. I wanted so much for him to be with me, to be my strength. A tear fell down my cheek as I softly spoke into his ear with a shaky voice "Father, can't you come with me?"

He held me tightly, his face against my neck, and I could feel the tears as they fell down his cheek. It was the first time I had ever seen my father cry. Then he pulled back and put his forehead against mine. His face was wet, but his smile firmed and his eyes glowed "You must do this without me and you must go now. Time is running out. You will find him in the castle Jayden. Do not underestimate him. He is strong."

He gave me a little nudge and with the tilt of his head he ordered me, "Now go!"

Even with his insistence and the need for urgency, I couldn't help but spend another moment staring at him before I turned to the house in the woods. I jogged towards the door, only stopping to turn around once I reached it. He had kept his eye on me the entire way, waving goodbye like my grandparents had every time I left their home. I smiled as my hand reached for the door knob "I love you Dad!"

Then, I turned my back to him and walked into the house in the woods!

CHAPTER FIFTEEN

Barren Land

I DIDN'T TAKE much time to observe the details of the home, aside from noticing that the interior was immaculate and warm. The floor plan was wide open and the beige carpet and fireplace were welcoming. Plants and flowers hung in every corner and adorned many pedestals. The door to the stairway was wide open and located just to the right of the dining area. I quickly made my way over to the frame and looked down the new wooden staircase. There didn't appear to be much light, but there was a green glow coming from the tunnel. I closed the door behind me and raced down the stairs with urgency.

I had forgotten about the compass that was wrapped around my hand until I reached the bottom of the stairs and it began to vibrate, tickling my palm. I had been trained in many areas, but never had I seen the compass until I opened that dirty duffel bag. I pulled my hand close to my face and opened my fingers. Inside my palm, the engraved tree on the compass glowed dark green. Then, without warning, a green beam of light burst out from the end of the compass and at the end of it sat a holographic tree; the Life Tree.

I sprinted toward the tree, sure that it was the direction my father had intended for me to take. The tunnel twisted, turned and split many times, but I continued to follow the map my compass laid out for me. Several hundred feet into the tunnel I got distracted by the "clunk, clunk, clunk," of loud footsteps that grew quiet as a beam of light met my eyes. I stopped in my path and shielded my eyes from the bright green glow "Patches, that you?"

The light dimmed and then broke from my field of vision and out of the darkness stepped my friends; first Desiah, then Patches, Chloe, Caiohme, and lastly Scraggs. Caiohme stepped up to me and wrapped her arms around me. She kissed my neck and spoke softly into my ear, so that the others couldn't hear "I just want you to know that I remember the way things were and I'm so happy to finally know just why I see so much in your eyes. I believe in you Jayden."

I kissed her forehead "I am glad to have all those memories back too. You fill a piece of me that no one else can and I have missed that on the days when everything else seems broken. I believe I can win too, with you by my side."

Chloe approached me next and I bent down to speak with her like I had several times before, but this time it was different. I had grown up around her, she was like my little sister and it was hard to know that visions of this war played again and again in her head. She stared into my eyes, as if to examine my thoughts, to know what resided deep in my soul. She smiled and hugged me firmly as she spoke "You're not afraid anymore and you shouldn't be. The people will rise and fight for you and he will fall. The beasts will know your name and there will be peace in Leotus. Follow Scraggs and follow your heat. I love you Jayden."

I kissed Chloe on the forehead as well "You are my sister. I remember watching you grow up and playing with you in the leaves. You are the eternal optimist and you bring so much joy to me. I am grateful to have you here with me today, but when the time comes you must hide. I love you."

Before Patches or Scraggs could approach me there was one loud explosion, then another, and another. I wrapped my arms around the girls, shielding them as each blast shook the tunnel walls with greater intensity. I turned my head in the direction of the explosion, toward the entrance, and was sandblasted by a sweeping cloud of dirt and cement particles. I shielded my eyes, but not before several granules entered my open eyelids. I feared that the tunnel may collapse under the weight of another explosion, but none came.

Patches grabbed my arm in the midst of the haze and pulled the three of us toward him. We followed the laser toward the Life Tree, which pointed away from the unsettled dust of the explosions. It reminded me of a laser light show I had been to when I was a young child, but this dust was much more suffocating. Patches hacked as he attempted to speak to me "Your father set those bombs to conceal the tunnel. It means the Farrians found the house in the woods. It won't take them long to learn of our whereabouts! We must move with increased urgency."

I stopped in my tracks and turned to Desiah "Will my father be all right? Did he have someone to protect him, something to protect himself?"

By that point the dust had begun to settle and I saw the holographic Life Tree resting on a shiny metal door. We had made it to Leotus, but nothing could have prepared me for what was on the other side. I looked to Desiah and could see the brooding expression on his face. His eyes sank and were wet with tears, his teeth sank into his lower lip and I could see the lump moving down his throat "In honesty, I cannot say. Your father is a smart man and he has survived many encounters with the Farrians, but he would always put your survival before his own. He is one man and you are the missing piece of their puzzle. All we can do now is fight to make sure that these sacrifices were not in vain."

He paused for a moment and looked toward the door "You cannot let what you see on the other side of that door detract from your confidence. We must walk through it and hold our heads high. I believe that we will win today and I hope that your father will meet us on the beach to celebrate our victory, but we must go now."

I walked toward the door with my right arm resting on Caiohme's shoulder and my left fingers intertwined in Chloe's. I was ready to open the door when Scraggs pulled on my pant leg. I knelt down and he spoke as frantically as he had the night he was cornered in Caiohme's room "Near the square is a home; beneath the home is a tunnel that will lead us under the castle and up the tree you found me in. Alcaeus, the homeowners, yourself and I are the only ones that know of its existence. We must get there."

I hugged him and tried to let him know he was appreciated, something I had not done enough to that point "Thank you Scraggs! If you think that's the best way for us to get in the castle, then all right."

I took a deep breath as I reached for the latch on the door and noticed there wasn't one. I looked over to Patches for answers and he quickly obliged "There is no getting past this door without your hands Jayden; it was made for you. Place your hands on its surface and it will open."

I did as Patches said; I released my grip on Chloe's hand and put my hands onto the warm surface of the door. Immediately, my hands began to tingle and I could feel the warmth move up my fingers and then my hands and arms. The door broke apart, the way that Havenbrook had when Alcaeus came for me, and entered my body as a pulse of energy. Perhaps the door was put there to remind me of something I had forgotten, our ability to consume energy from the various compositions of life. Like Alcaeus had given me life after the beast attack, it too was possible for me to restore energy and balance to the world.

As the door diminished, we stood face to face with a Barron land that the flames had robbed of life. Once a beautiful example of the coexistence of people and nature; the flames had destroyed Leotus to allow for something new to flourish. Our fate that day would decide how Leotus would be remembered. I wondered if someday Farrian children would visit the remains of a forgotten city and architects would dig for artifacts or if the Leonoids would tell stories of a great victory and resiliency to rebuild.

The exit stood among a rock formation, close to the same area where we arrived in Leotus for the first time, where Chloe ran up to me and tugged on my pants. Perhaps, subconsciously, her visions even led her to choose me that day. Whatever the reason, we stood in the distance of the castle again, this time without direction from the man in white. We stood their without the glamor of something beautiful and mysterious to catch our eye.

The fireflies' light had fallen dark and the glass of the lanterns was shattered or covered in soot. There was no more pasture to break the wind and the majestic animals that had occupied it were only evidenced by the bones scattered across the black earth. The flames had charred the trunks of the large trees and burnt the colorful leaves away. The square, which we had not noticed the first day amongst the tall grass and animals, was now visible between the black tree trunks. Details were not clear from a distance, but I assumed the beautiful gardens and flowers had withered away in the heat. Many of the homes laid in rubble and several that still stood were only shells of their former state. Few homes remained untouched and even they were covered in a layer of ash and soot. Smoke continued to rise from the square and pop up fires were common.

A plume of smoke and smog dimmed the sun and the majesty of the heavens. The day we first arrived in Leotus, the stars provided me a reminder of home and something beautiful amongst all the concern and questions. The Farrians had managed to take even that peace away from my soul. The smoke made the day appear dreary and I questioned whether it might rain or if it was only the smog of war.

The luster of the castle was no more. The white sand walls had been dyed gray and the gold balconies, which once shimmered under the afternoon sun, were black with soot. The vast beach that stood behind the castle walls was no longer littered with sea shells and crabs. Instead, debris covered the beach and floated on the water's surface like drift wood. The dolphins had disappeared for cleaner water and there were no birds in the sky. The land was desolate and all the beauty that Ex had given his life to save was gone.

I stepped out from the tunnel and onto the charred land. The ground crunched under my shoes and each step sent ash a foot into the air. The others solemnly followed in my steps, walking a few yards onto the barren land, until I came to a sudden halt. I heard them before anyone else, war planes heading our way from Fariah; the others followed my example as I hit the ground. When the plume of ash cleared I saw the human skeleton lying right in front of my face and watched the bombs fall on the square collapsing several more structures and sending ash and fire high into the air.

As I pushed myself from the ground I wondered if the fight had been taken elsewhere or if the citizens of Leotus had suffered the same fate as the charred bones in front of me. Chloe had promised that the people would rise and fight, but there were no Leonoids to be seen. Perhaps the fight was solely ours to win and those to rise were already by my side.

I rose to my feet and dusted the ash from my clothing and hair. My eyes burned as the tears tried to flush the granules from my vision. I closed my eyes for a moment and when I opened them I saw Scraggs run out in front of me. His pace was quick for his stature and he only slowed down to turn and shout "Follow me; we must get to the square! Then we can get into the castle from below."

I looked to Chloe, cautious as to why we would travel in the direction of an area that was just bombed. She nodded her head and took off running after Scraggs "Scraggs wait, wait for me!"

Caiohme ran after Chloe and I remembered the conversation Chloe and I had in the tunnel, where she implored me to trust Scraggs. Patches looked down to me "I will remain by your side whatever you chose Jayden."

I made my choice, thrusting one foot into the ground and then the other, sprinting until I caught up to my friends who's legs could not carry them nearly as quickly as mine. It took a moment for Patches and Desiah to catch up, but they were in great shape for their conditions. If we were to run through the open pasture, I did not want to risk being seen. For the first time since my return to Leotus, I used the knowledge I had gained my whole life. With ash in the air, running exhausted my lungs, and I breathed deeply for the oxygen to speak "Run tightly with me everyone. The winds are coming."

I threw my right hand into the air and the ash flew into the space around us. The ground shook and the wind picked up as we became the center of the coming storm. The cloud of ash began to rotate around us as we jogged, like the storm rotates around the eye of a hurricane. It hid us from those who wished to kill us, until we reached the center of the square. The fountains where Ex had first approached us stood as a landmark and a reminder that all was not lost.

As we reached the center of the square, I let my hand fall in exhaustion. The rotation slowed and the clouds began to fall apart. Ash fell on us like snowflakes in a winter storm. If I had not known better, I would have thought a volcano had erupted near Leotus. Scraggs was like a compass in the falling ash, an expert of the land, knowing exactly which direction we needed to go. He led us to the door of one of the few standing homes in the square, turned the knob, and walked right in.

Caiohme grabbed my hand before we stepped into the house "Where do you suppose he is taking us?"

Chloe answered Caiohme's question before I could speculate "Friends of ours are here, friends that will fight by our side."

Scraggs was several feet inside the home, but displayed how well his large ears worked when he turned around and gave us a better answer "In the basement is a secret tunnel that leads into the castle. Jayden, it will lead us into the center court, where you found me in the tree trunk."

I grabbed Chloe's hand and followed Scraggs into the house. The windows were draped with dark curtains and the lighting was poor. The smell of rotten food wafted through the air and flies buzzed above an overflowing trash can. As we headed through the living room and into the hallway, I noticed several colorful blankets strung over the back of the couch and chairs. Pictures hung on the wall, but were not clear in the darkness. Broken glass from the frames lay on the floor, shattered by the wall rattling explosions.

We made our way down the hall and to the second door on the right, lined up behind Scraggs. He knocked twice, paused, and then knocked three more times. The door swung open and I heard their voice before I saw their faces, a man and a woman's "Jayden, you made it, you finally made it!"

A sense of joy and relief resonated in their voices as they stepped up from the stairway and into the hall. I recognized their faces the moments I laid eyes on the two of them. It was the woman from the square, that had given me the poncho our first day in Leotus, and the man that had approached the table when I began to get angry. The secret they had so fiercely protected was no longer obscure.

The woman stepped forward with tears in her eyes. She approached me and wrapped her arms around me and wept with her face against my chest. Her husband grew emotional too, but held himself together with a smile on his face. When she was done, she grabbed my arm and pulled me toward the basement door "We saved as many as we could; they are ready to fight with you Jayden!"

I broke into tears as I looked down the stairwell. Packed from one side of the wall to the other and as far into the basement as I could see, stood healthy men, woman and children. Expressions of despair broke from their faces, replaced by the laughter and smiles of joy and consolation as they saw us standing there. What they didn't know as they waited for us to join them in the tunnel, was that they were the ones that provided healing for my heart and hope for the future.

CHAPTER SIXTEEN

The Hooded Man

THE LEONOIDS PARTED as Scraggs led the way down the basement stairs and into the tunnel. Each person greeted us differently as we passed by; some with a hug, others with a handshake, and a few with a simple pat on the back or shoulder. There were many individuals that I shared a tear or laugh with and others that offered words of encouragement. Children greeted me in much the same way Chloe had, tugging on my pants or wrapping their arms around my legs. I recognized several individuals from the visions of my childhood, but I made no effort to single them out, they were all there for the same reason.

At the end of the tunnel was a large room that had been made into a dormitory of sorts. Piles of blankets, clothing, and pillows formed rows of pallets for sleeping on the cement ground. The whole area stunk of human waste as a corner had been designated for that purpose. Empty water jugs and canteens littered the ground, along with food packaging and dirty clothing. The conditions had become deplorable and unlivable in such a short time, but they had stayed to fight.

In the far right hand corner of the room hung the rope

ladder that made an ascent upward, into the center court tree trunk. The flicker of light I had seen looking down the trunk must have come from a nearby bounty of candles that had long since burned out. Wax of many colors hung from the nearby pedestals like stalactites in an underground cave. The candles had been replaced with kerosene lamps, which provided a much brighter, constant light.

I gathered with my friends around the rope ladder and looked up; up to the prisoners, to Alcaeus, to Deseus, to Flora and to Katie. I looked up to Erebus and the Farrian army, who were ready to take our lives and destroy the Earth and Havenbrook, my home. I wondered if Carmine and Samarra were ready to fight and if Malachi was alive. I was ready to fight for Leotus, for my friends and family, for what was right. I put my right arm around Caiohme and my left hand on Chloe's shoulder. Patches towered above us from behind, joined by his wife and children. Scraggs stood in front of Chloe's legs as she ran her hands through the hair on his head. Desiah stood in the distance, looking on like a proud father. The Leonoids gathered in front of us, ready to take back what was theirs, awaiting my command.

I was not nervous standing in front of them. Everything that my father, Alcaeus and these people had done for me, prepared me for that day. I stood tall and spoke in a confident tone, my voice echoing off the room's walls "I do not ask that you fight this war with us, but I will gladly have you by my side if that is what you chose. I will fight for my home, for my friends and family and I will fight for Leotus. I will fight for you! You must search your soul and find what it is you will fight for. Will you fight for Alcaeus and these castle walls? Will you fight for your family and friends and all those who have fallen? Will you fight for your homes, for this land? Will you fight for what you know is right?"

I grew quiet for a moment, as what started as a whisper grew into a roar. The Leonoids consoled one another and talked about what was important to them. They all pledged to fight for different reasons, but they united in the fact that they would fight. One man's voice stood above them all, as he rose from one of the pallets on the floor and removed a hood from his head "Jayden, I too will fight for you, for Leotus!"

Jaws dropped and gasps of surprise turned to roars of excitement as the crowd parted to make way for an unexpected guest. His face was battered and dirty, but he was alive. I ambitiously stepped forward to greet him, but Patches pulled me back as Deseus made his way toward us. Patches did not speak gingerly. His voice was as loud as his size "Jayden, how can we be sure he is not a manipulation? Are you willing to wager our lives on it; Chloe's life, my life, Katie's life?"

I stepped back further and fell into Patches' body. A chill rippled down my spine and goose bumps covered my arms as I wondered how I did not think of something so basic. I pulled the device from my pocket which the white coats had used to test Caiohme, Chloe, and myself. I looked up into Deseus' eyes as he cautiously stopped in his steps. The joyous cheer and excitement turned to a still anxiety as I took a step toward him. He smiled at me as he revealed the palms of his hands to me "My hands have no Leonoid blood on them. These people, this town; these are my friends, my family, my life! I waited for your return to fight by your side and I am happy to see you cautious with whom you trust. It was I who came to warn you in the food court that night. It was I who did not have the integrity to reveal my identity. Now my home lies in rubble and our people are dying. I can no longer hide under a veil, like a coward, as others lose everything. I will show my face, I will fight. Erebus must die!"

Deseus smiled and let his hands fall to his side "Jayden, if looking into my eyes is what you need to do, then I will stand idle as you do so. My loyalty is deep and I call you friend, but realize there are traitors among us, even in this room."

It pierced me to know that the man in front of me, the one who called me friend, was the same person that had used the vines to squeeze the life from my body to make a point. I did not know if I could fight by his side, but I knew if he truly was Deseus, a God, then I could not fight without him and his knowledge of the castle. I tightly gripped the device and raised it up to the level of his eyes. Within a moment, a red beam blinded him, causing him to blink and shade his eyes. He pulled his hand away and looked sternly ahead into the beam of light, into my eyes, and I knew I didn't need the device. I could see his soul in his eyes; this was Deseus. The device only clarified what I already knew as it alerted us to his identity with a mechanical tone "Deseus, God of Leotus."

A roar of jubilation returned to the room as the crowd heard the results of the scan, only to be quieted by a stern "hush, shhh, shhh!" from Patches.

Leonoids stepped forward to join us as each of us greeted Deseus, but Patches was there to maintain a barrier of space between us and the unknown. The atmosphere calmed to gossip and chatter as Deseus put his palm on my shoulder and the others gathered in a circle around us. The tone became more serious as he began to speak to me "Farrian soldiers and beasts guard most of the common areas, corridors and entrances, but they should be little match against us. Erebus is holding his prisoners in Alcaeus' quarters. The most powerful Farrian's have joined to protect him; among them is a prophet at least as powerful as Chloe. He probably already knows of our whereabouts. Our time is short."

Due to his stature, I had forgotten about Scraggs presence until he spoke up in a quick, jittery tone "Their prophet knows nothing of our whereabouts. These walls were built by Alcaeus' hands to be a barrier from creation and magic. Only Jayden has the power to undo what has been done here."

Desiah must have been busy gathering keepsakes as the confrontation with Deseus occurred, because he passed out items to Caiohme, Chloe and I. To Caiohme he handed a white gold, heart-shaped locket and to Chloe a pair of emerald earrings "They were your mother's; she would have wanted you to have them. Fight for her!"

After he hugged both of them he turned to me with tears in his eyes and spoke before he handed me the items in his hands "The man you call your father has always been family to so many of us. He asked me to give you this picture if he was not able to make it here today; he has carried it all his life. I hope that you can see why he has sacrificed so much."

Into my hands he placed a picture that I had never seen, from a day that I didn't remember until that moment. I was young, three, maybe four years old. The winter had just begun in Havenbrook and the first snow storm had blanketed the fall leaves. The horses wallowed in the fresh powder and flocks of black birds headed south for the winter. The sun glistened on the snow, like glitter painted on the earth, and the trees stood like glass sculptures reminding us of our size.

Mom had left for the weekend to spend time with her grandmother, leaving Dad and I to fend for ourselves. I was upset, thinking I would have to spend the entirety of two days at his desk as he worked, but he surprised me. He pulled me from my snow fort that Saturday afternoon and proclaimed "let's go somewhere warm."

I conquered and he grabbed my hand and we walked from our cold home into the warmer climate of Leotus. He led me to a swimming hole, fed by a creek, with water as clear as the Caribbean. It was the same place I would later go to meet Caiohme during our forbidden visits. Before I had the chance to take my clothes off, he swept me up into his arms and jumped into the water. When we floated to the surface he was laughing so hard and was so happy that he made me giggle until I could hardly breathe. Just Dad and I played in that swimming hole and soaked in the sun for hours, until I was exhausted.

The warm weather cleared our mind of the cold coat of powder that blanketed Havenbrook, until we walked back into that world barefoot. We both quickly scampered over my snow fort and in the back door. We spent the rest of the afternoon curled up under blankets, next to the fireplace, watching Christmas movies. I eventually passed out with a blanket up to my chin, a candy cane stocking on my head, and dad's socks on my feet. I never realized dad had taken a picture to remember that day by. A tear fell down my cheek and onto the shiny surface of the picture. I flung my arms around Desiah tightly "Thank you Desiah! Thank you for being such a good friend to us and to my father."

In those moments I realized what was truly important for everyone to hear. I placed the picture in my pocket and cleared my throat, to which everyone grew silent. I smiled as I addressed them with a heartfelt tone "My friends, while I will not deny you the right to fight by my side, I ask that you remain here to comfort one another as we do what we have been created to do. I know the hurt associated with losing friends, loved ones, and your home, but there is still much to be lost. Look at those around you and realize that the strongest friendships can be formed in the darkest times and that love for one another is innate in who we are. You never know who may value your time or thrive in your strength. Your battle is here. Hold your heads high. Open your arms and hearts to an orphan. Offer a shoulder to cry on or an ear to listen. Laugh, smile and most of all, pray with each other, for each other! All else will fall into place as it was intended."

I wrapped my arms around Caiohme and Chloe as I stood beside Patches and his family "Now is our time, the day we were created for, the battle we have trained for! We will fight to reclaim your homes, to heal the injured, to rescue the imprisoned, and to save the human race. Pray that God will guide us, strengthen us, and fight on our side. Let today be a day of jubilation!"

We spent the next several minutes quickly discussing a battle plan, avoiding any visions or prophecies of the future. We discussed Carmine and Adrianna, and the hope that they would join us in battle. Improvisation was our strongest ally against a powerful prophet and it was how we intended to wage war. We would attack on as many fronts as possible, fighting with our individual gifts.

Finally, we broke our huddle, ready to finish what we had returned to Leotus to do. We hugged one another and shed tears over the division of our new found family. Deseus, Patches, Desiah, and several Leonoids that insisted on fighting, including the male homeowner, would take the ladder and capture the common area. Caiohme, Chloe, Scraggs and I would leave through the tunnel, rise from the pasture, and capture the castle walls from a different direction.

We parted from each other with one last warm embrace as Patches squeezed the air from my lungs and whispered his last guiding words into my ear "Don't fight with your heart Jayden, it will often lead you astray. Fight with your soul and let your conscience guide your actions. Keep the girls safe; they are as much a part of our future as you are. May God be with you brother."

Lastly, I reached my hand out and shook Deseus' calloused hand as he offered me his own advice "Be vigilant of those around you and careful who you trust Jayden. Remember that your greatest strength lies in your connection to the environment, it is what makes you more powerful than him."

I smiled and offered my own advice as I gripped his hand more firmly "Do your part and I will do mine. Protect Patches!"

With those last words my friends and I turned our backs to Patches, Desiah and Deseus and stepped forward into a crowd of Leonoids. As they parted we made our way toward the tunnel that would lead us into the open pasture. I thanked the people for their allegiance as we left and stopped to shake several hands and offer hugs. A girl, about my age, stopped to offer me the hope that none other had been able to. She offered up a mahogany cross, strung on a thin leather rope, reminding me of the roots my mother had instilled in me for so many years. Her words were simple, but complete "God will never abandon you Jayden. Through him all things are possible! Take it; you need the reminder more than I."

I thanked her and put the necklace around my neck as we forged forward, eventually leaving behind those who had escaped the Farrian wrath. I turned around only once as the tunnel curved and we nearly lost sight of our friends, to wave goodbye, to have one last look at the girl that had reminded me of God's power and love; she was gone!

CHAPTER SEVENTEEN

From the Balcony

AFTER A SHORT walk, we reached the latched vault door that would lead us out onto the Leotus prairie. Before I opened it, I wrapped my arms around both of the girls and kissed Caiohme on the forehead. I had come to Leotus fearful, thinking of Katie, of Havenbrook and of everything that I had lost; what I didn't remember was everything I had left behind. In that moment, I understood the term "roots and wings," I just didn't know where my roots where anymore. I smiled "I love you girls! No matter what happens today, I will always remember the times I had with the two of you. If the time comes where it appears we have lost, I beg you, turn around and run and allow me to lay down my life to save yours."

Caiohme squeezed me tightly, resting her head on my shoulder and then let me go suddenly, without any reply. She grabbed hold of the metal bars that climbed up the tunnel to the vaulted door and began to ascend toward the ceiling. Chloe stepped up to the bars and climbed until her face was even with mine and then showed me her carefree smile "Don't worry Jayden, your return to Leotus means we have already won."

Caiohme released the metal bars and put both hands on the latch, easily unlatching it. Her petite arms pushed on the door only enough to open it an inch or two, but then it fell closed with a thump. She was no quitter though. She pushed again, this time stepping up a row on the metal bars and pushing the door until the hinges bent and the metal fell into the burnt ground. A plum of ash and dirt rained down on us and hid the blinding sun from our eyes. Caiohme didn't climb out onto the land until she responded in a soft, but deliberate tone "Even if that moment did come, I would stand by your side just like I always have. I would rather die with you, than live without you forever. I have lived through years of emptiness and heartache, but finally I feel whole, I feel at peace. I need you, I love you!"

We stepped out onto the crisp earth, and I noticed in the distance was a survivor. Not a person or a beautiful beast, but a tree, my tree, the Life Tree. It was vibrant and had grown several feet in the short time since I had last seen it. The tree's leaves contained some of the only color not covered in ash. I could feel its strength inside of me, the life vigorously pulsing through it. I took off running towards it, followed by Caiohme and Chloe, but an explosion coming from the dining room knocked us off our feet. My eyes went dark for a moment and when I opened them I saw several dragons circling in the sky around us. The dragons set ablaze the Farrian army that was running toward us from a new hole in the castle wall. Our time to fight had come again; another battle had begun.

I stood up and helped the girls from the ground as one dragon swooped down and then another. On the back of one was Adrianna and on the other was Carmine and Malachi. Malachi wasn't alert, but he appeared to be alive. His survival sent a bolus of adrenaline pulsing through my veins as the power of the dragon's wings knocked Chloe back to the ground.

I helped her to her feet as Carmine shouted out "Get to Alcaeus, Adrianna and I will hold them back as long as we can! Go now!"

Beasts and men, bigger and stronger than I had ever seen, emerged from that hole in the castle wall with the speed and agility of fearless soldiers. Some were covered in scales and horns, but others were the pristine warriors of Greek mythology. Sheets of armor adorned the chests of the meek, but others wore only cloth and a sword. Many men shared the body of a beast and some merely rode on the backs of beasts, neither less dark nor evil than the other.

The warriors hurled boulders, arrows, and chains into the air, attempting to strike the dragons that cast fire onto their flesh. The beasts lunged at their wings, jumping high into the air, but fell back to the burnt earth, only to join those who had given their lives before them. Many men and beasts fell in those first few moments, never to walk on this earth again. Our dragons were winning the battle until the smallest of the soldiers cast his chain into the air and hooked it around the leg of the largest dragon. He ran, as fast as the wave's crash against the beach, and he grabbed the dangling chain. One man joined him, and then another, and another, until they had the strength to rip the fiery beast from the sky. As quickly as they had ripped the dragon from the sky, they spilled his crimson blood on the black earth, and I knew that the tide of battle was turning.

I didn't know if our friends would face the same fate as the dragon had, but we didn't have time to find out as the attention turned our way. Farrians that had focused on bringing the dragons down were now in pursuit of our blood. The remaining dragons spread walls of fire across the land, but I knew it was only a matter of time before the warriors reached us. They broke through the flames, fire eating away at their flesh and a thirsty stare in their eyes. I wondered if Erebus was among them, or if he would wait for us to come for him; I did not wait their arrival to find out. Instead, I did something I had not done in my years in Leotus; I used my gifts to save the people, the town and the life that mattered to me.

I left the girls were they stood, I knew I could now protect them from anywhere, and I ran for the Life Tree, for my tree. As I approached it, and the tips of its branches touched my skin, I threw myself into it and it cradled me with all its strength. I felt its energy pulse through my body as it connected with me, feeding me energy and life like an umbilical cord. For a moment it must have looked like I had fallen asleep inside the comfort of a cocoon, until I raised my head, opened my eyes, and commanded my army to rise.

The Farrians had men, beasts and the tools to leach the body of blood, but my army was more powerful. My army could destroy them all in moments. I jolted my arms into the air and the trees ripped their roots from the ground and converged on the Farrians from near and far. The Whisper Woods did not belong to them, it did not belong to anyone, but it would fight for me. I exhaled the air from my lungs, and what started as a wisp of wind turned into a force so strong that it cleansed the trees of their dead and tired limbs and pushed the soldiers and beasts to their knees. Lastly, I called the ocean, which cleared the beaches of the proof of our existence daily, to rise in the face of the cowards, ready to wipe our land clean. There, in front of Caiohme, Chloe, and myself, a wall of water rose higher than the tops of the trees as an army of evil lay helpless in front of it.

I could have let them all die, and part of me wanted to, for all the suffering and death they had caused my friends, family and the people of Leotus. I could have let that wall of water come crashing down, but I offered them something they had not offered my friends or family. I offered mercy. I broke free from the Life Tree and took several steps toward them. Several tried to rise from their knees and I called on the beasts of our land to come and cast them down. The dragons landed in front of me and Carmine and Adrianna carried Malachi over to join Caiohme and Chloe. I joined them, the six of us in front of an army of hundreds, and I cupped my hands around my mouth and raised my voice "I am offering you something you did not offer the people of our land. I am offering you the choice to run and never return here again or to face the same fate you delivered to many of our people. The choice is yours. I will not offer it again!"

It took the shame of one coward rising to his feet and running to encourage most to do the same. Still, many remained, not willing to cower and run from the wrath of the son of a Leonoid God. They rose and charged toward us and I still wonder, did they think that they might out run the water? We watched as the wall fell down over their heads and overcame the land, only leaving the earth we stood on dry. The water rose to the first level balconies of the castle and then it receded as quickly as it had come in.

As rain and water often do, the wave washed away much of the filth that had bestowed itself upon the land. A few corpses and some marine life remained, but much of the soot, debris and blood were washed away. In its wake, some of the plant life that had survived made itself visible as greenery rising from the ground. A few flowering plants even managed to maintain a colorful blossom or two. The bottoms of the balconies were cleansed and the gold shined brightly in the sun light. The castle walls were not the glistening white they once were, but the water had washed away enough soot to provide hope for restoration.

It was easy to lose myself in the silence for a moment. Thoughts of what Leotus had been and what it could be again. No one had to lose their homes; we could rebuild, better, stronger! I had seen natural disasters in the states. I had seen whole towns, the whole nation come together to rebuild New Orleans and Joplin. It could be beautiful again, it could be my home. A house on the beach and horses in the pasture; I could have the best of both worlds. As easy as it would have been to keep day dreaming, Malachi's flaccid body was an endless reminder of the circumstances that surrounded us.

For a moment everything had grown so still that I could hear the ocean molding the beach and the trees resettling their roots back into the soft ground. I closed my eyes and wished for the silence to last and I let the wind hit my face. I wished for any Farrian's that remained to flee and for there to be a time of peace again in Leotus. I wished for all the things Ex had worked for to come to fruition. I was soon reminded though that wishing is for the meek. You see, men can not merely wish for things to change, they must be the object of change. Good fortune is not simply the outcome of a wish, it is the work of strong hands and a courageous soul.

The noise returned as a rhythmic thumping, spaced evenly apart, but growing closer together. I looked out onto the plains and into the forest, half expecting the sound to be the evenly paced footsteps of a giant or a wild beast. As the thuds grew closer together, they also grew louder, and I recognized the rhythm as one palm meeting the other, clapping. Who might be applauding our victory I wondered, as I turned around to face the castle walls. I was silenced by what I saw; his clap grew louder and a thin grin turned into a smile that stretched the length of his jaw. Before I could find the words, he spoke "Bravo, bravo, bravo! I see that your senses, and better yet your abilities, have returned. It brings me shame that my son did not find proper use for his own strength; so much power wasted on a useless cause, an unworthy people! You have come back more powerful than I remember and it causes me to ponder just what it is you're fighting for Jayden."

He paused and stroked his fingers across his beard, breaking his stare with me to survey the land. He took in a deep breath of the burnt air, letting it consume his lungs for only a moment, and then he sighed and let his hands drop to his waist. He gripped the balcony with his palms, exposing the gold that lay beneath, and looked straight into my eyes as he spoke directly to me. His voice trembled with anger "This place, Leotus, was once my home. Your father's unrelenting love and forgiveness of the humans, and thus your birth and arrival here, is the cause for this fate. My son's blood and the blood of so many others is on your hands. Your people, your friends and family, your town will face a worse fate and you will bring me there or she will die! Bring out the girl."

On his command, two armed soldiers carried Katie out onto the balcony. They supported her body, holding her underneath each arm. Her appearance was intact, and she did not appear to be harmed, but it was obvious that she was weak. Her arms and legs were flaccid and her head hung loosely on her chest. As the guards released her, forcing her to stand alone, she crumbled and fell to her knees. She did not attempt to stand in the face of their authority, or even to raise her head, until she heard my voice. I did not attempt to curse the men, or even to enrage Erebus, but simply let her know I was there. I took a deep breath and rose my voice "Katie, I am here! I will find you and bring you home."

As my words reached her, she lifted herself from the ground and raised her head to look into my eyes. I saw a glow in her face that told me she believed every word. I reminisced for a moment of the last day we spent together; her sneaking up on me in the morning, the way the wind blew through her hair as we rode through the pasture, the gentle truths she whispered in my ear in the hammock and the way she sang and energized me on the way to the game. She had done so much for me, and that moment was my opportunity to save her, to save everything Alcaeus and so many others had fought for, had died for!

The guards lifted her from the ground by her shoulders as she fought them to speak to me before they carried her away "Jayden run! Jayden, Jayden, it's a trap! Jayden, don't..."

They gagged her mouth with a cloth and carried her into the castle before she could get another word out. I half expected Erebus to smile or laugh at the circumstance, but his face was stern as he spoke one last time "Do as I ask of you Jayden. Do not fight, do not challenge me, and you will have a home in our new land and she will not die! Defy me, try to stop what will be, and I will not stop until I take everything you care for from you. I expect you soon in the headmaster's suite. Oh, and Jayden, do bring your friends."

With that, Erebus turned his back to me, threw his arms in the air, and returned to the safety of our castle's walls. The bodies that were not washed away by the wave began to rise from the ground, as did the skeletons of the dead. A zombie apocalypse was upon us. I thought to myself how helpful it could have been to have read the CDC's guide to a zombie apocalypse. I pulled close to Caiohme and Chloe and noticed that Malachi, Carmine and Adrianna were gone. I looked up to the balcony were Erebus had stood and muttered the only promise I would ever make to him "I will never fight for you, but I will fight for her!"

CHAPTER EIGHTEEN

Inside the Castle Walls

AS THE SUN drifted lower in the western sky, Caiohme, Chloe and I stood in a pasture with the living-dead in front of us and Erebus behind us. I knew in my head what I needed to do, what I needed to fight for, but my heart was heavy. Should I save the family I had forgotten in Leotus, my blood line, the people who believed in me and the girl who filled a piece of my heart no one else could? Should I turn my back on everything in Leotus to save the girl who held the rest of my heart, to save Katie? It seemed the outcome was damned either way, but was there a way to have both?

I grabbed the girls tightly and kissed Caiohme's forehead. I wasn't prepared to lose anyone that day, so I knew the only answer was a fight, a fight I could not allow them to be a part of. I prepared to create a diversion, to give the girls an escape, to tell them to allow me to finish this fight alone, but I was too late. In that moment, it seemed Caiohme sensed every fear and emotion in my body. The same ground that we were created from, that little piece of my heart she held, allowed her to know me like no one else could. She fell to her knees right in front of

Chloe and I and thrust her fists into the ground, sending a shock wave outward in all directions.

The earth shook and the shockwave had its desired effect, but the energy was not only focused on our enemy. The dead, who Erebus had called on to wage his war, had either been obliterated or laid lifeless again in the fields. Branches were stripped from the trees and many trunks exploded. Further damage was done to the castle walls and I could hear the animals of the forest howl as the vibrations reached them. She was stronger than I knew and I could feel her grief and anger pulsing in my veins as she stood up. She grabbed Chloe's hand and looked into my eyes as she stood fully erect. I could not tell if she was angry, frightened or sad as a tear fell down her cheek. She spoke softly, but with a firm tone "We must go. We must save our home, we must save Katie."

I could see her pain as her lips quivered and her eyes welled up. I could feel the tugging on her heart as I stared into her blue eyes, into her soul. She had already given me her whole heart, but she knew mine was not fully hers. Alcaeus had brought us back together, restoring a bond that filled the empty places in our hearts that we had known for so long, but Katie still had so many of the pieces of mine. What Caiohme didn't see was that it hurt me too. I wanted nothing more than to be able to give her my heart, to finally fill that void, but what holes would that leave? I wanted to walk up to her and grab her hand, tell her that everything was going to be all right, that it would all work out, but that would have been a lie. I didn't know whether I could ever love either of them fully because they each were a part of me; take one away and there would be an emptiness to fill. I knew I couldn't have both, but I began to question whether I could be content with either.

I did not offer her an excuse or an emotional explanation of my feelings. I picked up one foot, and then the other, and followed in her footsteps toward the castle walls. I was a coward. She was braver than me, tougher than me and kinder than me; willing to fight for a girl who meant nothing to her because she meant something to me. I owed Caiohme so much, but in those minutes I offered her no words of gratitude or thanks. I did not even offer to lead the way.

We entered the castle through the new hole in the dining room wall. The exquisite beauty that we had witnessed our first night in Leotus was no more. There were no chandeliers hanging from the ceiling or fine table settings. There were no skating servers or dancing origami dinosaurs. The sweet smell of Lucula and glazed chicken was replaced by the stench of ash and decaying flesh. The floor was littered with crumbled stone and large debris from the walls and ceiling. Breathing was harsh on my lungs, as fine particles tainted the once fresh air. My heart literally hurt, as I wondered what had happened to the young girl and her mother that I had met in the buffet line the night before.

We made our way across the dining room floor, careful not to step on anything that would bring us harm or alert our enemy. As we neared Eurus Hall, Chloe stopped in her steps and I continued to forge forward, bumping into her back. She looked up to me and spoke under her breath "There are Farrians behind the dining room doors waiting for us; we don't want to go that way."

Caiohme continued to walk toward the doors. I thought to warn her, but maybe it was time to change Chloe's visions. Maybe it was time to fight when we otherwise wouldn't, to battle the unknown instead of trying to avoid what was preordained. I said nothing, but Caiohme was ready when those double doors swung open. The three guards standing immediately outside the door were crushed as Caiohme slammed her fist against the wall and it collapsed on top of them. She stepped onto the pile of rubble and walked over their lifeless bodies, not afraid of the soldiers down the hall.

She was fighting with anger, a passion I had not seen in her. I was sure she could defeat an entire army on her own, but the fight was not only hers. I focused on the beast that stood amongst the soldiers down the hallway, until I was able to get inside its head. He had the shape of a man, but his muscles bulged and his head was much more round than oval. Leathery, brown skin, that was hairless and filled with moles and warts, covered his body. His teeth were jagged, pointy and decaying. His eyes were round and bloodshot. His ears were large and drooped to the base of his jaw. His feet were bare and his pants and shirt were tattered and bloody.

Inside that beast was a rage that I had never known in my life, a hurt so deep it had turned his heart black. I could not find a kind thought inside of his mind and an adrenaline induced rage pulsed through his veins. He thirsted for blood and that was exactly what I gave him. I used his strength to lift the soldiers from the ground and to shatter their bones against the wall. I used his bare feet to crush another soldier's skull against the cold tile.

Getting inside the beast's head was more than control, it was a connection. I could feel the hearts of those men stop beating as the beast defeated them. I could feel their warm blood on my hands. I could sense their fear. I could feel the surge of pleasure the beast achieved with each kill, a darkness that tried to take hold of me. It nearly made me sick to have those feelings racing through my mind, but each time I grew weak I thought of all the innocents that had died, the blood on those soldier's hands; I thought of Katie.

The girls and I followed a trail of death and blood down the hallway, until the beast defeated the last of the Farrian army that had occupied Eurus hall. As we reached the stairwell that would bring us to the headmaster's suite, I commanded the beast out of the castle and back to the woods he had come from. The beast lowered his head and stammered through the dining room doors without a fight. I stood for a moment and reflected on what we had just accomplished and I wondered if we had become the same monsters that we were fighting.

My thoughts were not interrupted by a beast's roar, a soldier's boots on the cold ground or the cries of anyone I held dear. The girls were silent as they approached the door and drifted off in their own thoughts. Thus, it was not noise that broke my concentration, but pure silence. How was a land ravaged by war so peaceful? What had happened to the others, to Patches? What had Erebus done to Katie; was she alive? Fear crept into me like fog spreads across the plains, enveloping my thoughts until they were hazy.

Something unexpected happened in the next moments. Caiohme grabbed my hand and clasped her fingers between mine. She pulled in close to me and offered heart felt words. Her tone was soft, but loud enough to be clear to Chloe "I expected for some time now that our fight would come down to this, to Katie. I believe in fighting for what is right, for those you love, so I will stand beside you and fight beside you. I believe you are strong and smart and that you will have your way in this battle, in this war. I only hope that the benevolence in your heart will allow you to make the sacrifices necessary for the greater good. If my life comes between you and that cause, then sacrifice mine to save the others."

She stopped speaking to wipe a tear from my cheek. Her incredible bravery and love for others before herself was something I wished I could find in myself, if even for a moment. Her words brought me to tears, reminding me how greedy my own heart was as I worried how I could ever be content again. I responded with a response that showed my emotions "I could never let you die. I cannot imagine my life without you in it. Leotus needs you, I need you."

She dropped my hand from hers, looked me in the eyes, and

spoke with a voice that was much more firm "You have lived without me before and you can do it again, even if Alcaeus has to make you forget. You should not fight for me, or yourself or even Katie. You should fight for these people, for our home. They believe in you; don't give them a reason not to! The pain and hurt associated with loss is brief, but if you let a whole people die it will weigh on you for eternity. Fight for your father and all those who have perished. I love you! I believe in you!"

Caiohme was tough, but still tears began to fall from her eyes. Not wanting to show weakness in front of me, she opened the stairwell door and walked inside. I stepped toward the door to follow her, knowing that I should be the one to lead the way, until I felt a familiar tug on my pants. Chloe didn't look up to me scared and worried like she had the day we met. Instead, she looked up to me with a reassuring smile "Don't worry, Caiohme won't die and someday the two of you will be together. I just know it."

Chloe's sudden return to optimism made me wonder if her visions of the battle had shifted back in our favor, but I did not ask what she had seen. I bent over, wiped the hair from her face, and kissed her forehead. She giggled as I rubbed my nose against hers, reminding her of the Eskimo kisses we shared years before, "I love you Chloe."

As we traveled up the stairs we encountered many missing and cracked steps, pieces of debris and dead soldiers from both armies. None of the obstacles would keep us from our destination, but each came with its own degree of hardship and loss. Strangely, the stairs that weren't broken showed the castle's resiliency, as they radiated the energetic colors they had the first time I made my way up them. As I thought about the hardships the castle had endured, I was reminded of all the difficulties we had risen against.

Our trip to Leotus began with attacks from the Farrian beasts in darkness so deep it could consume a man's mind.

Though the darkness took the life of my brother, it made us aware of our enemy. We made it past the white coats and I survived the poison induced delirium of the spy ants. We endured a strong storm under the branches of a Leotus tree and Caiohme survived the death spiral of a dragon developed to help save us from the Farrians. We took shelter under the dragon's wings as baseball-sized-hail dented the earth; his blood a reminder of the cost all have paid for us to be here. We survived the Leucrocota in whisper woods, but the cost was paid with a new friend's life. We made it past the beast that Patches bravely stayed behind to fight. We defeated Samarra and escaped the Farrian prison, thanks to the unexpected rescue by a man I thought to be my foe. We made it through the battlefield, past the Farrian army, into the castle, and we now stood at the top of a staircase. We stood only steps from our enemy, from Erebus, with the future of both the humans and the Leonoids weighing on our hearts.

I did not hesitate any longer, stepping in front of Caiohme to take the lead. I was full of confidence as we reached the entrance door to the Headmaster's suite. I could win the battle and save the human race. I could defeat Erebus and return Leotus to Alcaeus and his people. I was ready to fight, to die if need be. I was finally ready to make my own sacrifices as I prepared to turn the knob. Then I thought, why ruin the surprise?

I raised my hands, closed my eyes, and pressed against the concrete wall that separated the headmaster's suite from the hallway. Stone that stood for hundreds of years crumbled before us. The wall did not come crashing to the floor in an avalanche of debris, but fell as small granules, like sand being poured from a bucket. As the dust cleared from the air and I opened my eyes, I was amazed and angered by those that stood before me.

CHAPTER NINETEEN

Dust to Dust

AS THE WALL fell and I saw Patches standing idly by Erebus's side, sinking his teeth into a crisp, green apple, I realized that ties to the enemy were deeper and more complex than I understood. I felt betrayed and inarticulate. His presence made me believe the war would not end until much more sacrifice had been made. Neither, Erebus nor Patches had any words for us immediately. They allotted us several moments to survey the room and determine our predicament.

I looked up into the eyes of Erebus as the dust settled. I knew that in the next hours the battle for Leotus would have its end, but I wondered, what of the war for the human race? The battle may have begun recently, but the war had waged since before my creation. A great city was built deep in the woods; tunnels were dug and technology developed. Children were born and families chose sides. Risk was calculated and the people of Leotus were led to trust one man's vision; a vision that I, a child of Alcaeus, would save the human race and return peadce to Leotus. Would the next moments put an end to the crimes the Farrians had committed, the very actions they hated the human race for, or would this war wage on until there was nothing left for anyone?

Several things caught my attention as I surveyed the room, but the only thing I kept my eyes on was Katie. It was the soft breeze blowing through the balcony door that first shifted my attention her way. The curtains fluttered back and forth in the wind, occasionally obstructing my view of her. She was still in her cheer uniform, causing me to wonder if Erebus had been holding her as I slept inside the castle walls. Her hair was messy and knotted and her skin was bruised and dirty. Her mouth was gagged and she was restrained by two large Farrian soldiers. Even as she starred at me she seemed absent, not attempting to break free or scream. I feared that she had given up, that she has lost herself in the confinement.

My stomach filled with knots and my heart with rage to see Katie that way. It made me oblivious to everything else around me; the noises, the movement, the other prisoners, even Caiohme. Nothing else mattered. I focused on Katie; I could save her. If blood had to be shed, even my own, I would stain the ground red for her. I took a deep breath and charged straight toward Erebus and Patches, towards the balcony. I screamed as one foot left the ground and then the other "Hurt her and I will kill you all. All of you!"

Before I planted my eighth step into the hard concrete floor, I ran into what felt like a brick wall and was knocked backwards, flat on my back. My vision doubled for a moment and as it cleared all I could see was the smirk that stretched Erebus' face. He shook his head as I pushed myself up from the ground. The barrier that separated Katie and me was not visible to the naked eye. There was no electrical charge or visible magic; it simply felt as if I had run straight into cement. I questioned whether the enemy could even hear the emotions I had expressed as I took my first steps.

I shifted my attention momentarily toward the other prisoners; toward Alcaeus, Desiah and Deseus. I wondered, as I
watched Desiah pace relentlessly back and forth, how Erebus
could be powerful enough to enslave such beings. The cage that
imprisoned them was deep blue and purple; it radiated with
energy and flowed like water moving through glass tubes. There
was something that caught my eye about the way it moved,
something majestic, something lively. The longer that I looked at
the bars the more relaxed I found myself, until my mind drifted
into a pure contentment where I found the answer to free us all.

The power was not Erebus' at all; he had simply borrowed it.
It all came to me as I remembered one of the basics of my high
school science classes; energy is neither created nor destroyed.
When the creationists built Leotus they left something very special behind; the energy. It lived in the walls and stairs of the
homes and castle, in the vines and the trees, in the creatures and
the ocean and even in the people. Erebus was not as powerful as
he appeared, he had simply sucked the life from Leotus for his
own purposes, but I planned to give it back to Leotus.

I looked to Caiohme, who had a tight grasp on Chloe's
hand, and hollered out to both of them to get back. I knelt
onto the concrete ground and placed the palms of my hands on
the ashy surface. I could feel the energy rush threw me like an
adrenaline high, empowering me for battle. My heart sprinted,
my pupils dilated, my breathing grew rapid and my senses were
strengthened. It was the same intense rush I had felt over and
over; as Alcaeus mended my broken body in front of the castle,
as the vines turned gray for me and as my life tree wrapped me
in her branches. My heart felt as if it might burst and my legs as
if they might run out from under me; still, I kept my palms to
the ground for as long as I could stand the intense high.

When I stood from my position I felt as if I might float
away. It seemed as if I was looking down on Erebus and that

he had fallen weak. No beast in the land had my strength. I felt more powerful than the father who had given me life, than the God's. I looked back at Caiohme, who too had begun to gather strength, but there was no time to wait for her help. Katie's life was in danger, Leotus and the humans were in danger. This battle was mine.

Just as I set myself to begin my attack on Erebus, I was reminded that I was merely a man, with the same emotions and fears controlling me. You see, as I took my stance I saw those two guards pick Katie up and dangle her from the balcony on which they stood. For the first time since I reached that room, I heard Katie's voice again. Not the playful laugh or the lovey tone I was used to, but cries of fear "No, please! Pick me up, pick me up! Jayden! Jayden help me!"

Erebus had struck one of the few places he knew I was vulnerable. He knew the flaws in my armor too well. I wasn't scared for my own well-being; I only wanted to keep Katie safe. I wanted to shout out, to tell her that I was there and that I would protect her. It was no use though; she would never hear me with Erebus between us. A thought crossed the back of my mind, actions are louder than words Jayden, and then I let all the built up frustration and energy erupt out of me.

I opened my arms and thrust them toward Erebus and a brilliant white light exploded from within me, consuming all space. Brighter than the sun, it blanketed everything with its brilliance, leaving nothing less pure to be seen. I took a step, fearing that I had destroyed creation itself, but then my step was met with the step of another. At first I saw only her feet and then her legs. Her hair shined golden in the white light and her smile glistened. Caiohme looked like an angel as she emerged. The sudden entrance of Chloe behind her only increased my joy. I hoped that Katie would emerge from behind them.

A look of astonishment did not fade from their faces as they approached me; I'm sure the same piercing gaze lingered in my own eyes. There was no time to greet them as the ground began to shake and a horizon began to emerge. The scenery changed the same way it had when Alcaeus had come for us. As the particles of life fell into place, flying by us as brilliant specks of color, I was overcome with a sense of excitement. I knew those fields, that sunrise; it was Havenbrook.

As everything fell into place and I turned around, I saw that my joy was not matched on Caiohme and Chloe's face. I am sure they were concerned and scared; another unfamiliar place, another path that did not lead home. I found it hard to hold in my excitement though as I thought of Main Street and Miss Mayfield's diner, cars and lights, street signs and even Mr. Fickler and the credit union. I could not wait to find my parents and to find Katie, hoping that those last moments at the castle had not been real.

I went to grab Caiohme's hand and explain our luck, when out from the shadow of a tree stepped a familiar face, Erebus. I recognized his features, but the image was not that of the man I had encountered moments before. His clothing was tattered and stained with ash and blood. He walked with a limp on the right side and supported himself with a walking stick. A grin did not occupy his face; instead there was firmness to his jaw that straightened his lips and flared his nostrils. He let the stick fall from his grip and began to clap his hands, as his lips opened to speak.

His tone did not come off flamboyant or exuberant; in fact, for a moment he seemed frightened "Beautiful illusion, wasn't it Jayden? To think, I wouldn't have been able to get here without your assistance; I had grown too weak to walk between worlds. The fields and trees, the open sky, the buildings and lights; I have not seen this world since we gave the humans a second chance. Finally, I feel at home. It all started here you know, here in Havenbrook. Your town is one of the few to hold onto what a second chance was supposed to be about; loving your neighbors, respecting the land, family and friends. It's a beautiful place."

He smiled and continued, his voice growing stronger with each sentence "It was I that enveloped you in darkness that first day, paving the way for your fear and distrust for those in Leotus. It was I that posed as Malachi at your first meeting in your room, to be sure that the two of you would never develop a bond, that you would always look to him to blame. It was I, disguised as a shaman, that Fariah trusted to bring a potion to cure your brother that night in the square, causing his death. I brought the ants to encourage you to flee Leotus. I killed your friend in the woods and brought the black beast to separate you from Patches. You are alive because I let you live. You made your way back to the castle because I paved the course for it. Everything, all of it, was part of my plan. You have always just been a pawn Jayden. Now I have what I want and I no longer need you or your friends."

He paused for a moment and ran his hand over the branch of an oak tree. I took a step toward him and fearlessly spoke "Your right, this is my town and it is home, but it is not your home. You call it beautiful, but all you want is to destroy it. Why don't you just go back to Leotus, have your way there and leave us alone?"

He laughed deeply as he stepped out from the shadow of the tree and closer to me "I don't want to destroy anything Jayden; you see, you have your facts wrong. I only want to fix what the humans have destroyed. I want to show them again what life can be, what they long for in their hearts. I want to sit on Earth's highest throne and be praised as their God. I will be the man they will thank for leading them out of this darkness. Not you or anyone else will stop me Jayden."

The anger built inside of me as he spoke. I could feel my

stomach churn and my hair stand on end. My body shook and my skin grew warm and moist. My voice shook as it roared from my mouth in a furious tone "They will never call you God! God is merciful and loving. God is the man we praise on Sunday and build churches and steeples for. God would never do the things you have done and I will die before I see you change one thing about my home."

He laughed again but his tone grew more confident and proud as he spoke in a more firm tone "Your God is an illusion. Just as I led you to believe that your friends and Katie were in danger at the castle, man provided you with false prophecy. You have met the God's in Leotus and I, Erebus, will be the most powerful of them. That is why I stand in front of you now as your father, Alcaeus, lay dead inside what is left of his great creation. That is why your friends have not come to save you. That is why I will have my way with these people, and they will call me King."

His strength grew and he became angrier as he pounded his fist into the trunk of an oak tree and it shattered before us "My son, Malachi, stood to inherit everything! He has followed me obediently. He has defied Alcaeus and waged war on Leotus. He should have walked with me today into your world, but he is not here. All his life he has asked of me the same questions you are asking of me today "Father, let us be kings in Leotus, let us take power from Alcaeus and leave the humans be. We can rule the heavens; we do not need the earth as well. He was foolish; he is not here because he fell victim to your story. He is dead because he grew to believe in the legend, to believe in you. He believed that you could save the humans, his sister, and all the people he had grown to love; if only he could see what he died for. Now, you will die and then your friends will die and the earth will be mine."

He paused, as the anger on his face seemed to break for a

moment. His voice dulled as he spoke again "Many would say that I stand alone, but alone there is no one to defy you or hurt you. Leotus is weak and leaderless now; soon it will fall. There will be no one to stand in my way and this land full of people will worship me. They will adore me. If they don't, I will destroy them and create a race of people that will."

I could not listen to his banter any longer. I intended to lay down my other abilities and fight him like a man. I intended to kill him. I planted my feet into the earth I had played on as a child and I charged toward him. Before I traveled ten feet, I was knocked on my back by a rippling force with a vibration so strong that it hit me over and over again. Unable to rise to my feet, I lifted my head and watched as a hole opened up in the sky.

Out of the sky poured our army, all of the people I had grown to trust, and some that I had doubted; Alcaeus and Patches, Carmine and Adrianna, Scraggs and many others. I was happy to see that my friends were not dead, but it was easy to see that the war had left its scars. Alcaeus led the group, limping across the hardened ground. It was the last man to step into Havenbrook that surprised me most; his walk, stronger than I expected, with a firm decisiveness in his eyes. He spoke in a full bodied tone that could not be ignored "I am not dead father. You see, I stand with friends, which itself cannot be devalued. You are a man alone, a coward. You say that no one can hurt you father, but tell me, who has your back now? Give up, come home and be judged like a man."

The air was tense and it was easy to see that the emotion was strong between Erebus and Malachi. He desired to have his son by his side, but was not willing to lose the war. The decision was his; cower and run or go home and face the people of Leotus. Erebus hesitated only moments before his decision was made.

He pounded his foot into the ground and the earth began to move. My knees buckled and I fell as a beast emerged from the dirt, shifting and buckling the land. Five beasts blotted out the suns light as they towered above us, woven together from the intertwined roots of trees and plants. Like the fibers that define our muscle, the roots built them into strong creatures. The beasts seemed confused for a moment of what they had become, looking around at their surroundings, at each other, but I knew it would not be long before Erebus controlled them for his own motives.

Before the beasts gained their bearings, Alcaeus called up his own army from the earth. The rocks gathered and formed walls between us and the beasts. Several trees pulled their roots from the ground. Their branches twisted and tangled and their trunks split, forming beasts smaller than those that had come from the earth, but just as strong. Wolves and coyotes emerged from behind houses and trees, growling and snarling. Horses met us and knelt, ready to be mounted for battle.

Erebus called for the winds to change and for the clouds to form and begin to pour rain. His army was half the size of ours, but they towered above us like bullies in the schoolyard. It was clear that this battle would be fought among beast and men and that the weather would play her part. In the end, only men would remain to decide the fate of Leotus.

I rose to my feet, mounted my horse and rode over to Chloe and Caiohme. As I reached them, I jumped to the ground and wrapped my arms around them in time to watch the beasts crush through the wall that Alcaeus had created. The battle had begun. The girls clung to me as I watched the towering beasts destroy our army. They kicked the coyotes and wolves into the broken stone walls. They snapped the trees in half, like toothpicks. I stood in shock as the beast nearest me crashed his foot down on Patches, returning him to the earth he had been raised from.

In the following seconds, several tears rolled down my dirty cheeks. I turned to Caiohme, grabbed her face and kissed her soft lips. It reminded me that not everything in the world is bad; some things are sweet, pure, and innocent. Some moments flood us with so much emotion that our stomachs float and our hearts skip a beat. Love can be so quick and empowering, making us feel as if we could do anything. I grabbed her shoulders tight "Take Chloe and run far away from here, run fast, keep running until you hit the edge of town. Then find a way to get home, get back to Ireland; I promise I will find you there. I will never stop looking until I do."

She flung herself against me and wrapped her arms tightly around my chest. Her soft words echoed in my ear, making me so angry, but filling me with the certainty that she was my other half "No! I will not leave. I will never leave you. I promised you that and I meant it. This is not just your war, it's all of ours and I will fight it with you."

She squeezed me tightly and kissed my cheek, then released me. "Chloe," she hollered, just in time to turn around and watch as the beast's fist came down on her younger sister.

No fear for the enemy pulsed through me in the moments that his fist sat on top of Chloe. No second thoughts raced through my brain. There was no "what if," or "this or that." Leotus had hardened me; only a hate for that beast, a hate for our enemy remained. There was no time to console Caiohme as she crippled to the ground in shock. I charged the beast and vaulted myself into the core of his body.

Everything seemed to slow down as I launched myself, and I had a moment to contemplate that those seconds could be the end of my life. I had come to accept that death had become more common than new life and I knew nothing should be taken for granted. I closed my eyes as my head collided with his body; beautiful images of the sun setting on a golden wheat horizon flooded my brain. The sun glistened off the field as the sky faded into brilliant pinks and oranges. If that was what the end looked like, I was ready to go!

Strange thing is I never felt the impact. You see, as I fell to the ground, I opened my eyes to see the fizzling flickers of an explosion falling back to the earth, like fireworks dying in the night sky. The beast no longer towered above us; what was left of him returned to the earth he was raised from. Dust to dust. I turned my head to the left to see Chloe running toward me, unscathed, without a scratch or bruise. My heart filled with joy and I knew I was blessed.

In the minutes that followed, what was left of our army gained a valuable edge and the beasts that Erebus had raised from the earth returned to the ground as one brilliant flash of color after another. I met Alcaeus behind the tree line as the beasts fell and he privately spoke words to me that I will never forget. His eyes met mine and penetrated deep into my soul, glistening with a love that can be seen as a new father looks into the eyes of his first child. I'm sure he knew all the struggles that were on my heart, because I could feel everything that he was experiencing.

I could feel the regret that was heavy on his heart for not having spent more time with me; for not having ridden together, thrown the football and talked about girls and life. I could see the faith he had in me, the belief that this earth and its people would survive. He believed I would lead them, that I would lead Leotus. I could feel his love for me; love that had existed since before he created me from the very earth that he created Caiohme from. Lastly, I could feel his pain, a deep cutting pain. His heart almost seemed to quiver as his eyes told me that this moment, this battle, would be his last to share with me.

I broke the gaze, refusing to believe what I had seen in his eyes. He leaned down and kissed my forehead and pulled me in tight "Son, I am very old and you are young. I have served my purpose here and now it is time for change; it is your time. I have heard my father's prophecy many times and I know what must be done. It is my time to return to the earth we come from and your time to lead."

Tremors shook my body and my voice cracked as tears gathered in my eyes "No, no its not! I am not ready. I need you. There is so much I don't know about you, about myself. Don't leave. Promise me you won't!"

He pulled me in tighter to his chest and his voice was unwavering in my ear "Always follow your heart and treat people right. Remember that not everything just is always fair. There will always be evil men; be firm in their presence and lead them with your kindness. Be courageous always, never cowering or being fearful for tomorrow. Show mercy to all, but be stern when you must. Do not let loss, or death, or the things of this world turn your heart cold. Lead the people of Leotus, not from a throne, but among them. Show the children how to be decent men and women. Show the humans how to find peace in their hearts once more. Always keep Caiohme at your side; she is the only one that will ever fully understand you, the only one that will ever fully keep your heart at peace. Believe in yourself. I love you son. Forgive me."

As the last of Erebus's army exploded into the sky and fell back to earth, I watched Alcaeus walk out from behind the trees and into the open field. The fighting ceased and those who lived looked on with curiosity as Alcaeus approached Erebus. Neither Alcaeus, nor Erebus, used their abilities as they came within feet of one another. Alcaeus knelt at the feet of Erebus. I tried to run toward them, to stop what was coming next, but it was as if my feet were made of lead, they would not budge. All I could do is scream "No, no, no! Get up Alcaeus! Get up and fight."

As Erebus raised a knife into the air, no one else tried to run and stop it, no one else even spoke a word. All of them watched as Alcaeus muttered his last words "Erebus, let it be done."

Erebus hesitated for a moment, as if it was a trick, as if there was something more to it. Then, without a second thought, he drove his knife through the back of my father. The blade pierced his skin and entered his heart. Without a gasp of air, or a last plea for life, Alcaeus fell. He fell first to his elbows and then flat on the ground. Immediately after he took his final breath, his body exploded in a blinding ray of light and a shock wave knocked everyone but Erebus and I to their backs.

A tear rolled down my cheek as I heard Erebus laugh, his words cowardly and filled with hate "stupid old man, now there is no one to stand in my way."

Had he forgotten about me, about the other sons and daughters? Had he forgotten about his own son? There was no more time to think, I could not let Alcaeus die in vain. Without realizing that I was able, I picked my feet off of the ground and began to run towards Erebus. I felt like I was running 100 miles an hour, but before I got halfway to Erebus a man emerged from behind the tree, on his left side, with a tight grip on Katie.

I could not hear her voice, her mouth was gagged and taped shut, but I could tell that this time she was real. It was Katie. I could see the fear in her eyes, but also the relief that came with seeing a familiar face. She tried to shake free, but her captor was strong and she was bound at the wrists and ankles. She appeared to be in good health, without bruises or scrapes. I hollered out to Katie the only thing I could, not wanting to make any promises I could not keep, "I love you Katie."

Erebus bent over and picked the knife up from the ground and I took a few steps forward. He took a step closer to Katie and put the knife up to her chest "Not another step Jayden, not one more. You know, I hoped that you could join me, that you could sit beside me and rule over the humans with Malachi and Carmine, like sons! I hoped that you could see the flaws in what Alcaeus has tried to do, in the belief that we can be content without power. Now you all will die and I will still have what is mine. You took my son from me and now I will take the only thing you have left from you."

Without hesitation, he thrust the knife into Katie's chest. I don't know that more than a few seconds went by, but it seemed like eternity as I watched the guard release his grip. She stumbled forward as blood stained her white, sequined tank top. Then, she collapsed to the ground and stopped moving. I am not sure what filled my heart first, fear of her death or the intense rage that I felt for Erebus. Either way, I ran toward her, trying to save her, but Erebus threw his hands toward me and sent me flying backwards.

I spent no time on my back as he walked toward me, immediately rising to my feet. He did not let me take one step before he made the ground under my feet move, like waves in the ocean, and sent me back onto my back. I hit the back of my head on a rock and my vision grew hazy for a few moments. As my vision cleared I found Erebus mounted on top of me, waiting for me to open my eyes to his grin. I watched as the others tried to intervene, but from his position he first sent Caiohme flying, then Malachi. His power seemed too much for theirs.

I was weak and he was able to hold both of my arms down with one of his. In his other hand, Erebus held tightly to the same dagger he had used to kill Alcaeus and Katie. As he continued to fight off those that wished to save me, his eyes did not leave mine. Unlike Alcaeus, I was able to see nothing in the depth of his heart or soul, only a deep darkness that hid his intentions. As Malachi made another attempt to free me, I was able to free one of my hands and mount some resistance against the dagger.

Erebus spoke as he inched the dagger closer to my chest. Most of what he said was a blur, but there were a few things that I recalled "Your father's blood, your blood, will free the people of Leotus from the fantasy that someone will bring them peace. I will bring them this dagger with your father's blood, Katie's blood and your blood, dry on its blade, and declare to them that I am their God. I will destroy Leotus, I will kill them all, and then I will finally be free from your father's fantasies."

My eyes shifted and all I could see was the blood on the blade of his knife. To know that he had hurt Katie, that he had killed my father, filled me with a fire that could have brought down Erebus and an entire army. I closed my eyes and my strength returned to me as I heard my father's words "Show mercy to all, but be stern when you must." I thought to myself, not even mercy could save a man whose son was not enough.

I closed my eyes again and images of Leotus filled my mind. I could not see my body, but I felt myself running. My vision fluttered between Erebus and images of Leotus. All I saw was what was in front of me; the castle, then burning homes, the stables and slaughtered horses. The images passed faster as if I was running away from Leotus. The whole while, I held Erebus' hand and the dagger far away from my chest.

The vision brought me further and further from Leotus, into whisper woods. I passed the creek, the house Desiah and my father had built and even the Farrian city. The images flashed faster and faster, deeper and deeper into the woods, until everything was a blur. For a moment all was black and silent and then I felt a thud and I opened my eyes to see that I was no longer a prisoner of Erebus, but that the Leucrocota had him pinned down.

He showed his teeth and snarled at Erebus, and I could

feel his anger inside of me. I could feel his heart beating and it seemed that his blood pulsed through me. As I blinked, in the darkness, I could see through his eyes. For the first time, I could see the fear in Erebus as the beast looked down on him. I closed my eyes because part of me wanted to be one with the beast. I wanted to feel Erebus take his last breath. I wanted to feel his heart beat one last time.

I don't know whether it was the Leucrocota or my control of him, but in the next moment he opened his jaw, dropped his front legs, and sunk his teeth into Erebus' neck. I tasted the blood in my mouth and I could hear Erebus scream and his last gasp of air, as if it was in my own ears. The beast kept his teeth in place until the last pulse could no longer be felt in Erebus' neck. Then he rose onto all four legs, took one last look at what he had done, and disappeared into the forest. I lost my connection with the beast as he ran back into Whisper Woods and I fell to the ground, my eyes shut and the world went black.

CHAPTER TWENTY

A Man Stuck Between

CAIOHME CAME TO help me up from the cracked ground, but I was so drained, physically and emotionally, that I nearly pulled her down on top of me. My eyes shot directly over to Katie, her body lifeless on the ground. None of it seemed real. I thought that I might fall to my knees again, but I placed one foot in front of the other, taking flaccid steps. Caiohme and Chloe offered to walk with me, but I told them I needed to go on my own. I was sure if there were tears left in my eyes I would have cried them; instead I walked without emotion. The world was quiet.

At no point had my spirit seemed more broken than in that moment. I had lost a brother I never knew, new friends, family and a great leader and father. To face the death of my best friend, a girl that had been there for me in the ups and downs, someone I loved, seemed like too much. In the distance I noticed Malachi, alone in the field, crouched down behind a row of trees with his face in his hands. He had lost Samarra and, as evil as the man was, I had just killed his father. Leotus had asked too much of all of us, it had taken too much. Great sacrifice was an understatement.

As I reached Katie's body, it was not the blood that caught my attention, but the intermittent expansions of her chest. The blood appeared to have dried, the wound clotted off. She was breathing. I fell to my knees and rolled her over "Help me, she is alive. Katie is alive."

Her eyes did not open as I turned her over, but her chest expanded and I could hear her breathing. Caiohme, Chloe, Carmine, even Malachi came to her aid, but they could not do anything I was not capable of myself. I put one arm under her knees and another under her neck and I picked her up from the ground; her body seemed as light as linen. I whispered in her ear "Katie, hold on. I love you! Fight for me. Don't give up, not now!"

Without waiting for the others I took off running. Not the type of running you probably have in your head, not state football game fast, but Leonoid fast. I did not care who saw me, if anyone could see me at all. The trees and buildings became a moving blur of color as I raced past them to the Havenbrook Hospital. I burst into the emergency doors, past the receptionist and into the emergency room. I laid her on the nearest bed and screamed for anyone that would listen "Someone, anyone! Please, come and help her!"

My heart beat intensely as sweat poured off of my brow. My chest expanded at 30 breaths a minutes. The nurses asked me what happened, but I could not get the breath to explain. All I could muster was enough oxygen to simply say "help her," as I fell to the ground beside the desk.

The others arrived as they rushed Katie back to surgery and stabilized me with some oxygen and IV fluids. I was not able to sit for long. I began pacing back and forth in my room, waiting for any news on Katie. I did not have to tell our story to anyone. Carmine and Malachi manipulated the minds of the land owners, witnesses, detectives, family and hospital staff to believe that an explosion had caused the damage and injuries. They explained that shrapnel had punctured Katie's chest and caused the cuts and abrasions we suffered.

Carmine had a passerby arrested for the incident, whom he told me had sexually molested children in the communities he had previously traveled through. Our community was a better place without him and no one would know any better. Malachi and Carmine disguised themselves as common men, firefighters from a neighboring community, in the right place at the right time. Because of their abilities no one would ever come to any of us again with questions of what happened that afternoon. The story stood and reporters searched for the "unsung heroes from a small Kansas town," before finally giving up months later.

News finally came from the doctors, 12 hours after Katie went back for surgery. Katie's parents and grandparents, my mother, the girls and I were all present as he approached us with a somber face. He managed a smile as he greeted us "I am happy to let you know that Katie is in stable condition. The wound did not puncture any major organs, but she lost a lot of blood. We are replacing the blood, her heart is pumping on its own, and she is breathing without any machines."

I let out a sigh of relief and we all rejoiced with hugs as the doctor paused for a moment. As the doctor attempted to continue, Katie's dad asked the only question I had "When can we see her?"

The doctor's smile faded as he again spoke "You will be able to see her after the blood has transfused, but I'm afraid I also have some bad news. Katie is in a coma. We have exhausted all medical means to bring her out of it. Her brain is functioning properly, but there is no guarantee that she will wake up. I'm sorry."

Katie's family had many more questions for the doctor, but eventually nothing more could be said. They declared that they intended to wait by her bed every day until she woke. I vowed to myself to do the same. Several hours later we were able to see her. Her clothes had been changed and the blood and dirt had been cleansed from her body. I was convinced that was the best anyone had ever looked in a hospital gown. Screens and cords monitored her as the wait began.

I sat at Katie's bedside for eight straight days as she continued in a comatose state. I asked the nurse to turn away most of my visitors, as I ignored the issues that had arisen since the death of Erebus. I rested in spurts, with Caiohme by my side, giving Katie's visitors' time with her. As the days passed the number of people coming to see me dwindled until only a few remained. I had few words for anyone, as I spent the nights at Katie's side, holding her hand and talking to her as she slept. I prayed more intensely than I ever had before, asking God to take me instead, to spare her life. I cried many times, but I never gave up hope that she would wake up.

Caiohme and Chloe were the only people outside of family that remained by my side every day. I introduced them to those I had interactions with as close friends from out of town that I had met on a family vacation. Friends and family grew to love them over those eight days. Chloe brought a child's laughter and her optimistic view to the situation. Caiohme sat with me, held my hand, cried with me, and kept me strong, just as she had in Leotus. She made me smile when no one else was able to and helped my heart to heal and forgive as we waited.

It was Caiohme that brought me tragic news on our second day in the hospital; Carmine had been delivering news from Leotus to her. There were stories that my father never made it back to the beach. She explained "They say that after he left you in the tunnel he made his way to a house in Leotus where women and children had taken cover in the basement. He protected them as wave after wave of soldiers advanced on the house. He was able to hold off the advances until the Leotus army made it to their location. He died saving a three year old boy who had run into battle after his father. Not one women or child in that house lost their life because of him."

Tears rolled down my eyes as I tried to come to grips with losing Alcaeus, my father, and possibly Katie. I hugged Caiohme "He was my father, the only father I ever knew. It seemed like he never had time for me, but his life revolved around protecting me. I'm glad to have the memories, but how can I ever stop missing him now? So many things I didn't say these last years; so many regrets."

On the fourth day Caiohme came to me; his funeral would be that afternoon on the beaches of Leotus. I would have asked her to stay with Katie, but I knew my father was like a father to her as well. I spoke to Katie's family, letting them know that I planned to try and get some rest and that I would be back soon. There was no need to tell my mother, she had never known my father or me to be gone, and my time in Leotus would be short. I kissed Katie's head and promised to return. Caiohme, Chloe and I made our way out to the countryside where we clasped hands and walked into Leotus.

As we walked into the town center I ran my hand over the girl's faces' and then over my own, disguising our appearance as one of the locals. Our faces again appeared dirty with ash, but there was not the sensation of filth on our skin. I made our cheeks appear more sunken, our noses and foreheads larger, and our hair several shades darker. Our clothes were tattered white robes, dirty with the soot of buildings that still burned. There was not time for praise or small talk. I was there to see my father one last time and get back to Katie. It was not the right time for me to return to Leotus, not the right time to lead our people.

No one recognized us as we walked past burning buildings and piles of rubble. The locals were out in masses trying to return to normalcy. Some trimmed trees and bushes while others pushed the rubble into piles. Carpenters repaired what could be repaired and several foundations had been cleared to start new. Debris was being burnt as other fires were being extinguished. There was heart in what they were doing, as they all helped one another to rebuild. These weren't just neighbors, they were family.

There were no bones or bodies to be seen in the rubble, the dead had already been taken care of appropriately. That day was not my father's, he was already home. It was an opportunity for the people of Leotus to have one last moment to say goodbye to his flesh, to the man he was. As we approached what was left of the castle I noticed that a mass of 10-12 men, woman and children had begun to follow in our steps. I hoped that they had not discovered who we were, as I urged Caiohme and Chloe to pick up the pace "Come on girls, we have a posse on our tail."

Travel on foot was more dangerous near the castle. No one had gone about the work of cleaning the debris up yet and it was so dense and widespread that we were forced to walk over and through it to get to the beach. As we neared the corner of the castle, I was reminded of our first day in Leotus and the darkness that enveloped us; it reminded me of the life tree. I turned around to see that the debris had not touched it and the fire had not burnt its leaves. The tree stood strong, a reminder of my own resiliency and a promise of brighter days.

As the beach came into view, it became clear that my father was a popular man. The crowd was large, hiding his memorial from view. Stragglers still made their way to the beach from all directions. It appeared that all the working men, woman and children from the square had sat down their tools to see him laid to rest. I wanted to watch my father be put to rest without the crowd, so I grabbed Caiohme's arm "Let's go up to the head-master's suite and watch the funeral from there."

She obliged my request. We made our way in the side entrance; there was no longer a door to keep the enemy out. Debris filled the hallway like it had when we battled the beasts to meet Erebus in my father's suite days earlier. Blood stained the floors and walls. We made our way up the broken stairs and into Alcaeus' room. The wall that had once separated the hallway from the room was now gone, making access much easier and the room much larger.

As we walked into the room, something on the ground caught my eye among the debris. I walked over to the shiny object and bent down to pick up the smallest of the obsidian horses from the ground. I ran my fingers over its back as if there was a mane to run my fingers through. The horse reminded me both of Alcaeus and my father. I hoped that they were both in a place where they found themselves as free as wild horses, able to run with the wind in their hair, not a worry in the world. I hoped that they were in a place so consumed by love that there was not room for hate or greed or the other vices of men. I smiled as I put the piece into my pocket to bring home with me.

We made our way out onto the patio and looked down onto the beach. I could no longer see the sand amongst the masses. The waves were littered with ash and debris; still, I watched them break against the shore for a moment, sure that there was a weed walker out there somewhere. A stage had been set up around my father's wooden casket. There were many carvings in the wood, most of which I could not make out, but I could see the symbol that was engraved on my compass, as it was carved largely in the center. The casket was closed and there were several chairs set up on the stage; one for Flora, one for a woman I did not recognize and two empty seats.

Flora kept pulling her robe away from her wrist and looking down at it, presumably waiting for Caiohme and I to show up. Little did she know; we were already watching from the balcony.

I figured that one of the chairs was mine, but it was not until I heard his voice that I realized who the other chair belonged to. It came from behind the curtains that still separated the balcony from the room "I knew you would make it back to say good-bye to your father, but did you really think those disguises would fool me?"

Deseus laughed as he made his way onto the balcony and greeted the three of us with warm hugs. He took my hand and looked into my eyes "I understand the need for privacy and your desire to not be overwhelmed at this moment in your life. I heard of your friend Katie, I hope that she is well. Personally, I am not much for big crowds, but I was asked to speak by your father should this day ever come. If you examined the crowd, you would see Desiah disguised among the locals as well; he was to speak today, but could not sturdy his emotions."

I spotted my father's one-legged friend in the back of the crowd, constantly allowing others to occupy spots in front of him, and I smiled. I patted Deseus on the shoulder "No one bet-ter to speak today than you Deseus. Just do me one favor, make today more about celebrating his time here and the things he accomplished than talking about his death."

He wrapped his arms around me and smiled "Your father's life was a celebration, a celebration of you, and I will make sure today is no different. I have stepped into a new role of leadership here in Leotus, but let me tell you, Alcaeus' role is not mine; it's what you are destined for. I will assume it for now, but you must come back home and help rebuild, develop relationships, and lead. Be what you were prophesied to be. Your father promised that you would bring peace and I believe in your father's prom-ise to our people. There are a few more things you must know."

I stopped him "Deseus, now is not the time. There are other things I must tend to at this point in my life. Perhaps, someday I will return, but for now you will make a wonderful headmaster. Now go, lower my father into the ground."

He hugged me one last time and released me from his grip "I will send for you should things get worse. For now, work on your abilities and look after these two beautiful women. Don't be afraid to visit, even if you feel the need to wear a disguise."

He hugged Caiohme "The people are calling you the queen." She blushed and smiled as he kissed her forehead.

Lastly, he approached Chloe and pulled a teddy bear from behind his back "Scraggs wanted you to have this Princess Chloe."

Chloe pulled the bear close to her heart and held onto it tightly as Deseus disappeared behind the curtains. He did not leave the room before he spoke one last piece of advice "Showing them your face would bring strength in these times of trial and keep the enemy in the shadows."

His words vibrated inside of my skull as I listened to each step he took through the hallway and down the broken stairs "...keep the enemy in the shadows." The crunching of rubble underneath his feet faded as the distance between us grew. I wondered if the Leonoids or the Humans could ever find peace. Unlike footsteps, it seemed that whenever one enemy's legacy faded away, another man's greed grew until he stepped into the role. Sure, there can always be peace for a time, but would we ever live in a world free from evil men. I doubted it.

I watched Deseus as he walked onto the beach. The crowd parted for him as he made his way onto the stage. As he whispered a few words to Flora, I watched her look up our way and a smile grew on her face. I did not do as Deseus wished though; I did not remove the disguise. This day was to be about my father, not about the three of us. Members of the crowd looked up and I'm sure they wondered who was standing on the headmaster's balcony, but for the most part the service started without the crowd noticing us.

Flora took the stage first, talking of how she had met my father only days after Alcaeus had created us. She reminded the crowd that it was my father who had brought her hope that the human race could change. She talked of the dream my father shared with Alcaeus for peace. She shed a few tears, grabbed an object from her pocket and placed it on top of his coffin. Quickly, Flora handed the stage over to a woman I did not know.

It turned out that the woman was the mother of the child my father had saved. Her speech touched me and brought tears to my eyes; it was a strong message of what humanity should be. The crowd kept quiet as her voice was frail and shaky "This man should be a model for the way we live our lives. From what I have been told, he committed his life to ensuring that his son would be able to save not only us, but the humans as well. Though he was not able to save my husband three days ago, he ensured that my son would be here to carry on our family name. He laid down his life so that a younger man could have his. Today we honor him."

As her words faded into the calm air a young girl escorted a boy to the stairs of the stage. His robe was as white and clean as the rose he held in his hand; a symbol of loyalty, unity, purity. It was then, that the white robes of the locals finally made sense to me. There was a moment of comical relief and smiles grew on all the people in the crowd, laughter was even heard, as the young boy ran across the stage "momma, momma, momma."

She swept him up into her arms as he met her midway across the stage. She walked him over to the casket with the flower in his hand and softly spoke a few more words "Say thank you and drop the flower on top."

The little boy smiled as he muttered the words he was taught "thank you sir." He paused for a moment, as if he might not be ready to let the flower go, but then he let it fall from his hands. For me, it seemed to fall like a feather onto his grave; a symbol of what we needed to become as a people, a vision of how we needed to get there. The woman took a seat, her child on her lap, as Deseus stood to speak.

The man I had come to admire wiped his eyes and cleared his throat as he rose to his feet and stepped up to my father's casket. His speech was nothing short of what I hoped it would be; short and joyous "It has been my pleasure to know this man. I have only a few words and then I, and his son, ask that you spend this day celebrating his life versus mourning his death. I know that this man lived his life according to the cardinal virtues, the same virtues he taught his son, prudence, justice, fortitude, and temperance. I ask you now to live your life by these same ideals. Look out for your neighbors, even before yourselves and we can build a stronger Leotus, a stronger existence."

He looked down at the casket for a moment and closed his eyes in a moment of peace. He dropped his own memoir on the casket and gave the sign for it to be lowered into the ground. At that moment, a huge flock of colorful birds gathered in the sky overhead, sending my father into the earth with nature's own beautiful symphony. As the casket reached the earth where it would rest, Deseus threw in the first handful of sand "Rest in peace my friend."

The stage was pulled back and a line formed full of citizens each clasping their own hand full of sand to say goodbye. Deseus looked up to us and smiled and we smiled back before he spoke his final two sentences. His voice was strong this time and echoed "I have spoken with his son and he is among us today. I believe he will come back and lead our people, but be strong as a nation in his absence and show him your gratitude now."

The crowd erupted in applause and cheer. I removed our disguises for a few moments and first one, then many, came to notice us on the balcony. I watched, as they dropped the sand that had built Leotus into his grave, and I was proud. I clasped

Caiohme's hand, and her Chloe's, and we raised them in the air to show our respect for the people of Leotus. The crowd roared and then we were gone.

For the next five days, Caiohme, Chloe and I grew closer. In the safety of a world not devoured by turmoil, we were able to enjoy the simple things together, growing to be more like a family. The girls kept my mind busy during the days, away from all the friends and family and questions. I took naps and rested with them. I shared my lap for Caiohme's head and my shoulder for Chloe's. We laughed at movies and funny videos together. I taught them to ride horses and we played in the creek water. I shared with them the hill that overlooked our land and the hammock my father built; nightly we watched the Kansas sun set.

We shared our desires to return to Leotus, to help the people, but also a passion for our home towns. We slept on the couches in my house and enjoyed my mother's cooking more than once. We tolerated the man she believed to be my father, the man the Leonoids had left her with, as a fake representation of who he really was. We ate junk food like we would never gain a pound and ran out to the pasture at the inkling of visitors. One night I stayed with them far past the sun set, looking up to the stars and pointing out the constellations, as we each enjoyed a cup of dark hot chocolate with marshmallows. In that moment though, I realized that I was giving more time to the girls than I was to Katie and I pardoned myself to return to her hospital bed.

No matter what happened during the days, my nights were spent by Katie's bedside. The hospital was much quieter at night and I did not have to deal with the continuous flow of family and friends. Her family would go home to sleep, entrusting me to call them if anything changed. I would lay there and read Katie stories, softly sing to her our favorite country songs, run my fingers through her curls and pray for her. Occasionally, I would lay my ear on her chest and listen to her heart beat; it was the music of life. The hospital would always remind me of visiting hours, but would never force me to leave. In the mornings, Caiohme and Chloe would find me asleep on Katie's stomach and would wake me to come home for breakfast. That was how my days went, one after another.

On the eighth night, after everyone had left the hospital and the nurse had reminded me of the visiting hours, I crawled into the bed beside Katie. I felt as if hope was fading. I felt as though our connection was slipping. All I wanted was to lie next to her. I drifted in and out of sleep as I rested my head on her chest. Several times the nurse came in to check on her, never asking me to move. Then, as the sun began to creep into the window, I woke from a dream where my father had come to me on the top of the hill, which overlooked our land, and promised me that everything was going to be all right. He reminded me to remember the virtues, and to follow my heart.

As the sun shined brightly in my eyes I opened and closed them. I stretched my legs, half awake, but still halfway asleep. Then, startled by a movement I jumped into a sitting position. I crawled out of bed and looked down at Katie, saying her name quietly "Katie, Katie are you awake."

There was nothing for several minutes, but I looked down on her without more than a few blinks, hoping that I had not only imagined it. After several minutes I hung my head and sat in the chair by the bedside. As I turned my back to her, I heard a voice so faintly whisper my name "Jayden."

I turned around to see her open her eyes and my body was overcome by emotion. My knees grew weak and I fell to the floor. I quickly used the bed rails to pull myself up. For the first time, in what seemed like forever, I was able to look into those beautiful green eyes. I screamed as loud as my lungs would allow "Nurse, nurse, come now."

I pulled the red cord on the wall to get the nurses attention as I bent over to kiss her "Katie, Katie!"

I was so overcome with joy and tears that I could not think of any other words than her beautiful name. Just to hear her voice quieted my nerves and lifted my spirit. As the nurses flooded into the room one after another they tried to push me out of the way, but I did not release her hand. They looked into her eyes with lights and asked her to move her fingers and toes. Everything was working like it should. One nurse phoned the doctor as another asked her questions.

The nurse smiled as she spoke, gratified with her work "can you tell me who you are hunny?"

Katie laughed as if nothing had ever been wrong "Of course, Katie! Why am I here?"

As the nurse began to explain the situation to Katie, Caiohme and Chloe made their way into the room. They were smiling to see Katie sitting up in bed and I smiled back at them, but I quickly whisked them away, explaining that the room was full and that I needed some time with Katie; They seemed to understand. As they walked toward the door Katie looked over at me "Who are they Jayden?"

I looked into those green eyes as I counted all the angel kisses on her face. I saw no reason to overwhelm her at that time so I brushed it off "Nobody Katie, nobody."

What I hadn't seen was that Caiohme was still in the door frame looking back at us. When she heard my words, she was so overcome with emotion that she could not hold the sigh in that preceded her tears. I looked up in time to see the first tear fall down her cheek and hit the floor. Then, she turned her back on me and walked quickly out the door.

I wanted to chase after her, to tell her I hadn't meant it that way, but I could not leave Katie's side. As the hours passed Katie came to know the story of the explosion and her injuries. Family and friends came into the room to share laughs and cries. I shared more hugs and kisses with her that day than I had my entire life. I felt so close to her, but I noticed something was missing as I was forced to lie to her about who I was and what I had been through.

When I left the hospital that night, I searched for Caiohme. I wanted someone to talk to about the whole ordeal, someone that I could share my real feelings with, without lying. Caiohme was not there. When I got home later that afternoon, her things were packed and she was gone. There was not a note or an explanation, but I wasn't surprised; I knew what I had done wrong.

Katie spent the next three days in the hospital and then she was sent home. It was a blessing to have her back in my life. I smiled as I heard her giggle again and as she shared jokes with me. My skin and lips tingled as she kissed me. My heart beat stronger whenever she was near. Still, I did not feel I could share my story with her. It seemed that even though a huge part of my heart had healed, another part lingered for the comfort and love of someone that knew the whole me. I waited for the mail everyday hoping a letter might come, but it never did. I stayed up at night, hoping that Caiohme might find me again, but she never came. As the days came and went life in Havenbrook returned to normal, but Caiohme never came.

Eighteen months after Erebus' death, I returned to Leotus to assume my role as headmaster when Deseus fell ill. The castle had been rebuilt and the town had returned to the beautiful place it was the day I first set foot in it. The Life Tree had grown strong and a deep peace and celebration settled in on Leotus. Pockets of Farrians remained deep in Whisper Woods, but many converted to our side every day. I spent days greeting the people of Leotus, shaking hands, exchanging hugs, helping build and embracing the beauty of the ocean. I met with Carmine and Adrianna many times, speaking of the future of Leotus. I never ran into Malachi; the locals told me they had not seen him since the war ended. I rode into the pasture and woods many times, hoping to find Caiohme and Chloe, but I never saw them.

As the town rejoiced over my return, a coronation ceremony was held at the castle to appoint me the headmaster. Deseus made his way from his sick bed, out onto the Headmaster's balcony, to appoint me to the position. Crowds gathered throughout the day outside the castle walls to see the Headmaster position handed over to me. My heart raced as I opened the sliding door to join Deseus and Flora on the balcony. I don't imagine anything could have stopped my heart in its tracks any faster than what I saw as I stepped onto the golden balcony. My eyes did not see Flora or Deseus, but immediately shifted to Caiohme and Chloe in the crowd. I almost broke as I saw her standing there with Malachi's arm around her. Instead, I let the tear roll down my cheek and stood strong as the new Headmaster of Leotus, waving to the crowd and trying to smile.